I0717950

IMMORTAL SOULS

TYROLIN PUXTY

IMMORTAL WORKS
SALT LAKE CITY

Immortal Works LLC
1505 Glenrose Drive
Salt Lake City, Utah 84104
Tel: (385) 202-0116

© 2024 Tyrolin Puxty
www.tyrolinpuxty.com

Cover Art by Ashley Literski
http://strangedevotion.wixsite.com/strangedesigns

All rights reserved, including the right to reproduce this book or portions thereof in any form whatsoever. For more information visit https://www.immortalworks.press/contact.

This book is a work of fiction. Names, characters, businesses, organizations, places, events and incidents either are the product of the author's imagination or are used fictitiously. Any resemblance to actual persons, living or dead, events, or locales is entirely coincidental.

ISBN 978-1-953491-78-7 (Paperback)
ASIN B0CWZTF95T (Kindle Edition)

To my wonderful, supportive, fun-loving family.

*For always enthusiastically listening to my bizarre ideas and believing
in me when I don't always believe in myself.*

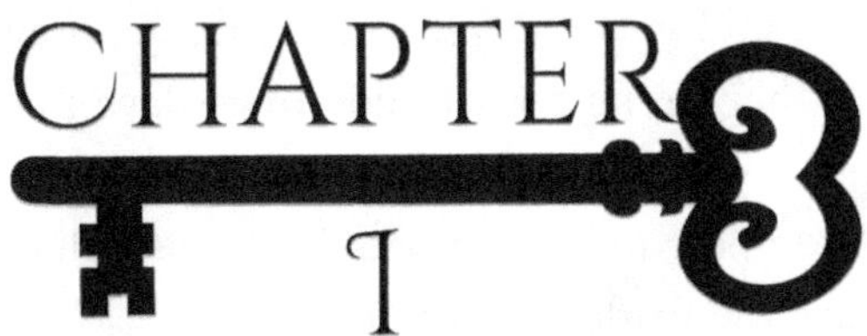

CHAPTER 1

And so we ran.

A chapter of my life I wrongly assumed was finalized and cemented firmly in the past, had come back to haunt me. I'd foolishly convinced myself that after endless chasing, hiding and imprisonment, I'd earned the privilege to be free.

But freedom was never my destiny.

Torture? Yes, *that* was definitely part of my destiny. Conflict? Uh-huh. An uprising? Apparently.

Caught in the middle of a war between mortals and immortals, my fate rests in the hands of gods I didn't know existed and an angry ghost-zombie hybrid hellbent on revenge. Then, of course, there's the ongoing issue involving my sister, who intends to publicly murder me in an attempt to restore power to the north.

My fate is in *their* hands, because I'm not a protagonist. I'm not a hero. I escaped my life as both a princess and a prisoner because I'm a spineless fraud who detests conflict—a sidekick in the lives of true heroes.

Heroes like Taylin. A young mortal from the north, who has similar androgynous looks and a tall frame. We share the gift of immortality; with only one of us able to possess it at any given time. She has a rather abrasive disposition, but in her heart of hearts, she's ambitious, powerful and loyal.

Then there's Rune. An immortal with the ability to regenerate quickly and repeat questions fifty million times until somebody adequately responds. He's kind, caring and diplomatic. He would make a peaceful leader—something we desperately need in this time.

Or even Zain. A hero to some, but definitely not to us. Hailing from the east and with the gift of the gab, the brawny immortal is in the midst of beginning a revolution to enslave mortals the way they enslaved us.

I can't compare to their impressive auras. All three of them could easily change the world, and yet, for some reason, it appears to be my responsibility.

Rune, Taylin and I shift uncomfortably on Nellabix, my childhood unihorn, who charges through the sunset fields and away from the shadows chasing the mountains. I'm sandwiched between them, Taylin at the head and Rune behind.

"Who do you think is coming after us?" Rune asks, his grip tightening around my waist.

"I can't be sure," I say. "Guards? Gods? Hybrids? We need to find a safe place."

"No such thing," Taylin mumbles, her pessimistic responses beginning to grate me. A little bit of hope, no matter how feigned, can go a long way. "We need a plan, Malin."

"Then make one!" I snap, relieved that the gush of wind dries the tears trickling down my face.

"We need to talk about it. Don't you understand what's going on? You've got a northern royal hellbent on restoring her throne. You've got Zain and Mitty out to slaughter the world. And you've got gods claiming the result will deeply impact their own abilities. We can either hide on an island until this settles, pick a side and fight, or run forever."

"Tell me what you think we should do," I say, the sleep deprivation catching up with my muddled thoughts.

"What I *think* we should do and what we *should* do are two very different scenarios," Taylin's voice is muffled by the wind carrying her tone in the other direction, so she repeats herself. "We're northerners. I'm mortal and you're immortal. This is our fight, whether we want it to be or not. I think we need to find allies that aren't associated with any corner. If Zain gathers his corner and other jilted immortals, all mortals will be killed or enslaved. It'll be an ongoing cycle, especially if your sister is involved in a power struggle. We'll need to convince Zain we're on his side and infiltrate the prison, freeing the immortals. Only we won't involve them in the revolution. A demonstration, perhaps. We can make this peaceful."

I consider her plan—wonderful in theory, almost impossible in execution. "And what allies are you referring to?"

"You're older than me, you should know."

"Well, I spent half of my life sheltered in luxury and wealth and the other half hiding in dilapidated shacks and bug-infested caves. My knowledge of the outside world is shamefully limited."

"What about all those beautiful books and libraries they spoke of in the north before it fell? Marble shelves and pages lined in gold?"

"They were mostly for show," I confess. "My brother was the reader of the family."

"That's extremely unhelpful! As usual!" Taylin adds, and I'm relieved I can only see the back of her head.

"I'm having trouble hearing back here," Rune shouts, "but if you're talking about corner species, my mother used to read me stories. Don't know how legitimate they are, but it's something."

"Like what?" I ask.

Taylin looks over her shoulder. "Huh?"

"I'm talking to Rune."

"Oh. Can't hear."

"Rune," I address. "What kind of beings?"

He doesn't respond, and I'm unsure whether he heard me or not. Eventually, he clears his throat. "Let's see. There were underwater beings. The felines in the forest. Ogres."

I haven't heard of the other two, but ogres definitely existed at some point in history. I think of Torg, the functionalist at the prison who strapped the world's most uncomfortable necklace to our bodies.

Tugging at the golden band fastened around my throat, I become paranoid that rumors of the application being nothing more than a tracking device could be true, especially with the shadows over the mountains approaching.

"I want to get this damn thing off," I say. Focusing on the trees ahead, I finally make a decision; albeit a small one. "We've been running for hours. We need to give Nellabix a break and work out our next move."

"Get what off? Our neck bands?" Taylin asks. "Didn't they say the gold gives us strength? And the tracking device threat was conjecture used to scare us?"

"I don't believe anyone anymore," I say firmly. "If we can remove them, we can examine them and take it from there."

"And that aids in our quest how?" I can't see Taylin's face, but I sense her eyes rolling. "One day you'll need to make your mind up quickly rather than distracting yourself with a minuscule problem."

"You're more than welcome to take charge," I offer.

"I'm not the immortal princess. This is *your* story. I'm only along for the ride."

Ignoring her comment, I gently squeeze my thighs into Nellabix's sides. "Nell, head for the trees. You... We all need a break."

I can't imagine how exhausted the enchanted creature must be, but it's deceptively tiring for us, too. Sandwiched together on an animal bounding through various terrains with no saddle or reins is challenging. My core is sore from holding on with my legs as we bounce up and down, my top teeth occasionally mashing into the bottom teeth unexpectedly.

"What are we doing?" Rune asks.

"Resting in the forest," I say. "Then you can tell us more about the other beings."

Mouth dry, I preserve the little energy that remains and welcome the cool shade of the trees as Nellabix weaves through the forest.

I've not seen trees like this before. Growing on an angle, their dark bark is stripped back, their long branches wrapping back around themselves, strangling the trunk. It doesn't feel particularly safe here. Nellabix must feel the same, as she doesn't slow down despite my gentle commands.

"Are you sure we should rest here?" Rune asks, his quiet voice surprisingly loud amongst the trees. It's like the forest absorbs all noise. Our breaths, our heartbeats, even our *blinks* are all exaggerated, externally taking center stage in this silent space.

"When have I been sure about anything?" I reply, mentally chastising myself for such a passive rhetorical question. "I mean, how bad could it be in here? Do you know anything about these parts?"

Cringing at the volume of my voice amongst the still trees, I nudge Nellabix a little harder when I spot a small clearing up ahead.

"Aiming for the clearing?" Taylin asks, her view much better than mine.

"Does it look safe?"

"Nothing looks safe in here," she attempts to whisper, her swallow a deafening crackle. "But it's not safe out there either."

"The lesser of two evils?"

"Perhaps. But you're right about needing to rest the unihorn. And my back is killing me."

Still highly alert, Nellabix struggles to comply with instruction, but eventually slows down to a cautious trot as we approach the clearing.

"It's like we're in a coffin for trees," Rune mumbles. "A forest morgue? A graveyard for nature? It's unsettling."

"We won't stay long," I assure as Nellabix comes to a stop in the center of the clearing. Her tail swishes and thwacks me in the side, her ears drawn back. I stroke her tenderly, wondering if she senses something beyond what we can see.

Taylin is the first to dismount, arching her back and pulling a strained face. She offers her hand to Rune. The jump from the unihorn is significantly higher for his smaller stature. When he lands, she offers her hand to me, which I graciously accept. I hadn't realized how stiff I'd become, my legs deep in slumber as I stumble to the ground.

Once I compose myself, an ominous sensation sends a lurch to my stomach. The grass is a sickly grey, not too dissimilar from the concrete prison cell we spent time in. Dread overwhelms my body, the impossible silence almost suffocating.

"Does anyone else feel like they're having a panic attack?" Rune asks semi-calmly, his eyes shifting from tree to tree. "Or a mental breakdown?"

"No," Taylin says firmly. "The trick is to be in a constant state of breakdown so you learn to function."

"We can't stay here," Rune says, keeping one hand on Nellabix.

"She needs to rest," I say, checking the unihorn's eyes. She's anxious, but I can tell she's tired and dehydrated. Pushing her to the verge of collapse isn't something I can gamble. "Is there any water around here?"

"No open lakes, but streams used to run beneath the earth. They might be dried up." Rune kicks at the grass. "But it's worthwhile digging. Which one of you is mortal at the moment? You'll need to drink too."

Taylin and I stare at one another, admittedly blasé about keeping track.

"Me," Taylin says eventually. "No, wait, it's Malin. Yes, Malin is mortal at the moment."

"We need to take notes or something," I say. "You might be right. I'm a little lightheaded."

"Get some water into you. If you can't find any, we'll swap."

The reassuring words are enough to invigorate me. It's been a trepidatious several months. Having been an immortal for the majority of my pathetic life, I abused my body in unimaginable ways. From starvation to sleep deprivation to deep wounds—none of them mattered. Sure, it was uncomfortable, but eating poorly was a lifestyle choice if need be. If I didn't want to sleep for a week, then I didn't. In the rare instances I wanted to be a hero, I could fling my body in front of someone and walk away with the knowledge my body would eventually heal, even if it left an unflattering scar.

Then, when I traded my immortality to save another, I had to relearn everything I knew about living. If I didn't drink regularly before, it was unpleasant but manageable. As a mortal, if I didn't drink regularly, dizziness and shredding stomach pains followed. My body felt like porcelain, each step a death trap. What if I tripped and landed on my temple? Dead. What if my heart decided to stop? Dead. What if I offended someone and they beat me to a bloody pulp? Dead.

It changed my whole personality. I've always avoided confrontation, but I never feared my own shadow. There was a time when I could walk anywhere with confidence, knowing that ultimately nothing could hurt me. Not permanently, anyway.

As a mortal, *everything* could hurt me. I didn't understand how people could live in a constant state of anxiety. Existing in a temporary vessel takes utmost courage and I have a newfound respect for all mortals who are working on their existential deadline. To be human means overcoming adversity and expectations on a daily basis. Why don't they realize just how amazingly strong they are?

Snapping out of my epiphany, I scope the immediate area. The clearing isn't particularly big, but I feel like we're sitting goldiducks. Taylin lowers herself to the ground and crosses her legs, cringing at the crackling sound of grass and twigs beneath.

"I doubt there's food here," she mutters. "We're probably something else's food."

"There's nothing malevolent here," I reassure. "The trees can't eat us."

My heart flip-flops at the notion, especially when Rune offers an unhelpful shrug.

"Be that as it may," I say hoarsely, "I'm taking Nell to find water."

"We shouldn't separate," Rune protests. He crouches and scratches at the surface of the ground. "We can dig here for water."

"All right. You dig for water, and I'll search for food," I say.

"But that's separating!" His eyes widen, a hysterical tone in his voice.

Damn it. What excuse can I find to get away from them for just a moment? I need respite.

"Look," I level my tone, "I need to relieve myself, all right? Nell can come with me. I won't be far. Just behind that tree."

"Do you want immortality?" Taylin asks.

"No. I won't be long."

That much was true. From a survival standpoint, I couldn't risk staying away for too long. From a personal needs point, I needed a week-long vacation. I wasn't used to being in such close quarters over a lengthy period of time with anyone. Oddly, I had more alone time in prison.

Leading Nellabix towards the trees, I seek solace amongst the silence. A frustrated scream is tightly bottled deep inside, and I want nothing more than to release it into the ether, freeing me of torment and anxiety.

I tug at the glowing neck band strapped to my throat. Nothing. I dig my nails into the slight gap between the band and my skin, searching for a clip or a lock. Nothing. A grunt escapes my lips, so I grit my teeth and try again. We don't have any weapons to smash this invasive brace.

Nellabix nudges my forehead with her muzzle in an attempt to ease my growing frustration. Succumbing, I sigh and wrap my arms around her wide, free neck. I can't cry. Rune and Taylin will undoubtedly hear each sob, each gasp. Instead, I crinkle my face into a pained expression and allow salty tears to silently slip from the corner of my eyes.

It's not as good as screaming, but it helps.

"I love you Nellabix," I soothe. "Thank you. I'd be lost without you."

She can't speak, but she echoes the sentiment with a tap of her hoof and another forehead nuzzle.

When I've regained composure and hidden all evidence of tears, I lead Nellabix back to the clearing. I expected to find Rune digging for water and chattily making random observations while Taylin stood guard.

Instead, I find them frowning at a pair of silhouettes. Unmoving, the shadows stand on opposite sides of a tree and whisper nonsensically. At us. Or at each other. It's difficult to discern.

I feel physically ill, in the same way Garu used to make me feel. There's a distinct prickle in the air, a shift in atmosphere, and a deep sense of dread.

"I didn't think they were real." Rune gulps.

"What? What are they?" Taylin asks, inching closer to Rune; not to protect him, but as if to protect herself.

"Shadow people. They're neutral."

"They don't *feel* neutral," I murmur. "I feel like they want to attack."

"That's only because they don't exist on our plane. They don't exist on any plane. The unease we sense is because they're darting from one time and space to the next. Odds are they don't even know we're here."

As if on cue, the shadows flicker for a moment before fully forming again.

I cautiously step closer, keeping my arm wrapped around the unihorn's neck, until we're close to Rune and Taylin.

"How do you know about them?" I ask Rune as a third shadow appears in the middle of the clearing, its chin tilted towards the sky.

"Mortal folk tales," he says slowly. "My village often spoke of shadow people. There was an old man who said he grew up seeing them from time to time."

"I think I heard of a story too," Taylin whispers. "There was a client who said her aunt took her own life after being haunted by a shadow man. I just assumed she was crazy."

The shadows don't approach us. It's hard to tell if they're even looking at us, as some disappear before our eyes and reappear in another location not far from where they originally stood.

"I guess...we sleep?" Rune says, a quiver in his voice. "Or rest. I can keep digging for water. And then...and then we rest."

"Or sleep," Taylin says, her gaze locked on the shadow flickering in and out of existence mere inches from her.

"It's definitely safe to sleep," I say unconvincingly. Slowly dropping to the ground, I curl up next to Nellabix who reluctantly lays, albeit tense.

Taylin and Rune follow suit, our breaths sharp and quick in the deathly still forest. I don't know why we all pretend to sleep. I don't know why we don't all admit how terrified we are and leave. But we creep closer and closer to one another, as the unnatural entities surround us.

Lost between nightmares and reality, I can't be sure any of us rest at all.

CHAPTER II

I somehow managed to convince myself to close my eyes for a short period, and within that time, I must've drifted into a form of sleep. It wasn't what one would call restful, but it was better than nothing.

A sharp stick pokes into my side as I roll over, and I instantly remember where I am. Flinging my eyes open, I'm relieved to find the shadows have dispersed, leaving behind three unsettled ex-cons and a suspicious unihorn.

Rune is already sitting up cross legged, digging at a small hole in the ground with a stumpy stick.

"Did you sleep?" I whisper, not wanting to disturb Taylin.

"Not a wink, but what's new there?" Usually he smiles to indicate his goofy sense of humor, but there's nothing to laugh at. Miserable, he prods at the ground with his stick. "I don't think there's water underneath here."

"Are the shadows gone?"

"Yeah. Think they stole my optimism too. They were awful. Maybe they were what we saw over the mountains. We didn't need to run after all."

"Is this supposed to be their territory?"

"They don't have territory, Malin. They're not part of this plane of existence. They're everywhere and nowhere. You can't communicate with them. You can't fight them. They're just...*there*."

The concept was foreign to me. How could something exist without existing? Although, somebody could no doubt argue the same thing in regard to the prisoners at the Immortal Cells.

My stomach growls rather aggressively, so I instinctively shield it with my hands.

"Your tummy was making sounds while you slept," Rune says, a weak curve forming on his lips. "I doubt there's food in this forest; it seems pretty dead. When Taylin wakes up, maybe we can move and forage."

"Sorry," I whisper.

"For what?"

"For my stomach."

"You're sorry that your digestive system made natural noises while you were unconscious?" Rune's eyebrows raise, revealing crinkles on his forehead. "Yeah, wow, you're a monster."

I smile at his non-judgmental approach to life. It's refreshing. A growling stomach back in the north was terribly offensive. It implied you weren't wealthy or taken care of. It's a trait I haven't managed to shake.

"What's it mean to be a princess?" Rune asks, as if reading my mind. "I'm assuming the polite panic over your bodily functions has something to do with your upbringing?"

My smile vanishes. Nobody can deflect Rune's questions. He simply keeps asking and asking until he's satisfied with an answer. I wonder if I faked a fatal attack if it would detract him?

"Um, well..." I fumble over my words. "Can you clarify what you mean?"

"What's your role? Your responsibility?"

"That's a damn good question," I utter under my breath. "I don't know. I didn't live up to expectations or fulfill obligations. I quietly rebelled by associating with mortals."

"Cool." Rune, bored with his water search, throws the stick over his shoulder. "Were you next in line to rule or something?"

Shifting uncomfortably, I glance at Nellabix for some sort of reassurance. The amount of times I skipped out on political classes to go riding with her instead was unprecedented.

"Technically, yes. Me, followed by my sister Adalin, and then my brother as a last resort."

"Women were given priority over men to rule?"

"Yes. In the north, women are depicted as the dominant sex. The creators of life. The peacemakers. I didn't agree with that notion either. Like mortals and immortals, I craved equality between the sexes. Nobody is above anybody else. Quite frankly, my brother would've been the more fitting child to take the throne."

"A noble notion, but equality never has and never will exist," Taylin's slurred voice interrupts. "You can't change society."

Sometimes I prefer it when Taylin is unconscious. I wonder if her dreams are as pessimistic as her reality.

"Of course you can," Rune argues. "Look at society now."

Taylin sits up, her hair wild and her eyes puffy. "What about it? The powers that be are the ones who did this. It took a war and powerful leaders to alter an already damaged system. It's easy to destroy a society but nearly impossible to build it up again. I mean, let's discuss these so-called species that are probably nothing more than legend. You mentioned underwater people or felines or ogres. I'll entertain the notion that they exist *somewhere*. The fact they don't interact with any of us is no doubt due to the fact they destroyed their own society."

"Or somebody destroyed it for them," Rune says. "I understand you think we're all inherently evil, but some people are only victims of cruelty. It doesn't mean they're incompetent or bad. And why are you skeptical of their existence?"

Taylin shrugs. "Doesn't make sense. We'd know about them."

"You're only young," I interject. "The very fact we've been working beneath gods that we didn't even think were a possibility means there's a lot we don't know about."

My addition only miffs Taylin. She throws herself back onto the ground and rolls over, arms folded.

Rune smirks at the tantrum, then redirects his focus towards me. "I think the underwater beings are definitely real."

Pulling my legs into my chest, I shift into a more comfortable position. "Why? Specifically, why the underwater beings, of all people?"

"Consider all the rivers, lakes, streams, oceans, seas. They're practically inaccessible. Even for an immortal, traveling to the depths of these places is a difficult and uncomfortable task. There's too much to explore with the added risk of carnivorous creatures. Underwater beings could be in solitude deep below, living their lives in peace."

"And you're proposing we attempt to find them?" I laugh, not because it's funny, but because I now understand Taylin's negative attitude.

"Yes!" Rune continues with his boy-like excitement. "My mother said they could sense great hardships and courageous souls. They would rescue fishermen lost at sea or children who fell overboard. Who is more noble than us? Who has been through worse hardships than us? It's worth a shot, isn't it? The three of us can't stop Zain on our own. I'm not saying the underwater beings will want to join a war that doesn't affect them, but maybe they can do *something*."

"You're better off convincing those creepy shadows," Taylin murmurs.

"Maybe I will!" Rune says petulantly. "I'll ask everyone and everything! I don't want a war. Few people do. And when Malin takes back her throne, everything will be good again."

"Yeah, put the indecisive one in power." Taylin's commentary is beginning to bug me, so I do something completely out of character—I grab a handful of sticks and rocks and throw them at her. It's enough to startle her into a sitting position. "What's that for?"

"I'm sick of you putting me down!" I shout, wincing at the sound. I've adjusted to the intense silence, but mostly because we've been speaking in hushed tones. "I've told you; if you have better ideas, *you* take the helm. If you're not going to take the lead, then shut up. Nobody wants to listen to your toxic negativity. We're trying our best."

Her eyes narrow as we all hold our breath. I'm the mortal one right now. She could easily strangle me to death within seconds; a feat I wholeheartedly believe she's capable of. Instead, she scratches her head and exhales.

"I'll back off. I just think you shouldn't be wasting time on underwater beings who probably don't even speak our language. We know ogres exist, don't we? Wasn't that Torg guy at the prison ogre-ish? Maybe he was a mixed species, but he has an in at the prison. Ultimately, our goal is to stop Zain from infiltrating. If we can manipulate the ogres through Torg, then it might be enough to dissuade Zain, at least for a short while."

That sounds like the most sensible plan—and I *hate* that I didn't think of it.

Rune seems oddly disappointed, his shoulders slumping forward. "Well, sure. But if we come across any large bodies of water, we might have a *little* look, anyway? You know, just in case?"

"Sure." Taylin's tone is dripping with sarcasm, but she forces a gentle grimace. "If the opportunity arises, sure."

Mollified, Rune beams. "Great! So is everyone awake? Can we eat? Can we leave these awful woods?"

"There's nothing to forage here," I lament. "Probably best to make way."

"Go have another look, would you?" Taylin urges. "I'll help Rune dig a little quicker. Just in case there is some water beneath the earth."

Suspicious of her eagerness to dispose of me, I reluctantly call for Nellabix and head towards the trees once more. Immersed in the cool shadows, I scan the immediate area, but nothing resembles food.

In the deathly silence, Taylin whispers to Rune who responds in an equally hushed tone. I can't quite make out their words, only the harsh S's.

She...she sent me away to *gossip* about me?

A more assertive person would burst through the trees and demand an explanation. Meek Malin? She waits just out of earshot for a decent amount of time to allow them to finish their conversation so she won't intrude.

What a pathetic leader I'd make.

Jilted, I return to the clearing with Nellabix, the last of my already small ego completely diminished.

"No food," I announce gravely.

"No water." Taylin shrugs. "Guess it's time to go."

"We should spare Nell," I say, concerned for the lengthy time spent without hydrating. "We will walk beside her."

Taylin's lips curve into a sneer. "She's a unihorn. Aren't they supposed to be...I don't know. Special or something? She doesn't *need* water, does she?"

"You of all people should have learned that just because we don't *need* something to survive, doesn't mean we should go without," I snap, pleased to find I have *some* sort of a spine.

She shrugs again, the flippant response boiling my blood. I can't stand it when she's in this mood. I'll blame it on poor sleep and let it pass, for now.

"Right!" Rune claps his hands together and rubs them enthusiastically. "Anybody know where the ogres reside?"

My eyes widen. "You're the one we've been listening to about this stuff! We thought you knew!"

"In fantastical theory, maybe." Shifting his eyes awkwardly, he pats Nellabix. "In stories they lived in valleys between mountains."

"So back towards the prison?" Taylin scoffs. "So we'll go in one large loop?"

"I don't think that's right," I say, desperately wracking my brain for some useful information. "The mountains around the prison don't have wide valleys. Ogres are big—they'd need more space for their civilization. There are mountains towards the south. Granted, I don't believe there are as many, and they're snowcapped. It might be worthwhile investigating."

"Snowcapped?" Taylin repeats. "Are ogres known for living in the cold?"

"I know Torg was a mixed race, but his skin looked pretty hardy," I attempt to recall his visual appearance. "He wore short sleeves even in that freezing prison. Besides, it doesn't mean the valleys are covered in snow."

Taylin and I turn to face Rune, expecting him to deliver an insightful answer.

He strokes his fingers through Nellabix's mane and clears his throat. "I remember something about rocks!"

We groan in unison, throwing our heads back in defeat. This is utterly, utterly pointless.

"This is why I thought we should try the underwater folk first," Rune says timidly, avoiding eye contact. "At least we *know* they're underwater."

"Do you know how much water there is?" Taylin cries.

"Obviously not enough." Rune motions at the ground then clicks his tongue, clearly as thirsty as the rest of us. "I'm sorry I'm not as helpful as you'd like, but I'm doing everything I can with the limited knowledge I've received. At least it's more than what you've done."

Wow. Even Rune is grumpy. Maybe those shadow people really did leave us in a bad mood.

Too aggravated to respond, Taylin storms out of the clearing, Nellabix trotting behind.

"I'm sorry," Rune says, but it falls on deaf ears. He repeats it several times, but Taylin refuses to answer, focused only on weaving around the tight cluster of trees and getting out of the suffocating forest.

Hopefully sunlight will give us some clarity.

Only...it's not morning when we emerge from the depressive area. It's twilight, the beautiful light and dark blue hues mixing together in the sky above.

"Can those shadow people mess with your perception of time?" I ask nervously, not particularly fond of traveling in the dark.

"I don't know." Taylin narrows her eyes at the vast countryside.

"We couldn't see much in the clearing. Maybe our body clocks are just confused."

"Body clocks and body compass," I mutter. "Which way do we go?"

Rune jogs ahead, slightly uphill to gain a better vantage point. It's picturesque from here, the grassy hills likes waves, the blossoms in the trees losing their petals in the gentle breeze. I stay with Nellabix and Taylin while Rune stands atop the slope. He points in the direction of the prison, which is still distressingly visible. Granted, it's a speck in the distance now, but it still sends chills up my spine. I feel like at any moment, the guards could haul me back in.

"Let's make a final decision," Rune says. "Look for ogres near the prison or walk south towards the mountains and potentially underwater beings. Won't be the coastal ones, but we might find some in the lakes."

"I can't bring myself to go anywhere near the Immortal Cells," I say through gritted teeth, desperately pushing away the mental images that keep flashing in my mind's eye. "Not yet. It's too soon."

"Then we go south and hope for the best." Rune turns his back on the prison and takes the lead, much to my relief. Although I've been on the run for a lot of my life, I never learned any basic survival skills. I didn't need to while I was immortal. I never learned to read a map, I never learned to cook anything special, and I never learned to create fire out of nothing. Nobody ever showed me how to. When you're a rich, spoiled princess everybody does everything for you. No wonder my kind are all but extinct.

"Do you know where you're going?" Taylin asks Rune, who confidently strides forward.

"Nope. We're just moving forward."

The sentiment warms my heart, even though my body is beginning to freeze as the night draws closer.

Sometimes that's all we need to do. Just keep moving forward.

CHAPTER III

The terrain changed drastically, albeit slowly over the next few days. What was hilly and lush is now flat and dry. With no sign of life in this brown desert, Taylin and I consistently swapped immortality so that the other could rest their body and cope a little better without water and rest.

"My body feels like the scenery," Rune's husky voice cracks on every second word.

"You brought us here to die, didn't you?" Taylin says, resting her upper body on Nellabix and dragging her feet.

"You're not currently the mortal one," I remind, my mouth struggling to formulate words. I'm used to pain and discomfort, but this is becoming unbearable. My aching calves and lower back feel like stone, each torturous step forward adding to the pulsating throb.

"Do you need to switch now?" Taylin asks. "Or can you give me another hour?"

"I can give you another two hours," I say, feeling rather altruistic. There's something about misery that prevents you from wanting to feel better. It's the lack of belief that you *can* feel better, so you succumb to the endless pain.

"It's not far. I know it," Rune encourages. "By the end of the day, I promise we'll find patches of grass. And not far from that will be water. We can rest in the dewy blades, hydrate and relax. We will discover tasty, filling food and be energetic by morning. It's happening. Positive vibes, girls!"

I'm sure a healthy mind aids a healthy body, but it's easier to let the darkness win.

"My legs feel like they're quivering," Taylin says.

"Mine too," I say. "Muscle weakness. Maybe we should sit down."

Taylin has already beaten me to the punch. She tugs on Nellabix to stop and drops to her knees. Rune and I walk ahead. I figure the further I can push, the sooner we'll be home free.

Everything about this place is egregiously deserted, the dark surface somehow absorbing the pleasant colors usually found in the sky. Everything is dead, a maze of cracks trailing on the ground.

"It just keeps going," I murmur. "Shouldn't we see something up there? *Anything?*"

"Malin, Rune," Taylin yells, her voice tight. "Everything is still quivering."

I glance over my shoulder, Taylin kneeling stiffly, her eyes wide. "It's just your muscles. Are you all right? Let me help you up."

"No." Taylin wraps her arms around Nellabix's front leg. "I think it's the ground rumbling."

Rune grabs my wrist and forces me to stop. "Malin. She's right."

Maybe being mortal prevented me from feeling the earth groan beneath us. Maybe I was just too exhausted. Whatever the reason, I only just now notice the vibration beneath our feet, ever so slightly rocking the earth.

"Is it a quake?" Taylin asks. "I suppose it's not like any buildings will collapse on us, so we are safe, right? We just need to ride it out."

"I'm not worried about anything falling on us," Rune says, his optimism replaced with unbridled fear. His grip around my wrist tightens. "I'm concerned we might fall through the earth."

"Where do we go?" I whisper, as if hiding my intentions from the angry grumbling. "Do we stand still? Do we run?"

Something shifts beneath us as we clasp onto one another to maintain our balance. Taylin from afar holds onto my unihorn, who is neighing uneasily.

"It's okay," I quell.

Nobody believes me.

With a maddening crack, Rune and I are flung forward as the

earth below opens its hidden mouth. I frantically grab onto the side of the crumbling surface, Rune digging his nails into my legs as he hangs from my numbed body. I haven't got the energy nor the strength for this. I peer down at Rune's horrified face and the bottomless pit that awaits us.

"Malin!" Taylin screams, speedily crawling towards us.

"Stay back!" I instruct, trembling to hold my body weight—and Rune's—as the earth continues to eat away, disintegrating in my hands. I attempt to pull myself up and hold on with my elbows, but Rune's additional weight makes it impossible.

"Malin!" Taylin's words run into one another as she recites a quick incantation.

"Nellabix," I grunt. "Take care of—"

My words are replaced with a shriek as my muscles give out and I free fall as Rune releases his grip on my legs. We plummet through the darkness, the rumbling intensifying.

As I flail in the abyss, a burst of energy embraces my being, Taylin's bequeathed immortality reminding my body it may not shield me from pain, but it'll prevent me from the sweet release of death.

Part of me wishes she'd kept it to herself.

"Land on me!" Rune shouts. "I'll heal quicker! Aim for me!"

"I can't see you!" I cry, scrambling midair for something to hold on to. Cold air pushes up from below, Rune's small target impossible to find.

His hand clumsily bats at my ankle, followed by a heart-wrenching scream and thud. Within dreaded moments, I tense my body and brace for impact.

It's so much worse than I ever could've anticipated, and I genuinely wish I could've died rather than deal with the excruciating pain.

My lanky body only half lands on Rune, arching my back in such a way that I probably would've been better landing flat on the ground. I can't tell if every bone shattered, but it certainly feels like it.

Air is forced from my body; my lungs, kidneys and heart mangled internally as they push against my ribs.

I sob, *once*, then realize I'm in too much anguish to follow through. I can't breathe. I can't move. I can't talk. I can barely think. Rune shifts beneath me, but I see nothing in the darkness.

Minutes become an eternity, Rune's quiet grunts getting louder and stronger over time.

"Malin?" he eventually croaks. "Are you all right?"

I don't answer. I *can't* answer. My body died. It's my immortality which leaves me to suffer.

"It's okay," he says when I don't respond. "Take this time to rest. I think one of my lungs has healed. Think it was punctured from impact, but I can inhale now. I can't imagine yours healed yet. Are you cold? I was freezing. The landing must've stopped my heart. This is good in the scheme of things. I thought for sure we would splatter. Maybe we didn't fall far enough. Good thing, too. Would've been hard to heal as a pile of goo. Can I gently rest my head on your body? Maybe the gold from my neckband will give you extra strength to heal. That is, if they really do help. Maybe *that's* why we didn't splatter!"

His muddled words provide no comfort. I consider giving up my immortality in this very moment, letting it disappear into the air and gifting me sweet relief. Anything has to be better than *this*. Eternal anguish combined with somebody who (despite their good intentions) *will not* shut up.

He continues to narrate his actions, very lightly placing his head on one of my legs, causing me to scream. He swiftly lifts his head and abandons the mission, instead opting to sit beside me while I moan and writhe.

"Please hold on," he whispers after what feels like days. "I know what you're thinking. I know you want to give up. And you're lucky because you have the option of doing so. But *please* don't leave me. There's no afterlife for immortals. I'll never see you again. You will heal. You will heal. You *will* heal."

Will I though? I could easily be a paraplegic for life. Not all immortal wounds heal. I attempt to move my toes for validation, and as predicted, they don't budge. There's no coming back from this. Although the pain is a consistent scream throughout my body, I work up the energy to move my mouth.

"How long have we been down here?"

"A while," he says solemnly. "I haven't left your side."

"I know. Rune, my body is dead. I can't move it."

He doesn't respond. We remain in the darkness, unaware of our surroundings. I'm freezing and I wonder if it's because my heart hasn't started beating yet. It might never beat again. Or maybe it's just because we're so far underground. I don't care.

"Malin?" Rune clears his throat. "Did you always know you could bequeath your immortality?"

"What do you mean?" Ow. I can't bring myself to speak again. It's becoming all too much.

"Northerners could always relinquish their immortality, but did you know you could give it to somebody else? Or was that something you just did in the moment?"

I consider the question, my brain scrambled from both the accident and dehydration. "From memory, it was always theoretical. In a moment of panic, I didn't want Taylin to die so I..." I suppress a cough, knowing the pressure on my chest wouldn't be worth it. I squeeze every muscle I physically can and hold it down.

Rune shifts beside me, his tone brighter. "I'm just thinking. If you can give your power to somebody else, why can't I give mine to somebody else? I heal automatically, so theoretically I should be able to project that ability onto you!"

A flutter of hope sparks within, but I suppress it like my cough. What a silly thing to hope for. There's no way I'd be that fortunate, given my history of bad luck. "You can always try."

"I will! Immortals were taught to hide for so long that we don't understand our own abilities. Maybe we all have something special to share. All right. Um. I have no idea how to do this. What's that jibber jabber you and Taylin always say to one another when swapping?"

I'd laugh if it didn't hurt. "Ancient northern dialect. I've given her the immortality without incanting, though. I believe it's more about the intent."

"Teach it to me, anyway. I need all the help I can get!"

Reluctantly, I comply, listening as Rune says the incantation over and over until he gets it right. I can't see him in the darkness, but I sense him hovering his hands over my body, mumbling the northern words.

He holds for seconds, minutes...maybe an hour. I can't be sure. The little guy refuses to give in though, his hands occasionally bobbling and tapping my body.

I'm not sure if it's tiredness or delirium, but I'm beginning to feel a little better. My chest doesn't throb when I breathe in, and the stabbing sensation in my lungs is gone. Carefully, I wriggle my toes, shocked when they abide.

Rune exhales and removes his hands. "I'm exhausted."

"Don't stop," I croak. "Rune, it's working."

Silence. There's a shuffling sound and I assume he's stretching or relieving himself.

"Rune? Are you there? I feel better! I can't believe it—you're a genius! This could help so many people, immortals and mortals alike! Can you spare another ten minutes? I think I'll be able to get up soon!" Cautiously, I consider shifting my right leg and laugh hysterically when it moves on command. It still hurts like hell, but *I can move.* "Rune! I can feel my legs! You're amazing!"

Silence again. This isn't a conventional Rune response. The boy is always talking, always filling the gaps. Something must be seriously wrong.

My heart starts beating again, thrumming against my chest as I roll onto my side. Everything aches, but I pull myself onto all fours and eventually onto my knees. Dizzy and disoriented in the darkness, I edge myself slowly towards a wall so that I can stand.

"Rune?" I whisper, reaching out my hand.

Nothing.

Fear overtakes initial concern. Leaning against the filthy wall, I shuffle forward, one heavy step at a time. My exhales are loud, nervous, so I fight to keep as quiet as possible. It was nightmarish to be sprawled motionless on the ground, but at least I had Rune by my side. Wandering blindly and aimlessly is substantially worse.

"Maaaaa-linnnnnn."

The familiar haunting voice sends chills throughout my mangled body. Frozen against the wall, I can't bring myself to glance over my shoulder where the sound came from.

"Come on, why won't you look at me?"

"It's dark," I say hoarsely. "I won't be able to see you anyway,"

"Oh, I think you will. The wonderful thing about manipulating energy? I can project myself even in the darkest of places."

Reluctant, I turn and find the strange hybrid of a woman, still dressed in her navy uniform, a bitter expression permanently etched into her otherwise attractive face. She's right—her body is somehow outlined even in the darkness, her face alight with a dull glow.

"What did you do with Rune?" I ask, knees weak at the thought of confrontation, but I'll hurt her if need be.

"How should I know?" She looks up. "Quite a tumble. This would *almost* satisfy my need for revenge if you were to be imprisoned down here forever."

"What do you mean?"

"These sinkholes aren't an act of nature. They were created. Which means whatever lives down here has your friend, which means there's a way out for you." She pauses. "I saw him heal you. That is a *very* interesting progression. Will definitely aid in my revenge. Maybe there's even a chance to kill those vile gods so I can become the one and only."

I don't know how to respond to such a ludicrous suggestion. Gods only recently drew my attention, and I don't know enough about them. I certainly don't want to hurt or offend them, considering they have abilities beyond my understanding. This transparent immortal, who was killed by a god, and is somehow transporting and stalking my every move leaves me beyond confused and concerned.

"What *are* you?" I ask, tabling etiquette.

"I don't know," she says, her eyes locking intensely with mine. "I'm not alive. I'm not dead. I'm not here. I'm not there. Nothing matters. Everything matters. I need help, I need nothing. I must go. I must stay."

I blink and she vanishes, as I return to the all-encompassing darkness.

"Where did you go?" I ask, unsure whether I'm addressing the strange, invisible girl or Rune. When nobody replies, I continue to drag myself along the wall.

I lurch forward when the wall ends, an empty space in place of my only support. Working up the courage to continue trudging forward, I shuffle one foot forward to ensure I'm not about to walk off a cliff. It's as if I'm turning a corner, the cool air fresher from this angle. I search for more walls, but either I'm in a wide corridor or an empty space. Trusting my instincts, I continue in what I assume is a straight line, listening intently for any clues to my whereabouts. My gut tells me not to yell for help, despite wanting to scream Rune's name.

Whatever lives down here can see better than I can. It can probably hear better too and it definitely can navigate the tunnels. I can't show any vulnerabilities or weaknesses, no matter how unbearable the pain in my bones and muscles might be.

I attempt to transmute my fear into anger, to look more threatening when the time comes. If something has Rune, I'll need to fight. The thought sickens me, but I won't leave him behind—especially not after he worked so hard to heal my wounds.

I'm unsure how long I walk for. My slow pace could very well have me moving in circles, but the increasingly cold air alleviates my doubts. It's only getting stronger, which means I'm getting closer...to *something*.

As I inch towards *something*, I pause at the sound of grunts, groans, or growls. It's difficult to distinguish, but it's unfamiliar. When it stops, I step closer, my sharp breaths deafening in the grim silence.

The threatening sound surges once more and I stop again.

"Stay still, Malin," a low voice whispers. "These aren't to be trifled with. They're not like us."

Rune. That *has* to be Rune. He's nearby, but I can't decipher which direction. I spin in place, arms out to grab his, but I'm met with emptiness.

"Rune?" I ask, my whisper matching his. "What has you?"

I need light. It's the only way. Going against my better instincts, I clear my throat and speak up. "My name is Malin, Princess of the North. Please show yourselves. You've taken my friend captive by mistake."

There's a strong possibility I've sealed our fate for the worse. Sure, princesses hold some clout, but not the ones from the north. Not with our arrogant and violent history.

The delayed response is troubling. Sometimes silence speaks volumes.

Then, a sudden spark and I shield my eyes from the blazing flames. The heat offsets the cold breeze trailing down the tunnel—an expansive, endless tunnel I can finally see.

But that isn't what surprises me.

Rune stands tense, lips pursed together, his hands hidden behind his back. By his side are two tall beings I've never seen before. Broad shoulders and snouts in place of noses, the proud-looking creatures have yellow eyes with a glassy sheen. Black hair hangs limply, brushing against their bare skin; dark patches conveniently covering the reproductive organs on their anatomy. They're humanoid and hold the torches confidently, but their faces are strangely animalistic.

"Doggans," Rune says, reading my astounded expression. "I think. They don't speak our language. They don't speak at all."

"Do they..." I try not to address Rune and instead turn my gaze towards the doggans, hoping eye contact is inoffensive. "Do you understand me?"

With their free hand they point in unison at the cave drawings. There are various interpretations of their species, performing day-to-day activities like digging in the tunnel and feasting on animals that are either poorly drawn or entirely unfamiliar to me.

I scan the wall, hoping to find information that can aid me. Behind Rune is a drawing of the surface, a big hole and a humanoid falling. I motion at the action.

"Yes. This is what happened to us," I confirm. "Rune, shift your head please."

He hunches and I flinch at the rest of the picture—a decapitated, shattered humanoid drowning in its own blood. Crude illustrations of the doggans surround the dead mortal, spears in their hands.

"Oh," I moan, unsure how to respond. "Yes. No. I mean. We aren't mortal. We can't die. That's why, that's why…"

"They're carnivores," Rune utters out the corner of his mouth. "The drawings behind you depict them eating the dead mortals."

I choose to believe him and refuse to turn around, instead keeping a close eye on the doggans. What's worse, I don't know if they're threatening me or questioning me. Do they understand why we're alive? What is their level of intelligence?

"We mean no harm," I say as calmly as possible, hoping they don't notice my quivering chin. "We want to return to the surface, if that's possible."

The warrior-like figures glance at one another, either speaking telepathically or utilizing a very subtle form of body language. They nudge Rune forward and motion for me to follow.

We continue down the tunnel, albeit at a faster pace now that there's light to guide the way. The walls are covered in drawings, showcasing mundane activities and explicit scenes. A little flushed, I keep my head down.

As we approach the end of the corridor, we are greeted by a circular room adorned in glowing red rocks I've never seen. They sparkle against the flames, even decorated on the floor to create small but pretty patterns.

In the center of the room stands a womanly figure, her hair much longer than the others and her gaze far more intense. Her snout-like lips curl into a small smile as we halt before her.

"Welcome, immortals," she says, her voice low.

"You speak!" Rune exclaims, wincing when one of the doggans slaps him across the face. I daren't utter a syllable or move a muscle.

"Only royalty has the approval to learn the surface dialect. I have never needed to utilize it, so excuse any errors." She turns to me as if waiting for validation, but I don't want to be slapped by the untamed guards. "Northerner. We thought you were but a myth. I have great respect for your people."

My lips part, stunned by the revelation. *Nobody* likes the north. When she seemingly awaits my response, I gamble my chances. Perhaps I have permission to speak. "There's a few of us left."

"The northerners are wealthy, esteemed and powerful. I long to be them. I wish for their jewels, their luxury, their grace. To be in your presence fills me with delight." Her eyes flash at Rune. "*Not* the likes of you. Your corner are inhabited by timid, weak farmers. We usually feast on your mortals; not that they have much flesh. We open the sinkholes and trap them in the darkness. What an awful surprise to find you alive, barely injured, practically flourishing. What use are you?"

"He's a healer!" I interject, concerned for his wellbeing. He'll never die, but I dread to think of him in pain. "He heals my wounds and his own. If not for him, I'd still be crumpled in a heap."

"A slave?" Her eyebrows raise, her disgust quickly transitioned to intrigue.

"No. A friend," I say, glancing at the violent guards. It's possible they could turn on me at any moment. "We are friends."

"Friends," she repeats slowly, as if trying to find a word in her native lexicon to relate to. "You are not dressed how I would expect. The stench is unsettling too. Are you from the prison?"

Is honesty the best policy here? Do I risk the truth? I turn to Rune for reassurance, but he offers a small shrug, decidedly quiet.

"The Immortal Cells, yes."

She takes this admission onboard, her nostrils flaring. "A man tunneled through here. He was also from the prison."

My breath halts as I think of Zain. "Was he of eastern appearance?"

"I do not know. We are closer to the central parts and I know only of northerners from drawings and stories. The remaining surface species I have little interest in. This man was dark and filthy from digging. He was, what's the word? Unhinged. He spoke to me as if I would abide by his rules. I did not like him. But he was strong and fast and accustomed to the dim light. He fought his way out of here."

It *has* to be Zain. "May I ask what he wanted from you?"

"He rightly assumed we have little respect for mortals. He said an uprising was imminent. He tempted me with the promise of hearty feasts and banquets if we joined the revolution. I was appalled. *Nobody* manipulates me. *No.* We remain underground for a reason. We have no interest in involving ourselves in surface matters. We are content digging for jewels and keeping what's left of our culture intact." There is a hint of sadness in her glowing eyes and I'm ashamed to have never educated myself on the history of our land. "He was awfully frustrated by my refusal to participate. I said I would not offer ourselves up for war, not now, not ever. He was strangely confused. I set the guards on him, but he was evasive."

"How..." Rune clears his throat, darting his eyes at the guards. When they don't hit him, he continues. "I mean, this man has the ability to pull the truth out of people he speaks to. He can con anybody. It's part of his corner's ability. Why didn't it work on you?"

"I haven't the faintest clue what you are referring to," she says dismissively. "Perhaps this is a surface issue. Perhaps it is a language barrier. I do not care. Now be quiet and speak only when spoken to, or you'll be responsible for healing every bone in your body."

Rune shifts in place, literally biting his tongue to show his compliance. Irked, she glares at him and redirects her attention to me.

"You should teach your healer manners. Northerners have always respected etiquette. That's what I've been informed of." She turns her back and strides towards the back of the room where a throne made of unpolished gold resides. She takes a seat and points at smaller seats that are far less glamorous and crafted from stone and rock. Cautiously, I follow and lower myself onto the wobbly seat, checking Rune who remains in place with the guards. This must be invitation only.

"You seem to be thirsty," she says, snapping her fingers. "We have a stream that runs through here."

"Parched," I confess, relieved by the offer. "Thank you."

Two doggans emerge from the darkness, holding a jug and wonky handmade stone cups. They pour the water for us and run back to wherever they came from. I reach for the cup and squint my eyes at the walls of the circular room. There's slight movement and I only now notice that we are far from alone. Dozens of doggans have gathered, their backs pressed up against the walls. Have they been here this whole time, or is their species impressively stealthy?

The water greets my lips, refreshingly cold. It's the best water I've ever tasted.

"Are you joining this absurd revolution?" she asks, a thoughtful finger resting on her chin.

"Goodness, no!" I almost splutter. "We're tracking the man you met in an attempt to stop him. The fewer allies he has, the better. We've seen war destroy our corner. We don't want it destroying the entire land. Mortals may have imprisoned us, but it came from being mistreated by immortals."

"You empathize with mortals?"

"A little, yes. My corner treated them terribly. I want us to be equal."

"Equality never has and never will be sustainable," she says bitterly, snout turned up. "Mortals are egotistical, panicked monsters.

Limited lives lead to power struggles and selfish actions. Are you unaware of this?"

"Some mortals are kind," I say sheepishly, clasping at my cup for comfort. "Most are scared."

"The ones we've had dealings with are *evil*." Her words drip with disdain. "Those of us foolish enough to live on the surface were forced into breeding with animals to create hybrids that would act as ultimate guards at the prison. We are strong fighters, but we have no desire to use our abilities for violence. We wish for an easy life here. It's how we've survived."

I sip my drink, pretending to swallow even though I've finished. I genuinely can't foresee how this will end. The leader speaks in cold tones and I sense she's only using us to gain information. She's transparent about her stance on surface dwellers, so there's no incentive to help us. The only thing going for me is the fact that I'm northern—an attribute that has never yielded positive results.

"I apologize for our intrusion," I say, even though the onus is clearly on them. "It is unthinkably malevolent the way mortals have treated your kind. I would not wish that upon my worst enemy. But I do not wish to inflict pain on anybody. We are very short on time, especially if you have already met with Zain. His revolution will happen quickly, and blood will be shed. I can't let that happen again, not after what happened to my corner. Is there any chance we could ask for directions?"

She processes the request and crosses her humanoid legs, covering the patches of hair, leaving her appearance all but naked. "Directions to where?"

"To leave, I mean, to return to the surface."

My answer hangs in the air, a universal hatred directed towards me. There's no indication the pack of doggans can fully comprehend surface language, but their eyes glow in tandem with one another, my response toxic in their sanctuary.

The leader never breaks eye contact, her elegant position never compromised, her authoritative tone never diminished. She is a woman who knows what she wants and understands who she is. "And what will you offer in return? Will you lead the mortals to our location? Will you rescue our hybrid children? Will you offer me tremendous wealth from your corner? How does your leaving benefit us?"

"What is the benefit of us staying?" I blurt before I can think. "We're immortals. You can torture us if you feel the need, but our healer works quickly and from a distance. We will not be your slaves; we experienced enough of that as prisoners. You say you do not fight, but *we* will if circumstances call for it. We cannot die, so we will ultimately win. We will leave one way or another, without being indebted. After all, you purposefully dragged us down here."

I can sense Rune cowering behind me, each doggan inhaling sharply as they await their leader's response.

Despite the flash of rage in her eyes, there's a glimmer of respect. As she stretches out her long fingers, I only now notice how black her claw-like nails are. Perish the thought of being on the other end of them.

"Tell me your name," she says.

"Malin," I address as politely but as firmly as possible. "Princess Malin. The healer is Rune."

"I do not care to learn his name," she says with a wave of her hand.

There's a rumble above and a slight quake. She stares up at the ceiling and growls, her low grumble chesty and ominous. The other doggans join her, focusing above. Uncertain, I consider getting up from my seat, but I pause when the unique species growl whilst inhaling.

A few moments pass, the rumble ceases and the growling stops. The leader clears her throat and centers herself.

"Excuse us. We sensed a mortal above. As a pack, we have the ability to manipulate the earth, allowing it to open up and swallow whatever movement above. It seems we have secured a tasty meal for the evening."

I cringe at the thought of Taylin and Nellabix falling victim to the same fate. This woman has made it perfectly clear that she doesn't care for mortals, so negotiation to keep Taylin alive will be difficult. I can only hope she was smart, or alternatively, selfish enough to run far away from this place.

"Can you sense who or what fell through?" I ask as nonchalantly as possible.

"My sense of smell is decent, yes. It is one lone mortal. *Drunk.* That vulgar poison is exceptionally strong. Most likely exiled from a village. He was probably too inebriated to even comprehend his death. Shame. There's something tasty about blood that screams."

I almost sigh in relief, but suppress the urge. No doubt the mortal's death is tragic, but I'd rather it be a stranger than somebody I know.

"Fetch the body," she orders the guards towering over Rune. "It has fallen some distance from here. I want to eat it while it's still warm. I detest stale food."

Somewhat desensitized from the prison, I push away the visual image and ignore the bile that creeps up my throat. "We would hate to distract you from your meal and take up more of your time."

"Time is endless." She pauses. "I request that you remain here until I have finished eating. I do not make the best decisions on an empty stomach. You are entitled to water and the use of this room while we eat. When I return, we shall discuss our next course of action. I understand as a royal, you are not accustomed to being spoken to this way. But you are in my territory now. Is this clear?"

"Crystal," I respond through gritted teeth. It's the most amicable choice given our current situation.

Mollified, the leader rises from her throne, signaling at the others to join her. "Leave some light. Surface people have terrible eyesight."

A snarling doggan approaches Rune and aggressively shoves the torch into his hand, almost burning him. One by one, they line up behind the leader whose name I never learned, marching out of the circular room and into the inky tunnel.

I stand from my uncomfortable seat and rush towards Rune once I know we're alone and drape myself over his body.

"Are you all right?" I whisper, trembling with mixed emotions. "I was so worried about you."

He pats me on the back with his free hand, the top of his head only reaching my shoulder. "I'm so sorry I left you. I wasn't even sure if you could walk. The healing worked?"

"It did!" I exclaim, wiping away a stray tear. "Can you believe it? The amount of people you'll be able to help!"

"It is a promising thought," he agrees humbly. "What now? Should we try to leave before they finish eating?"

"We can't navigate through here alone. We don't know who we'd bump into. I think we have an accord; if we stay we might remain on civil terms."

"Or they'll imprison us."

"Nothing we haven't faced before," I say, somewhat stunned by the ferocity in my voice. He doesn't respond and I somehow feel like I've scolded a young child, so I wrack my brain. "Hey, I don't know if it's the glow from the torch, but it's pleasant seeing you with your natural skin tone. Without all those drainings, you definitely look healthier. You know, for a man who fell through the earth."

He beams, clearly relieved by the change of topic. "You're not doing too bad yourself. Blue skin doesn't look good on anyone. Um, I need to ask you something."

"Anything."

"Our voices carry in this place. When the doggans dragged me away, I heard you calling out to me...then I heard you talking...to someone. Do I need to heal your brain?"

"Oh!" I almost laugh. "That horrible, weird, dead immortal showed up again."

Rune blinks.

"You know. The one that showed up after we were released? She was saying how a god killed her but she's come back wrong?

Remember? Or do you need *your* brain healed?" I joke, although I'm beginning to question my own sanity.

"Malin," Rune says carefully. "I've never seen this girl. There was that day in the field you were staring at something and you said something out of context. Are you telling me you were talking to someone then? I thought it was an external monologue of sorts."

Utterly humiliated and panicked, I tuck my chin to my chest to conceal my flushed cheeks. "It's nothing."

Rune extends his hand to mine when I turn away from him, fretting over this girl I've imagined. "Malin, you need to share these things."

"No. I'm going crazy. Immortals can't die and then come back as invisible beings defying space and time."

"Why not?" Rune asks. "We've encountered shadow people and doggans in a matter of days, all by going off the beaten track. Who knows what else is out there?"

It's meant to be a comforting statement, but it triggers me negatively.

Who knows what else is out there, indeed.

CHAPTER IV

Doggans either take an extraordinarily long time to eat, or they've forgotten about us. I hope it's the latter.

Rune sprawls on the ground, too anxious to use a seat without permission while I energetically use the free time to decipher the drawings on the walls.

"Thanks again for healing me," I say over my shoulder, feeling spritely and clearheaded. "No wonder you're always so chatty and bubbly. You must feel this great all the time."

"Not right now," he says hoarsely. "Healing others is tiring."

"You'll be back to your cheery self in no time," I encourage, disinterested in his negativity. Very little could kill this good mood. "So, you'll find this intriguing. They've drawn themselves as hostages, forced to breed to create those horrible hybrids. It's very confronting and grotesque. It appears she may not have been exaggerating. Can you believe those vicious creatures at the prison share DNA with these dignified doggans? It's horrendous."

"*Great,*" he mumbles.

I stop at a drawing of a tall, androgynous being adorned in jewels and a flowing dress. The doggans are bowing, their weapons by their side.

"They really did worship northerners at some point," I address Rune, but he's decidedly apathetic. "Nice to think we had some allies. Perhaps it was before my time."

"You said yourself you were sheltered. Who knows what went on behind your back?" He's blunt, but he's right. "I don't mean to be so rude—"

"—no," I dismiss. "It's true. I'm not proud of the way I lived my life. I'm still not. I have a lot of growing to do. A lot of learning. I can never redeem myself, I'm sure. I was never cruel, but I was never a hero. Sitting in silence automatically places you on the enemy's side. If you want justice or change, you need to speak up. Resorting to violence is not something I'll even condone, but I wish I'd made more of an effort to stand up instead of running away."

"Running away helped you survive. If you hadn't, you might not have learned your lesson. You're exactly where you need to be." Even with a monotone voice, Rune's pep talk is inspiring. He would make for a good motivational speaker.

Rune sits up, dark rings beneath his eyes. "I'm hungry."

"Me too," I admit. "I am under the impression they'll only offer whatever is left over from the mortal. Should we make a run for it?"

His eyes shift to the tunnel as if waiting for a guard to spring out and beat us for considering such an option. That is, of course, if they can even understand us. "Not a great strategic move, especially if they're meant to be allies. I know they're not going to fight, which is great, but would leaving abruptly and without permission be in poor taste? Would that be to our detriment later?"

"I'm prone to holding grudges," that sleek voice answers from the shadows, her face glowing as she steps closer to the flames. "Fumbling around my home as means to escape, especially without saying goodbye would certainly cause irreversible offense."

"Theoretical," I interject. "Sorry, we just weren't sure when you would return. We had no intention of leaving."

"Mmm." She responds as if she doesn't believe me, too bored to argue. Wiping her snout with the back of her veiny hand, she misses several stains that have dripped into the patches of hair that cover her breasts. "I commend your patience. It was a while. I think clearer after a meal and a massage."

"Massage?" I clarify.

"Yes. It is customary for my guards to use the spine of the mortal to relax my tense muscles. We ensure to use all of the mortal so as not to waste it. I refuse to decorate with bones, however. I find that extraordinarily tacky and morbid. We use them for tools instead."

I shouldn't have asked. This woman has no qualms about over-sharing.

Stretching her lanky arms above her head, she groans. "I'm weary. There's nothing for you here, so you best leave on one condition. If the north is restored to its former glory, I demand to be included in trade, to enjoy your variety of wealth. I'm tired of my people being forgotten. In return, I'll ensure these tunnels will not be used for war. No underground surprise attacks. If we see somebody attempting to utilize our tunnels, we will inform you. Agreed?"

I hesitate. "There's no promise the north will ever be restored, but I promise we will not harm your people. If I take the throne, you will definitely be included in our trade. Unity is all I want. Instead of jewels, could we discuss a better food substance for your kind instead of luring mortals to their death?"

"I am willing to discuss options, yes."

"Then we shall do that once the war has been decided."

Agreeable, she tilts her head then points to the narrow tunnel behind us. "Those conditions are fair. We are temporary allies, and you shall be informed if the enemy returns. I wish you all the best on your conquest. Behind you is a steep incline. As you progress, you'll find a stream of water. Follow it and you'll eventually reach the surface. There is a short vertical climb, but not unmanageable. Consider yourselves free."

We don't know how to respond. Freedom has been such a foreign concept that any mention of it feels suspicious or laced with malicious intent. Rune fidgets in place, waiting for me to make the first move.

"Thank you," I eventually say. "I look forward to our next encounter. Hopefully it will be during a time of peace."

"It better be." Her eyes glow. "I want jewels and better meals." There's no change in inflection. No humor. She means what she says.

Unable to find the trust to turn my back to her, I wave at Rune to join me by my side. He scrambles up, and together we side-step towards the narrow corridor.

"You seem trepidatious," she says. "You need not be. We are non-violent. We will not attack you on the way out."

Non-violent? I suppose sneaky traps and hitting Rune for talking are defined as something else down here? That said, despite not knowing her name or if she even has a name, I believe her word is everything. It is most likely how she defines herself.

Feeling less need to be on guard, I force a polite smile and turn my back, even though it goes against my better instincts. Rune lifts the torch to light the way as we step into our apparent freedom ahead.

I hold his hand, feeling a little braver with him next to me. I spent so many years alone on the run, but having a familiar face helps me be more courageous. If I can't do something for myself, then I damn well will do it for someone I care about.

We continue through the tunnel in silence, our breaths getting a little louder as the incline begins. The floor is damper, a tiny stream of water trickling down.

"It's cold," Rune says, as we heave ourselves up a particularly steep part of the tunnel.

"It is. It must mean we're getting closer to the water, and hopefully outside."

"What do you think Taylin is doing?"

My stomach churns at the very thought. "I genuinely don't know. How long have we been gone for?"

I feel Rune's fingers tap against my hand as he calculates. "You were paralyzed for a long time. Days, I'd say. Added hours to walking, talking and waiting. Under a week, perhaps."

That's far too long. "She's mortal."

"She has your unihorn."

"She's mortal," I repeat. "We left her in a deserted land with no instruction, no direction. What will she do? Where will she go?"

"Taylin is tough," Rune reassures, his face serious against the glow of the torch. "A survivalist. She's young, but savvy. I'm not worried about her."

"Not even a little? How are we supposed to find her?"

He doesn't respond immediately, careful with his words. "As a survivalist, she wouldn't have stuck around. There was no championing her way through, no way to rescue us. My bet is she would've gathered the necessary energy needed to get to safety with Nellabix. She's had time to gather herself. She knows we were heading to the water. That's where she'll go."

"She's a mortal!" I protest again, this time sounding like an obnoxious child. It's the only way to feel heard. "I don't think you understand! She can't swim underwater for long. Why would she bother trying to find them if she thinks we are lost causes?"

"Because it's what we would've done," he replies, his voice tight. "I know she's difficult and cold at times, but she's a sensitive soul. She also has a lot more faith in you than you realize. She will believe we can find a way out. She'll wait for us at the closest body of water. I know it."

I wish his optimism was contagious, but I'm caught on the one thing he said: *She has more faith in you than you realize...*

I have a hard time accepting that admission. Taylin, for the most part, thinks I'm a joke. She thinks I'm incapable, indecisive and incompetent. At least, that's always the vibe she's given me.

I can't dwell on it. The important part is moving forward. Moving upward. Literally.

"Guard that torch with your life," I instruct. "This climb will be incomprehensibly difficult without that light."

"No pressure," he says, tightening his grip around the handle.

Our feet slap against puddles of water, the quiet bubbling only getting louder. It's absolutely freezing. My nose begins to run as we ascend, but there's a flicker of hope inside of me. Each step brings us closer to the surface.

"Do you think this water is healthier? Would there be magnesium in this?" Rune asks, but I have no clue what he's talking about. Water is water as far as I'm concerned.

"Maybe," I reply, knowing he'll keep repeating the question if I don't answer. I slip on the surface, frantically clinging to the wall but I've already pulled a back muscle. Wincing, I continue forward.

The stream gets stronger until we find ourselves wading through as it reaches our calves. Up ahead is a dead end and water falling vertically through a patch of sunlight.

"We made it!" I pick up the pace until I'm near the exit. The water soaks my skin, leaving my teeth to chatter against one another. But I don't care. We're so close. We just have to climb a wall.

"Question," Rune says reluctantly, inching towards me. "How are we supposed to climb that?"

"We'll give each other a boost!"

"Uh-huh…" Rune strains his neck as he looks upwards. "And how tall do you think we are? These cave walls are slippery with nothing to hold on to. I hate to say it, but we've been had."

"No we haven't." I chew on my lip, staring up at the exit. "Yes, I see your point. That's very high. Maybe this isn't the exit she was referring to. There could be a few."

"Or she's led us into another trap so they can eat us."

"Rune!"

"Sorry," he says sheepishly. "Without Taylin, the sarcastic commentary was lacking. Does it look like there's another way out? Or does she wrongly assume we have talon-like claws that can scale cave walls? She mentioned it being manageable. Manageable under what conditions?"

I run my fingers along the slimy surface. There is literally no way we are getting up this wall. Once again, the window of hope is slammed shut.

"I don't believe she did this deliberately," I say. "Maybe it's ignorance."

"Well this torch won't last much longer." He motions at the

flame. "But hey, at least we have water and some...strange looking derryfish if we need food."

"Raw?" I scrunch up my nose, sneering at the tiny black creatures gently nibbling at our feet. "Even cooked, they're hard to swallow. I can chew them for hours and they always get stuck to my teeth."

"Better than nothing."

"Their little lips feel nice on my skin, admittedly."

Rune smiles and shifts in the water. "Glad they don't have teeth. Very suction-y."

"Very," I say slowly, not fond of the idea formulating in my mind. "They're very sticky fish, aren't they?"

He seems to catch on relatively quickly. Testing the unspoken theory, he shakes his leg in the water and the derryfish remain stuck to his ankle, unyielding. "Certainly stubborn at the very least."

I cringe at the thought. "How quickly and painlessly can we attach these to our fingers?"

"To climb? You think it'll work?"

"It's potential grip."

Rune twists his face. "I suppose we eat them to survive. This is also technically a tool for survival..."

He bends over and curses as he attempts to pull a particularly stubborn one off his leg. I watch his muscles tense as he finally tears its pouty lips from his skin. Pulling it out from the water, Rune grimaces as the fish writhes between his fingers, struggling to breathe. Poor tiny thing. It convulses once more, then goes limp. He passes me the torch and apologizes as he rips off the tail.

"I plan to suppress this memory," he mutters, poking his finger through the body like a glove. Approaching the exit, he taps his finger against the cave wall, the dead fish lips on the tip of his finger instantly sticking. "A bunch of these could work."

"One on each finger and thumb?" I ask.

"Big toes too," he suggests. "I feel awful doing it."

"I know. Me too. I spent most of my life as a vegetarian. Meat was for emergencies. If it helps, derryfish don't have the ability to feel pain."

"I believe they recently disproved that."

"Well...it's an emergency!" I reason.

He nods in agreement, but it doesn't ease our discomfort with the process. Quietly and as respectfully as possible, we catch the little, yet powerful fish and fashion them into suction cups for our fingers and toes. I hope this works. Not just so we can escape, but also to justify killing dozens of innocent animals.

"They don't live long anyway," I say almost to myself as I slip the last one onto my right thumb. "Thirty days average."

"They can live up to two years though. The average is brought down by—"

"—predators like us, I get it! Let's speak no more of it! You go first."

I crouch to play the torch against the wall, far away from the water as I watch Rune bend, then leap. He flattens his palm and his makeshift gloves stick to the wall.

"What now?" he grunts.

"You'll need to use your biceps and kind of pull and slide upwards," I say, much preferring this supervision role than doing it myself.

Listening to my instruction, his entire body shakes as he pulls his petite frame upwards. Using his feet to grip into the wall and ease the pressure on his arms, he groans expletives as he ascends.

I feel like a proud mother, which is instantly replaced with dread when I realize I'm up next.

"How are you doing, Rune?" I shout upwards as I lose sight. "Please reply. I don't want a repeat of earlier!"

A breathless laugh trails down the opening. "It's beautiful up here. I'm not sure if I'm soaking wet from sweat or water, though. Hurry, Malin!"

His bubbly tone inspires me. Copying his movements, I scale the wall, relieved by my upper body strength. Because of my height, I move a little faster, but it's by no means easy. I remind myself to only gaze upwards, as falling down is *not* an option.

"You're almost there, Mal!" Rune peers over the hole, resting his bare hands on his knees. Splashes of water restrict my vision and almost choke me, so I tuck my chin to my chest and continue.

Within moments, a familiar hand wraps itself under my arms as I cling to the side, pulling me to the surface. Panting, I rest on my back, blinded by the midday sun warming my chilled flesh.

I tear the sacrificial fish from my body and relish in the soft moss that cradles my tired, sweaty, aching body.

"It is beautiful here," I agree, once I open my eyes.

It's a vision of paradise. A cluster of flowers and trees surround us, the soothing waterfall trickling from the rocks and down into the hole we climbed out of. Do the doggans know this place exists? The fresh air, the colorful scenery, the healing sun? Why would they choose tunnels over sanctuary? Are they *that* scared of potential conflict? Do they detest the light? Are they gluttons for suffering?

"Different species, I guess. We may never know," Rune says, as if reading my mind. He can't wipe the smile from his face as he appreciates the private enclosure. "Maybe they sneak up here for a holiday."

"Rune. I was just thinking that. Are you a mind reader?"

"You're easy to read. Your face, not your mind," he clarifies. "I'm more observant than others care to note."

"Or maybe projecting your healing abilities unlocked additional advantages."

He shrugs without a care in the world. "I doubt that. Anyway. I don't want to leave, but we need to find Taylin."

"And Nellabix," I add, then sigh. "There's countless directions. This will be like finding a needle in a haystack."

"Go with your gut instinct."

"Because that's worked so well in the past?"

"It has. We could be in a much worse position than we are now.

You said the right things to appease the doggan leader. You encouraged me to heal you. You're more capable than you know."

I don't know how to accept compliments, so I smile coyly and clear my throat, which doesn't need clearing. I pull myself to my knees and grab onto Rune as we hoist ourselves up. Channeling my apparent gut instinct, I point in the direction of the waterfall. "Let's find the bigger source of water. That's where Taylin is."

Together, we leave the heavenly backdrop of nature and follow the drizzling waterfall gently draping over the rocks. It's not much of a hike compared to our tiring vertical climb, so we navigate upwards until we reach the top.

There's more greenery up here, flowery vines wrapping around trunks and hanging from the cliff side. If I wasn't immortal, I'd convince myself I was dead.

At the top of the waterfall is a bubbling stream that we follow forward; images of Taylin and Nellabix magically sitting at the end of it only manifesting false hope.

An hour passes, the scenery becoming less saturated as we approach a large lake. We spend the time conversing and appreciating the cool breeze. The weather couldn't be more perfect if it tried.

We come to an abrupt stop at the lake, an island centered in the water. The island looks like a giant elephantano rock; the ears, the trunk, the body, the legs...it's too natural to have been carved, but it's also made to perfection. Hanging vines and moss color the smooth stone, adding an extra layer of realism.

"It's magnificent," Rune says, his eyes glistening. "Even the eye is indented. Did somebody craft this?"

"I don't know how," I reply, awestruck by the structure.

"There were stories of powerful beings turning troublesome animals and people into stone. Everything used to be a lot bigger millions of years ago. Do you think this could be a real elephantano?"

A traumatic memory flashes in my mind's eye of the god Sharnique, frozen in her eternal rock tomb in the tower in the

Immortal Cells. Could it be that the gods lived close by, or at the very least, visited? And if so, why would they turn an innocent animal to stone? Or is this one silly coincidence?

"I want to say no," I say, my voice tight. "But it might've been the gods."

"I thought that too," he responds softly. "We don't know if they're the villains, do we?"

"It's safer to assume everybody is against us." I push aside the negativity. "All right. Search for signs of Taylin and Nellabix."

We check for footprints as we begin circling the lake to no avail. I *knew* my gut instinct was off. Rune has too much faith in me.

Pausing for breaks to rest our legs and rehydrate, we soon find the sun setting and the moon taking its place, the silver orb bouncing off the lake's reflection.

"I hate to say it, but it might be time to rest for the night," Rune says. "We can look tomorrow."

"We've nearly walked the circumference of the lake," I complain. "I'm the worst."

"No you're not. It's early days." He spots a grassy patch and plops down, groaning and closing his eyes. "Starting to feel my age."

I join him, letting out my own old-lady grunt as I pull my long legs to my chest. "If we ever, you know, stop the revolution and are able to live a quiet life, I'm going to sit in a warm bath for twelve months. Then I'm going to find the softest bed and remain in that for an additional twelve months. Then I might learn to garden."

"We'll live in a big house together," Rune continues. "Just for company, you know? I can't imagine not having you in my life now."

"Which corner of the land would we live in?" I ask.

"Not mine. I love it, but too many memories. It's time to start fresh. We could find a new corner. Or a new land across the water. Find others like us. Or find others who know nothing about us—even better. It'd be magical."

"How would we spend our days?" I like his concept of this ideal life. It feels like he's telling me a bedtime story.

"Music. You mentioned you used to sing. Read, educate ourselves. So long as we're warm, comfortable and loved. That's all I want."

I reach out and grab Rune's hand, squeezing it gently. He's such a sweet soul. "Me too. What about a family?"

"You are my family now."

"I know. But children. Would you have them?"

He considers the question. "I honestly don't know. Would I settle down with a mortal or an immortal? Would the child be mortal or immortal? How would I cope with an aging family who would die? But on the other end of the scale, would I want to bring an innocent being into the world where there was prejudice against them? Where they'd live for an eternity watching friends die naturally? It feels like a punishment. Sometimes I feel like I'm being punished. I don't like outliving people I love."

It's not something I can fully grasp. I lived mostly with other immortals, scorned for associating with mortals, so those attempted friendships were strained. "But what if you settled down with someone like me? Others like us? We could live happily ever after. If there is such a thing."

"And there's the rub," he says with a smile, closing his eyes as he lays back. "If there is such a thing."

CHAPTER 3

I wake up in the middle of the night, confused as to where I am—a sensation that has become all too familiar. Rune is spooning me from behind to keep warm, his breath soothing on my shoulder, but his occasional twitches are semi-alarming.

Desperate to relieve myself, I carefully roll out of his arms and search for privacy, despite him sleeping like a log.

I trek through the long grass, searching for the perfect place.

Only, the perfect place is not what I anticipate.

Hidden in the weaving blades is a lanky northerner, pale, bloody and bruised.

I crouch down and jostle the still form. "Taylin? I can't believe it! Taylin?"

My heart sinks when I can't spot Nellabix nearby, but there will be time for questions afterwards. I go to lift her, but am worried I'll only enhance any injuries she's sustained.

"Rune! Rune, wake up!" I shout. "I found Taylin!"

Startled, he yells something nonsensical, stumbling towards us in the dark. When he finds us, his eyes are puffy from lack of sleep. Motionless, he frowns. "That's not Taylin."

"What are you talking about?" I snap, infuriated by his idiocy. "Of course it is."

"Then your eyes need healing. Look closer."

He must be sleep walking or delusional. Of *course* it's Taylin. I mean, she's wearing silky, silver robes that she must've found after we were separated. They've seen better days, but it's a luxurious type of fabric.

Her hair might be a little lighter than usual, too. And despite a northerner's tendency to appear more androgynous in comparison to the other corners, I can't see any evidence of her breasts, her shoulders slightly broader and her chin slightly wider.

"It's Wylin," I gulp. "Rune, heal him please."

He's crouching before I finish the sentence, hovering his hands above Wylin's gash. It's next to his temple, a fatal blow for a mortal and potential brain damage for any immortal. But with Rune, I have faith.

After several minutes, Wylin's eyelids spring open, staring up at us in horror. He scrambles back into the grass as if we were carnivorous animals primed for attack.

"It's me, Malin," I say calmly, raising my hands to show I'm unarmed.

"I know," he says hoarsely. I wonder why he doesn't just run if he's so scared, but I glance down at his ankles which are swollen and bruised.

"I'm not going to hurt you," I say. "I promise. What happened?"

His stoic grey eyes fill with tears as his lips begin to quiver. "I betrayed them."

"Adalin?" I snort, thinking of my hideously evil sister. "Or your siblings? Dalin? Cheralin?"

"All of them!" Wylin shouts, covering his face with the inside of his arm. "I'm a disgrace!"

"Because you refused to sacrifice me?"

"Because I went against the main plan!"

I can't empathize with him, and it's evident in my tone. "And you're crying in the shrub because you didn't agree with their twisted sense of morality? They're narcissistic, pugnacious, malevolent beings! You should be proud that you're not one of them!"

"They're my family!"

"Adalin is my sister, and she attempted to murder me! Since when does family mean anything?" I motion at Rune. "I've known Rune for a few months and he is more like family to me. Blood isn't always thicker than water. Especially when there's more water in our bodies than blood."

He wipes his face, then rocks back and forth in place. "I know. *I know I know I know.* It's been a long time. Listening to the toxicity over the years and their plans to regain the throne and, and...*they're so cold.* When I saw you at the prison, it was like everything made sense. There was normality in the world again. I didn't have to convince myself anymore. They bludgeoned me when you left. Tried to convince me to give up my immortality and die, rather than forever be burdened with unfixable wounds. Garu distracted them long enough to help me get away. I don't...even know how I got here."

"Me neither," Rune says, inching closer to Wylin to continue healing. He places his hands lightly on Wylin's broken ankles, who winces at the gentlest touch. "Physically, I mean. How did you even run on these? They're mangled."

"I don't recall my feet being this bad when I left. Maybe I fell. I'm having trouble remembering. I have a pounding headache." He squeezes his eyes closed, as if it will somehow trigger a visual image.

"A head wound will do that," Rune mutters, smiling as the swelling visibly reduces. What an amazing gift he has.

"Do you think healing his wound will reinstate memories?" I ask, folding my arms and keeping my distance. I'm too frustrated by Wylin's regretful confession; the deeply suppressed animalistic side to my nature wanting to pummel him for thinking he betrayed vile betrayers. How foolish can he be? It makes me distrustful of him. He could turn on me at any moment due to his guilt. Or twisted loyalty.

"Who can say?" Rune's focus doesn't deter. He seems to enjoy what he's doing. "Healing others is a new concept to me. I would assume so, but what is done is done. I'm just aiding in breathing new life into the body. Theoretically, let's pretend he'd been shot. Regeneration doesn't clean the bloodstain from his shirt or instantly close the hole. It's a slow, arduous process. I spent an hour or more on your body which was practically dead. I'm learning as I go."

"How are you healing me?" Wylin asks, his eyebrows furrowed.

He looks absolutely bewildered and fidgety, anxious to run away as soon as possible.

But I won't let that happen.

"People from his corner regenerate quickly. Part of their quirks," I answer for Rune. "He recently learned to project his ability."

"Like how you projected onto that mortal?" Wylin clarifies. "By bequeathing your immortality?"

"Yes."

Wylin grins, an unnatural expression on his perpetually concerned face. "Your brother worked that out too. What seems to be an utterly selfless, average ability can have the most beneficial side effects of all. Fortunately our siblings have yet to figure that out."

Rune rests his arms, the three of us staring at one another, chippets and songbirds peacefully filling the silence.

Wylin checks his feet. The swelling is reduced, but bruises and broken toes are still evident. He'll have to crawl away at this rate. "The feet don't feel as cold! Thank you! Could you keep going?"

"If you tell me about my brother, yes." It's difficult to remain emotionless. I haven't spoken to or heard from my brother since the north collapsed. I wasn't even sure if he survived. We were never close as he was much older and enjoyed traveling, but I always respected him. He treated everyone with great compassion and fairness; the way a leader should. "He's well?"

"He's alive," Wylin corrects, glancing at Rune as if to encourage him to continue healing. "He's an extraordinary being, Malin. He discovered that once you bequeath your immortality, you are forever linked to that person energetically. Telepathy, tracking, sensing, feeling, exchanging. So many elements he's exploring."

"Liar," I protest. "I haven't experienced any of those things!"

"Have you tried?"

The simple question shuts me up.

"Leighton is discovering new, divine aspects of our genetic makeup," Wylin continues, but I'm quick to interrupt.

"Leighton?" I repeat. "You have my brother confused with

someone else."

"No I do not. He, ouch!" Wylin grinds his teeth as something in his foot snaps back into place as Rune works. "He denounced all evidence of his northern heritage, including his name."

"And how do you know this?" I'm blatantly skeptical. "If you've been living in underground tunnels with my sister and your siblings, how can any of this be feasible?"

"Nobody said I *stayed* in the tunnels for all that time. I can be just as inquisitive and adventurous as anyone else. Adalin used me as a messenger, sending the least favorite out on potentially dangerous treks. It was during those times I'd return to your brother."

"Where is he?"

"Have you forgotten your northern manners?" As Wylin's body heals, his arrogance emerges. "I don't appreciate the abrasive tone, Malin. I understand your reluctance to be civil due to what happened back at the prison, but if you remember, I helped you get away. Clearly, the broken image of me here isn't enough to convince you that I've cut ties with my siblings, as difficult as that is for me to process. The guilt, the shame...I don't know how to overcome it, but I intend to."

I struggle to find a polite way to respond, so I awkwardly sigh and tilt my head. "I'm sorry. It's been a difficult few days... months...decades."

"Yes, it has been." He looks me up and down. "You called me Taylin when you first found me. Is that the mortal who looks like you?"

Begrudgingly, I nod. "Yes."

"Why don't you try sensing her? Your brother showed me how to do it. Would you like that? Alternatively, would it aid in you trusting me? That manic look in your eye has me worrying you're only healing me to hurt me again."

"You know that's not what I'm like!" I snap, offended to have been accused of such a malicious act.

"Things change. I bet you never thought your own sister would try to murder you for personal gain. We never truly know what a person is capable of."

I hate that he's right. After all, we're all capable of benevolence and malevolence. We all have our limits and our breaking points. I've never considered what mine might be.

"How can I reach Taylin?" I ask, ignoring his last comment. "She's mortal currently, and I'm concerned for her."

"It's no different to giving her your immortality. Breathe. Focus. *Intent.* Tune into your mind, body, soul. Take mental note of any images, sensations or thoughts you receive. No matter how silly you think they may be, it will ultimately lead you to her."

It *sounds* simplistic enough, but theory has always been my forte. Executing any idea is my downfall. Too on edge to close my eyes, I stare at my hands instead, unable to breathe successfully into my stomach. I can only get as far as my chest, which is tight and uncomfortable.

"It gets easier," Wylin reassures. "I promise."

"Rune makes it look easy," I mumble.

"It's not," Rune says with a light laugh. "Feels like my energy is tearing out of my body, but I am determined. You can't doubt yourself, not even for a second."

He's right. Whenever I've transferred my immortality, it was never a question in my mind. I just did it because I *had* to. Just like now.

With an intense spark of staunchness, I visualize Taylin, sensing my energy drift into her body. There's a strange tingle...then the aches, the misery, the loneliness.

"She's lost," I hear myself say. "Physically she is safe. Just sore. Maybe a little sick. Yes. My nose is running."

"Track her," Wylin's distant voice encourages. "You can view her location. Delve deeper."

The experience confounds me. I'm in two places at once, two *bodies* at once. I'm neither Malin nor Taylin, yet I am both.

A pool of muddy water flashes in my mind's eye, my hands

covered in bloody scratches. *I'm not supposed to drink this. My body will be terribly sick. But I need something.*

"Water," I murmur. "She went to source water."

Where did that unihorn go? It abandoned me. I suppose I'm lucky to be alive after the attack.

My eyes fling open, mortified by the inner monologue.

"What did you see, Malin?" Rune asks gently, as I frantically attempt to return to the split mental state.

"She said there was an attack. Nellabix is gone, Taylin's hands are sliced to pieces!" I run my fingers through my hair, squeezing my eyes shut. "I need to find her!"

"Not with that attitude," Wylin says, seemingly bored despite my near hysteria. "Settle yourself."

"I can't!"

"Then you won't be able to tune in again. Simple as that."

Simple as that. Anything is easier said than done. It's easy to tell someone to be calm when they're calm. It's easy to tell someone to breathe when they're breathing fine. It's easy to tell someone to get over something when it doesn't impact them.

I *don't trust Wylin.* I don't like the way he digressed when I asked about my brother. I don't like how his mood shifted from an anxious wreck to passively peaceful. He could be as sociopathic as his siblings for all I know, testing the waters with me. The last thing he needs to see is me successfully utilizing this ability.

"Fine." I clench my jaw, ignoring Rune's scowl. "I'll tune into her when I've regained composure."

I can almost hear the voice in his head. Re-*gain? When did you* ever *have composure?* His facial expression says it all.

Rune lets out an exasperated sigh and lowers his hands. "I wouldn't suggest walking far on those feet. Same with your head injury; you might still be dizzy. But I've healed the major problems. Your cells know what to do now."

Wylin gently rolls his ankle, pulling a face when it cracks. "Thanks, Rune. Truly. The thought of being permanently disfigured is abhorrently depressing. You saved the day." He stands gingerly, testing his feet. He can stand, but Rune is right. He'll need at least a couple of days of rest before he's ready to travel far.

"You're somewhat eager to get going," I observe, trying to push aside the mental image of Taylin, alone and hurt. I can't even bring myself to think about Nellabix...

"Obviously. I'm a fugitive, according to your sister and mine. Why would I want to stay out here, uncovered, unprotected?"

"Where are you trying to go?"

"Back to your brother. He's nestled away safely. I'm happy to live out my days there as far as I'm concerned. No more vindictive wars. No more petty battles. Just peace and quiet."

"And where *is* this place?" I narrow my eyes when he smirks.

"I wouldn't dare break confidentiality by telling you," he replies, his abrupt change of tone unsettling. "I still don't know if I can trust you."

"You don't know if you can—" I shout, then stop myself. Why he is purposefully aggravating me, I don't know. It amuses Rune at first, who only scrubs the grin from his face when I glower. "You're clearly as abrasive as the others, which has no doubt rubbed off on you after all these years of isolation with them."

"I'm just reciprocating your tone, Princess Malin," Wylin replies innocently. "You set it. I simply follow it."

I take a moment to process the accusation, wondering whether I had unintentionally made this exchange so uncomfortable or if Wylin was merely a master manipulator.

"Tell me where my brother is residing," I say, mindful of a politer tone.

"I genuinely can't tell you," Wylin says, his own voice softer. "I promised not to tell anybody. But I can take you there if you'd like."

My stomach somersaults at the very notion of meeting with my long-lost brother, who has allegedly proposed new methods of enhancing our abilities. My dull eyes light up as I'm ready to dive in and say yes.

"What about Taylin?" Rune asks, still on his knees and resting in the long grass. "And Nellabix? We haven't forgotten about them, right? And our quest?"

"*Quest*," I scoff, the unpleasant northerner in me emerging. "No, of course I haven't forgotten about them, but we are presented with the rare opportunity of meeting our allies."

"Allies?" Rune repeats. "Wylin just said they're secluded away from war and battles. If we go there, we might miss our chance to help the mortals and stop the revolution. I hate to say it, but your brother is low on the priority list when there are people who need our help. Right?"

I have no way to reason with him. Is it selfish to choose your heart over duty? Then again, is this war *really* our duty? Why *can't* I hide away with my family?

"Well, make up your mind fast," Wylin says unapologetically, "because I'm not going to wait around for long. I want to get out of here as soon as I can."

"Good luck with those ankles," Rune mumbles, covering his sneaky statement with a cough. "Buddy, soon isn't as soon as you think."

"It's still an ultimatum," Wylin counters, massaging his ligaments. "You can't search for her *and* come with me. Not unless she's geographically nearby."

"Malin..." Rune whispers. He looks like a child next to Wylin and me, his petite frame and boyish round face only sending me into a guilt spiral. "Taylin wouldn't leave us."

Wouldn't she? Maybe not Rune, but I get the impression she would abandon me if she needed to.

Swallowing hard, I think out loud. "Maybe you could stay behind while I go with Wylin. Taylin needs you to heal her."

Rune's jaw drops. "You're suggesting we split up?"

Concealing my nervous shakes, I lift my chin. "My brother has found a way to further develop our abilities. It might help us long term."

"We don't have long term to consider!" Rune yells, the sudden volume silencing the chippets. "This is happening at a rapid pace whether you like it or not! If you go with Wylin, you have nothing to ensure your safety. For all we know, he followed us here and will lead you back to your maniac sister! And I won't be there to help you."

Wylin darts his eyes awkwardly, uncertain how to respond, the way one might feel when walking in on a lover's quarrel.

Great. Another pivotal moment, another choice, *another* decision. One that feels wrong either way. Weighing up my options, I attempt to use an authoritative voice.

"There are many difficult decisions in war. We will rest during separate intervals and I will reconnect with Taylin to secure her location."

"Then you'll leave me," Rune says bluntly. "After all that we've been through, you'll leave it to me to find Taylin with no way to ever contact you again because of secrecy. It sounds like a swell plan, Malin. No wonder you couldn't handle taking the throne. You're nothing but a selfish coward!"

He slaps his hands on the grass and stands, returning to his original camp.

His words cut into my soul, a never-ending loop in my mind. An out-of-character statement only worsened the blow. He must've truly meant what he said.

"For what it's worth," Wylin begins, "I think you're making the right decision."

"That's because you're northern," I retort. "We don't have a good track record of making the right decisions."

He shrugs. "Who does?"

Not one for rhetoric questions, I lay down in the grass and roll onto my side, eager to rest until sunrise, even though I know the only dream I'll have is the once even-tempered, optimistic Rune reminding me of my biggest insecurity.

Selfish coward.

CHAPTER VI

"Wakey, wakey, sunshine and steak-y!"

The familiar ditty throws me back to memories of my childhood when my brother would pounce onto my unnecessarily wide triple bed and bounce on his knees to rock me awake.

"Sun's up!" He'd announce, a factual statement I could have at any moment learned once I opened my eyes. Only I didn't enjoy opening my eyes so early. Had it been anyone else but him, I would've thrown the pillow over my face and ignored them until he grew bored and walked away.

My brother? He was so infrequently home that despite my tiredness, my eyes flung open with gusto, delighted to see his glistening silvery irises and cheeky smile.

"And," he'd continue, "I brought home some pacon to go with eggs!"

"Pacon?" I'd repeat hoarsely, the rare meat sending me into instant salivation mode. "Where did you get that?"

"Places," he'd say mysteriously, before pulling off the satin bed sheets. "Get up, get up! The day's a wasting!"

"Will you tell me about your travels this time?"

"Ah, my whimsical stories?" He would press his lips together, eyes narrowed as he contemplated. "The people I meet and the adventures I have and the places I visit would be severely frowned upon. Our little corner is content with our limited knowledge of the land. I'm afraid I might stir things up or start a conflict if I told you. Kids are impressionable. Like cute little mortals. Maybe when you're older and you've chosen which end of the spectrum you're on. Which *side* you're on. You'll either be a rogue rebel struggling to find your purpose in this eternal damnation or you'll, well, you'll be just like our dutiful, single-minded parents. When you know who you are, you'll find me...and I'll show you the world."

I never understood what my brother meant...until now.

With the sun rising and Wylin and Rune fast asleep, I realize how vital it is to reconnect with him. If we had any chance of extinguishing this revolution and appeasing the gods, then I needed resources, information, and power—all things my brother could show me. It wasn't a logical choice, but it was a sense of knowing.

I glance over at the two men, their mouths slightly parted and their breaths slow and relaxed. Now was the perfect time to tap into Taylin without any distraction.

Attempting to mimic their calm trance, I breathe deeply and close my eyes, focusing all of my energy on our lost comrade.

An electrical bolt hits me, the current running through my body as my mind's eye sees the world through Taylin's perspective.

Muddy and bloody, she lays next to a dam, humming sadly to herself. Too tired to quench her thirst, her lips remain cracked and dehydrated despite the endless source before her. Unless it's...tainted.

That's why she's sick. She drank it and threw it straight back up again. Hunger pangs cramp our stomachs, the mortal body shutting down.

All right, this is bad. She's wounded and unwell. But *where* is she?

Intent, intent, intent. Narrowing in on her location, I have a bird's-eye view as I hover above Taylin's body. Zooming out, I find her several miles in the opposite direction from where we are. It's at least a day's travel.

But she might not last a day.

In that moment, I know what I must do. Scrambling up, I rush to Rune and shake him awake. Flustered, he raises his fists, dazed and confused.

"Come on," I press. "We need to help Taylin."

"What about your brother?"

"She's dying. You must heal her."

Rune lowers his fists and rubs his chin, eyes red from interrupted sleep. "No. I'll stay here and keep an eye on Wylin. I won't let him leave. I thought about what you said, and you're right. We can learn vital information from him. Give Taylin your immortality."

"We're not natural regenerators like you. Immortality doesn't ensure instant healing. It just means we don't die," I counter, my words running into one another.

He peers over my body towards where Wylin remains fast asleep. "We could take him as our prisoner. Or I could re-break his ankles."

Frozen, I try to analyze his tone. "I can't tell if you're joking."

"Me neither," Rune says, chuckling at himself. The boy's gone mad. "I was thinking..."

"You've thought a lot for someone who has been asleep."

"That's when I think the best! Anyway. If you can tap into energies, why can't I distant heal?"

"Aren't you full of revolutionary ideas?"

"Yes! Go to Taylin. Let me toy with this concept and keep a watchful eye on Wylin so he doesn't scurry off. Go while he's asleep. You've got longer legs than me, so you'll cover more ground without me."

I gaze deep into Rune's eyes, desperately trying to gauge his true thoughts. He seems genuine. He seems confident. Nodding once, I stand, I pause...then I sprint.

I ARRIVE at the body of water before dusk, drenched in my own salty sweat and out of breath. I never stopped running, but I covered more ground than I would've with Rune—he was right. At least it was flat terrain most of the way.

"Taylin?" I yell, my body energetically buzzing as I hone into her whereabouts.

She doesn't respond. I can sense she's too exhausted, but she can hear me.

When I see her pale body crumpled in mud on the edge of the water, my heart breaks. I can't believe I even, in a moment of weakness, considered abandoning her.

Hurrying over, I crouch down and transfer my immortality, wishing I could keep a little for myself. My heart is working overtime at the moment.

Taylin's eyes flutter open, her lips pale and cracked, dark rings beneath her eyes. "There's nothing...nothing in the water. No fish. Nothing. Water...like poison."

"Just rest," I whisper, holding her tight, unaccustomed to seeing her so vulnerable. Despite the warm breeze, she is freezing cold. Another night, and we might've lost her. "Just rest."

PATIENTLY, I nurse her, wondering what on earth is wrong with this water and whether there's a way I could filter it. It looks pretty murky and stagnant. Or, we could be allergic to this part of the land regardless of a decent filter. As a mortal, I'm not going to risk it, despite how dry my mouth is.

Taylin begins to stir after a couple of hours when the sun has completely vanished, taking the warmth with it.

"I...tried to find water...like you would've," Taylin says hoarsely.

"You did well," I reassure, sweeping her greasy hair behind her ear.

"I didn't..." She shakes her head, her face twisting into an ugly expression as she holds back tears. "I lost Nellabix."

I forget how to breathe, dreading the answer to my question. "What happened?"

"We ran from the sinkhole. But these, these *things* surrounded us. Nellabix was amazing. She scared a few off, chased some off. I had no weapons. I used my hands to punch, scratch, whatever I could. Another sinkhole opened. I fumbled, I fell...then Nellabix..."

"Did she fall in?" I ask dryly, thinking of the doggans and their love of meat.

"No, no. The creature bit into her neck and three others jumped on her. She ran off, with them on her back. I lost sight as I chased her. I don't know where she is or where she went or if..."

Despite Taylin's grim outlook, there's a glimmer of hope in her story. Nellabix is strong. She is wonderful. She is no doubt out there looking for all of us. I *know* it. I repeat this notion to Taylin.

"I hope so," she croaks.

"What were these things that attacked you?"

"I don't even know. Animal but not animal. There are so many humanoid species out here I never knew existed."

"I know. I can't believe I always thought there were only five due to the corners. We either lived in denial or wiped them from history books. If it's the latter, I can't help but wonder *why*."

"History tends to dismiss anything that is difficult to explain. If it doesn't fit the narrative, it disappears," Taylin says, finding strength within her immortality to sit up. "How did you find me?"

I take a moment to process her story and then give her the digested version of our experience, stopping to answer any surprised or suspicious questions.

"So we need to get back to Rune and Brylin?"

"Wylin," I correct. "The sooner the better, yes."

"I mean, I do feel a lot better. Do you think Rune can truly distant heal?"

I shrug, too tired to authentically care. "We're capable of more than we understand. That's why we need to get going if you feel you can walk. I don't want to miss my chance to reunite with my brother. And I definitely don't want Rune following through on his threat of hurting Wylin. It's been a tense, confusing day."

"It's because you didn't have me there to be the antagonizer. You both tried to take my place. Dynamics were all off."

I force a smile, semi-appreciating her humor, if she actually knew how to joke.

We help each other up and begin the arduous trip back to Rune, each taking turns to carry one another as we stumble through the night.

⚇

WEARY, we arrive a little after sunrise, hungry and aching.

Stunned is an understatement.

I expected Rune to be holding Wylin hostage. Or that I'd find one of them terribly injured. Or most likely, Wylin vanished into oblivion and Rune absentmindedly explaining why.

Prophecies have never been my forte. Instead, I find them both sitting around a poorly constructed campfire, chewing on what must've once been a bird or a burrower. They're conversing amicably, enjoying their disgusting meal.

When Rune spots us, his face lights up. "Taylin! Malin! You're all right! I bet you're starved! We saved some for you." He waves a leg above his head. "So it worked? Did my distant healing work?"

Limping, mostly from exhaustion, Taylin approaches Rune and lightly slaps his hand. "Something worked. You need to fill me in."

He helps her sit as I curl up beside them, groaning as I finally rest my throbbing legs. Rune offers me a piece of breast, which I reluctantly accept. I whisper a thank you for its sacrifice, hating myself for eating it. I wasn't a vegetarian in recent times—you can't be when you're surviving in the wild, but I always wind up with tremendous guilt.

My heavy blinks lull me into slumber, Rune's energetic voice comforting. Taylin was safe. Wylin would soon escort me to my brother. It seemed that maybe there was light at the end of the tunnel...

⚇

"Malin."

Somebody shakes me until I rouse. I scramble up, bleary-eyed and thirsty. Rune is standing and pointing at Wylin who slowly hobbles from camp.

"What's happening?" I ask, my throat sore. Judging by the daylight, they let me sleep until late afternoon.

"He's not waiting anymore," Rune says. "He said come now or not at all."

"That was sudden," I mumble.

"I'm learning northerners are a little manic and spontaneous." There's no malice in his voice, even if his words are rather insulting.

"*Thanks*," Taylin scoffs sarcastically, still sitting. It looks like she's been asleep too, eyes puffy and hair wild. She seems to be in much better shape than earlier, no doubt thanks to Rune.

I call out to Wylin, who ignores me. I wish he'd given me proper notice. I have no idea how long we'll be trekking for, but I must take advantage of this opportunity. It doesn't take us long to catch up to him, as he hobbles through the grass which easily reaches our hips. The blades are annoyingly itchy as I bat them away and pause to scratch at my skin.

"Are you sure you don't want to wait another day?" I ask. "You look like you're in pain."

"We can't wait another minute." He winces. "It's imperative to our survival."

When I press him for more information, he dismisses me with a grunt. Understandably, it's difficult to speak when in pain, but there's a hint of panic in his eyes. It's worse when we make our ascent up a steep incline towards a small mountain. He declines our help, stopping only for a minute to adjust his robe and catch his breath.

"We need to reach the rocks," he says between sharp inhales. "We'll hide behind them."

"Why do we need to hide?" I ask, wiping the sweat from my eyes and longing for something to tie my hair back with. It's well overdue for a cut.

"Later," he says, propelling himself up onto the rocks, my stomach lurching as I watch his weak ankle twist on impact. "*Ow.* Hurry."

We hit a flat surface as Wylin motions for us to join him. Crouching behind the rock, I watch as he massages his ankle, relief flooding his face.

"Stay here for a moment."

"Why?" I ask, lowering my voice.

"Because your brother sent me a message telepathically. We had to leave."

I stumble over nonsensical words, my mind littered with dozens of questions. I try to start with the most relevant one. "What was after us?"

"I think the most accurate question would be, *who* was after us," Rune says, carefully peeping over the rock to look down into the fields. "Friends of yours?"

I join Rune, feeling physically ill at the sight of Dalin and Cheralin riding on the back of a unihorn through the fields. At least they're not on Nellabix.

"They've been tracking me," Wylin whispers. "Not out of love. They don't trust me. They never have, but especially since the incident at the prison, my sister vied for me to be tortured."

A picture of elegance as their robes drape over the unihorn, the two triplets scope the field. They don't have any interest in our current location, instead fixated on the elephantano rock across the water. Cheralin points at it and the unihorn comes to an abrupt stop.

"What are they doing?" Taylin asks.

Practically holding his breath, Wylin frowns, most likely deciphering a mental message from my brother. "Discussing methods to unleash the animal from its stone prison."

"Are you inferring that thing is real?" Rune bounces with excitement.

"Yes and it is the perfect ammunition for those seeking power and control. No cause for concern, though; my siblings don't have the resources currently to do that."

We observe the elegant northerners as they continue through the fields. Once they're far enough away, Wylin exhales. He is overly perplexed, trembling as he leans against the rock to help him stand.

"Are you all right?" I ask gently.

"Tired. Hungry," he replies abruptly. "Eager to get out of the elements. Follow me."

Complying, we follow, anxiously checking over our shoulders from time to time to ensure they haven't spotted us.

As day turns to night, and then darkness fades into light, Wylin only allows short rests. I'm filthy. I'm exhausted. I'm thirsty.

"How much longer?" I ask, my calves throbbing as we continue up the mountain. "We've climbed all day and night."

"Close." He doesn't intend on using what's left of his energy to talk.

I struggle to believe him. He said we were close last night.

Eventually, the ascent levels off and Wylin leads us to the entrance of a small cave. With the exception of Rune, we all duck and pull back hanging vines, cautious not to accidentally thwack the person behind us.

A soft lullaby of distant voices travels through the cave which transforms from a stony cavern into a mossy oasis. Broken stone columns are assembled in the grass, a blue glow lighting the cozy area.

"What is this place?" Rune asks the question I've been waiting to ask.

"Sanctuary." An awe-inspired smile stretches across Wylin's face. "One of many."

He's right. This truly is a sanctuary.

Something about the atmosphere settles my nerves, despite the incessant daydream I have of reuniting with my brother. I envision many variants of him. I picture him exactly the same as he was in my childhood, vivacious and welcoming. But then images appear in my mind's eye of a man turned stoic and cynical, distant and cold. Some scenarios have us hugging and holding back tears, while others depict an awkward encounter, with him barely recognizing me. It could go either way.

"Wylin!" A flinty voice welcomes. A beautiful, curvy woman with lavender hair wanders into the clearing, her locks curling at her waist. I've never seen beauty like this. Thick strands of hair are twisted into roses, the unnatural purple perfectly matching her inquisitive eyes. Her plump lips are the color of her flushed cheeks, and her silky mauve robes accentuate her pregnant belly.

I haven't seen a pregnant woman in a long time. Immortals don't have a biological clock, so it is rare to see a mother have short breaks between children. They can wait a thousand years before even thinking about conception. A twenty-year gap between children is considered very short. When I was on the run, I found myself hiding in villages rife with disease and poverty, so pregnancy wasn't commonplace. Without the north buying all the luxuries of the land, economy suffered.

"Sierra," Wylin greets fondly. "I've brought company."

"I can see." She rubs her stomach, her tone difficult to decipher. Clicking her tongue, she speaks in a language I do not understand. Wylin responds in the same dialect, clicking his tongue and using consonants that are nonsensical.

There's a pause, a moment of understanding and Sierra whistles. Seven other woman appear, each one as striking as the last. They all sport colorful hair which matches their eyes and robes. From deep crimson to vibrant yellow, they looked like something out of a children's book. Their long hair has intricate stylings, from plaits that interlock with one another and weave to create an impossible do, to up-styles that look like crowns and bows.

But the most surprising thing of all? Every single woman is pregnant.

I quickly glance at Rune and Taylin who look equally surprised, but probably not for the same reason. Rune, no doubt, is merely enamored by all the pretty women. Taylin probably can't believe how styled their hair is.

"You must be Malin," Sierra says, stepping forward to greet me. She offers a hand and I accept it, in awe of how soft her skin is. "You're the sister. The good one, we trust."

I don't know how to respond. I've never considered myself good at anything. "I think so."

"May you humor us and share why you're looking so dazed?"

"Oh." I lower my gaze, the heat of embarrassment warming my cheeks. "I'm sorry. I just haven't seen a pregnant woman in a long time, let alone a room full of them."

"Ugh." Sierra rolls her eyes and grunts, half of the women sharing her sentiment while others giggle lightly. "We're always pregnant."

I'm quick to forget my embarrassment. "Pardon?"

"Pain. In. The. Ass. I hate it. The infliction is part of the survival of our species. We're pregnant with ourselves in case this vessel dies. A lifetime of nausea, lightning crotch, pelvic pressure, fuzzy eyesight, sinus infections and ligament pain. I'm often tempted to kill myself just to start over."

"Oh, it's not *that* bad," the one in blue interjects, rubbing her belly and smiling. "I love it. The sensation of the little one kicking me. The happy hormones. The thick hair."

"You're annoying and weird," Sierra snaps back, a cheeky glint in her eyes. "Before you ask, no, we're not technically immortal. When we are reborn, we forget our past lives. Some genetic memories are retained, but we are not quite the same person. The baby is born slightly older than most species, so that it can survive on its own if need be. Mortal newborns are bloody hopeless on their own, aren't they? Our species is young, but capable. If we die in battle, the new us crawls out and grows quickly, starting the cycle over. A cycle of womanly misery and discomfort."

"Drama Queen," the yellow one torments. "Swollen ankles aren't ideal, but it's fine."

"That's because your bump isn't huge," Sierra retorts. "I wouldn't even know if my ankles are swollen. I can't see them. I'm still trying to find a method to give birth without having to die to do it."

"Sure," the yellow one continues. "Go against thousands of years of our kind's evolution to accommodate your own personal vendetta."

"I'm serious!" Sierra's intensity goes from semi-serious to full-blown rage. "I will get this thing out of me. Maybe I can have a mini me. And then I'll be skinny and nimble and you'll all be begging me for help to pick up the things you've dropped."

I have so many questions; questions that may not be well reciprocated given the current tone of the conversation. Fortunately, a curious Rune beats me to it.

He raises a hand. "Hi. I'm Rune. Um, so are you the only ones of your kind? Can you make more of yourselves or a perhaps few at a time? Twins? Triplets? A litter?"

"We are all that remains," the lavender one replies solemnly, as the others fixate their gaze on their bare feet. "If a newborn is killed before they are old enough to carry, then the line dies with them. Only one woman in each generation can reproduce a few before dying."

Her response hangs in the air, the grave implication leaving us in silence until Taylin speaks. "Who was the bastard who killed your kind?"

A bemused smirk twitches on the lavender's face. "We are all villains when war is at hand. I cannot bring myself to hate those who were only defending themselves, even if it means a great loss for our own. All's fair in love and war." She touches her stomach tenderly.

"I've always hated that saying." We turn to face a tall northerner with a remarkable tan, dark ruffled hair and stone-grey eyes. He flashes his incomprehensibly perfect teeth; a feature I don't recall him having before. His clothes are out of fashion with anything from the north, sporting a mish-mash of styles from the central and western areas. His blue shirt has buttons and a crinkled collar, his pants black and tight-fitting. He belongs nowhere and everywhere.

"Leilin?" I ask, unable to control the quiver in my voice.

"It's Leighton now," he says warmly, his brows knitted, and his voice heavy with concern. "Malin? Oh, sweetheart. Honey."

He's at a loss for words as he scrutinizes my body. I guess I'm looking far worse for wear than I realized. As he approaches with his arms outstretched, I find myself bubbling with emotion. Without warning, I burst into tears, finding comfort in his loving embrace.

"It's been awful," I sob, wetting his shoulder. "I've been homeless and starving. And the prison. Lei, the prison was a waking nightmare. I've missed you so much. And Adalin, she tried to kill me. My own flesh and blood. And Nellabix, I don't know where she's gone. Lei, it's, it's—"

"My darling girl," Leilin, I mean, *Leighton*, hums. His hypnotic voice has always soothed me. "I can't begin to imagine the terrors and torment you've endured. Take some time with us here. We can offer a warm bath, fulfilling meals, and most importantly, support. Share with us what you need to so that you can heal from the trauma. I'm here for you now."

I don't get a chance to show my gratitude before I'm interrupted.

"Leighton," Wylin says through gritted teeth. "There's a war coming. We can't enable this. We need to get to it."

"All warriors need rest," *Leighton* replies calmly, stroking my hair. "And soap. Lots of soap."

I laugh through my snotty mess, my last bath having been in the tower at the prison. Prior to that, I genuinely couldn't say. I became desensitized to my own stench.

Lei leads me from the clearing, motioning for Rune and Taylin to follow. Through an archway of vines is a small cave room where a tiny pool surrounded by rocks greets us.

"A hot spring," Lei says. "Please, use this at any time. We'll fetch you food."

"Is there only one?" I ask meekly, not quite prepared nor desperate enough to share a bath with Rune and Taylin.

Lei throws his head back as he laughs. "There's six scattered. Let me take your friends to them. Soak. Relax. Indulge. I'll check on you in twenty minutes."

It's hard to argue with my brother. He enthusiastically pats Rune and Taylin on the back, something Taylin is visibly unimpressed with. They leave me alone with the hot spring, steam dancing above the clear water, coaxing me over.

I need little encouragement. Once I'm left to my own devices, I strip down and step in, the warmth tickling my pores, the water clearing the dirt.

Resting my head against one of the smoother, flatter rocks, I fall into a micro sleep and revel in this brief moment of luxury.

CHAPTER VII

I'm abruptly awoken by my own snore. Snapping my mouth shut, I open my eyes and stare awkwardly at a pregnant woman dressed in black sitting across from me. I don't remember seeing her with the others. She looks older—not in a decrepit way, but certainly much more mature than the others. Her silky black hair is tied up to resemble a crown, her dark eyes absorbing any pigment from her pale skin.

Uncomfortable, I try to shield my nudity with my hands.

"Needn't worry about hiding anything," she says, her amused voice contradictory to her rather intense expression. "Once you become a mother, you don't care about those sorts of things. A breast becomes a tool instead of an asset. It's something you couldn't possibly understand until you experience it."

"Have you ever experienced it though?" I ask, still covering my chest. "Doesn't your kind give birth then die? Wouldn't that mean you've never breastfed?"

Her lips curl into a smile. "I'm special. Each generation has what we call a grandmother. We can birth up to five children to ensure the survival of our species. We do not know how it works, or how one woman is chosen, but it is our evolution. I'm often tucked away, hidden from the world. I'm to be protected at all costs. I'm the wet nurse for any newborns, the provider for our new little people. Underrated and entirely priceless." She sniffs, her tone swiftly shifting. "Your brother suggested I collect you. He thought you'd prefer a woman to intrude while in a vulnerable position. You were asleep, so I didn't wake you. Patience has become my best virtue."

She uses her bare feet to lift my clothes from the ground, dangling it from her big toe. "Should we be concerned about your visit?"

Genuinely confused, I contemplate the answer as I reach for my clothes from the safety of the bath, failing in my attempt. "What do you mean?"

"It was a surprise when your brother, a *northerner*, chose to reside among us permanently. He denied his heritage, changed his name. Now here is his sister, another northerner who we believe to be mortal, joined by an immortal from the central. Corners don't generally mix. Neither do immortals nor mortals. Either the land is in big trouble and you're seeking shelter, or you're here to destroy what's left of us."

"We're definitely not here to destroy you," I reassure. "My brother hasn't told you anything?"

She blinks slowly in response. "It seems not much has changed, then. Your brother pretends to respect us. Clearly he doesn't. Otherwise we would be privy." Sighing, she thrusts her foot up and I catch my dress midair. "My people do not have abilities like the corners. We do not possess classic immortality either. That leads to the incorrect belief that we should be of little value, of little threat, of little use. We don't tend to make the history books. We're second class and can be wiped out in the blink of an eye. So my kind, and various others, hide. Away from the main corners. Away from the ongoing wars, unless we're dragged into them. So my question to you is this: is there a war coming, and are we going to be involuntarily pulled in to fight?"

I'm too tired, too naked and too wet to best respond. "We're attempting to prevent a war. Your other questions can be answered by my brother, I hope."

She lifts her chin and ceases eye contact. "Hmm. Is it true you did not know of our existence until just now?"

I don't know why I'm made to feel guilty about my answer, but my heart sinks. "It's true. Not just you, but other species too. My kind were very sheltered in our wealthy bubble. It's taken homelessness and prison for me to learn of others. I plan to rectify this. If I can ever find a place to call home again, I'll educate myself."

"Don't bother." She stands, shrugging her slender shoulders. "If there is a war, we'll all be dead, forgotten for eternity. A species of pregnant women aren't made to fight. We're made to love. Create. Remind others that life is precious and special. That's something immortals can't possibly understand. How precious can life be when it never ends?" She exits through the vines while still talking, ending the conversation before I have a chance to reply.

I dry myself on the fabric left for me on the side and get dressed, reintroducing myself to the stench. I should ask my brother if I can wash my clothes next.

Outside, Lei leans against a column, narrowing his eyes at the black-haired woman as she storms past him. He attempts to engage, but she's not interested.

"Lei?" I ask in a hushed tone.

Folding his arms, he sighs. "I see you met Greta."

"She's not entirely happy with you."

"What she doesn't know doesn't hurt her." He snorts. "At least, so I thought. Turns out, it's extremely hurtful to learn that nobody knows about your species because you're considered unimportant. What a repugnant notion. This is why I traveled when you were a child. I learned so much about our land outside of our conceited bubble. There are truly magical beings out here who deserve to be heard. I'm writing a book, did you know? Whether it reaches the masses is up for debate though, especially given this climate."

"That's extremely noble," I say, "but what are we supposed to do? About the impending war? About our sister? About the gods?"

"Gods." His eyes seemingly flicker, a wistful sigh escaping his lips. "Ahh. Nothing more than immortals who honed their craft to perfection."

Surely sleep deprivation didn't make me mishear that. "Sorry?"

"That's my belief based on my research. Think about it. Gods are immortal. Gods have incredible powers. Rather than upend any corner leaders, they sailed away to live peacefully."

The strange thing is, it *does* make sense. "A god I spoke to implied they didn't want a war because it would impact their powers."

"Of course, it would. Theoretically speaking, at least. Power comes from the land. Power comes from other beings. Kill the land, kill its people and it'll weaken anybody who has harnessed it to such a high level. We don't know how connected they are. What I have discovered, is the more I use telepathy with Wylin, the more I feel his emotions and any physical distress he may be in. It makes me feel awful. I get tired, I ache, I cry. Times that by a thousand when you're a god connected to multiple people and throw into a war. Intense stuff. It probably wouldn't impact them if they weren't born on this land. That's why I think they were immortals who sailed away. But I could be wrong. We may never know."

Another thing I admire about my brother—he doesn't let his ego get the better of him. There has never been a need for pretense, as he is humbled by how astounding and vast life is. The more he knows, the more he realizes he doesn't know, which only inspires him to find the answer. Even if he somehow obtained the ability to know everything about everything, he'd still proclaim there was something to learn.

It's a relief to see he hasn't changed.

"Anyway!" He claps his hands together. "My former fugitive sister. Fancy a feast?"

"A feast? What is this foreign concept?" I quip, almost salivating at the thought of a hearty meal. "Show me the way!"

Through another archway covered in vines is a long stone table where the women are serving fruit, salad, and servings I don't recognize. Rune and Taylin are squeezed together at the end of the table, both with wet hair and hungry eyes. The woman in black is nowhere to be seen. Wylin is at the opposite end, in fresh clothes and sporting wet hair himself.

Lei leads me to the end of the table, and as I sit, he helps the women prepare. When everybody is seated, we all reach for servings that appease us. Rune grabs one of everything, and I follow suit. Taylin is a little more reserved and picky, scrunching her nose up at various fruits.

I can't believe my luck, swallowing anything I recognize in record time. I'm cautious of the other foods, not wanting an allergic reaction to sully this magical moment.

It's a picture-perfect scene, as we converse and laugh merrily, enjoying the food and the company. It feels like a happy family reunion, which I suppose it is. Having my brother around makes me feel safe and secure, reminding me of my childhood.

I take in my surroundings, forcing myself to remember every sight, every scent. These memories are one in a million. And I want to mentally relive the unadulterated joy for as long as I can.

"I'm stuffed." Rune pats his bulging stomach. "Can't recall the last time I've been spoiled like this. Thank you!"

"You're welcome back any time," the woman in yellow says as she stands to clear the plates. She disappears with the other women, chatting vivaciously and leaving behind a grumpy Sierra who was too nauseated to eat much.

"I'm not moving," she announces, even though none of us thought to ask why she stayed at the table. "The girls thought you'd want a private conversation. I won't listen if that's what you want, but I'm too sick to stand right now."

Lei grins and reaches over to rub her shoulder fondly. "It's fine, Sierra. We have no secrets."

"Greta would disagree," Sierra snorts, tossing her hair over her shoulder. "What happened? She was so filthy she said she refused to eat with our guests."

My heart sinks. I take full responsibility for the delicate exchange with the woman in black. Lei is quick to dismiss the topic. "I'll make amends later. Tomorrow is a new day. How would our guests fancy a comfortable night's sleep? We need you feeling fresh if you're keen to expand your abilities. I predict it'll come in handy."

"How do you know?" Wylin says through gritted teeth, as if we wouldn't be able to hear him. Sitting stiffly, he acts as if we're not around. "You told me yourself; not every immortal has the ability to expand their abilities."

"They don't. But looks like Rune has already learned to heal others and Malin tracked Taylin's location. That's only a few steps off from total possession. They will excel."

My eyes nearly pop out of my head. I must've misheard him. "Possession?"

"Oh, yes," he says calmly. "With the right training and willpower, we are capable of wonderful talents. Telepathy is only level one, and it's no walk in the park. Navigating through somebody's messy mind to get a message across is beyond irksome and tiring, even when you've mastered it. Possession is even murkier than that. I digress. Let's get you to bed."

Lei claps his hands together enthusiastically and stands, helping Sierra to her feet as she curses under her breath. She waddles away with a tense Wylin, while we follow my brother through the vines and a mossy tunnel. Ahead is a fallen marble column, with a large nest made of moss and flowers sitting atop it. I fail to see how it will be as comfortable as a normal bed, but it can't be much worse than anything I've slept on recently.

"We don't have many guest rooms," Lei says with a hint of remorse. "I hope you don't mind sharing. The nest is large enough to comfortably fit five or six people, though."

"We don't mind," Rune jumps in. "Body warmth is always a positive. We're just grateful for your hospitality."

"Good man," Lei says, patting him on the back. "I'll leave you to it. Call out if there's anything you need, but I strongly suggest catching up on sleep."

I step forward, lowering my voice. "Lei, it's Cheralin and Dalin.

They're close. They're working with Adalin and a god to kill me and reclaim the north. Then this prisoner, Zain, he's beginning a revolution to overthrow mortals."

"Hush, little sis." He places a calm finger to my lips. "Tomorrow. Rest now. Feel free to change into the fresh clothing the girls left for you on the side." With a reassuring smile, he leaves us to our own devices. Lavender tunics await us, the clean fabric heavenly against the skin. It must be even nicer for Taylin and Rune who didn't get a change of clothes like I did when working in the tower.

"This is nice," Taylin says under her breath, closing her eyes.

"Right?" Rune is quick to jump into the nest, nuzzling into the middle. "This is actually way more comfortable than it looks!"

Taylin opens her eyes and glances over her shoulder, stooped over. She's been uncharacteristically quiet since dinner. "Malin?"

"Yes?" I mimic her uneasy tone.

"I understand he's your brother and all, but don't you think this is rather peculiar? This set up? Talk of learning how to *possess* people? That didn't sit well with me."

I hate that she has the audacity to question my brother's motives, especially considering how kind he's been.

I hate that there's a nagging voice screaming in the back of my head, only I can't quite hear the words.

And I hate that Taylin might be right.

CHAPTER VIII

Maybe I'm overtired. Maybe that's why I can't sleep. Or maybe it has something to do with Taylin and Greta's comment about my brother.

Or, most probably, it has everything to do with the creepy girl who keeps appearing to me, unbeknownst to everyone else in the vicinity.

"You're back," my croaky voice greets. I'm getting somewhat accustomed to her spontaneous visits. I'm on the far end of the nest, away from a tossing Rune and a turning Taylin. It's as if their bodies never allow them to rest.

"Maybe I never left." She keeps to the shadows, her chin to her chest, pacing back and forth. "You've reunited with your brother."

"Sort of." It's strange how in this moment, I am comforted by her familiarity. She's become an old friend of sorts.

"You have reservations."

"Yes, but that's not exactly a new trait of mine."

"I've noticed." She pauses. "Do you know what you are?"

I contemplate the question. "In regard to?"

"Do you know what you are?" she repeats.

Glancing at Rune and Taylin to ensure they're asleep, I clear my throat as I answer. "An immortal, sometimes? A northerner? A prisoner...even if I'm no longer in a physical prison, I still feel...*trapped*."

"Hmm. So you still label yourself, tying your identity to this existence. It's interesting how you perceive yourself. I'm fading, Malin. I truly don't understand what or who or even how I am. I think I'm dead."

"You can't be dead," I say, perfectly aware that if Rune or Taylin stir, they'll think I'm crazy for speaking to myself.

"Immortals can't die, but I died," she reminds.

"All right, let's say you defied the impossible, and you died at the hands of a god. You can't have an afterlife. Immortals don't have one; it defeats the purpose of living forever."

"Then what am I?" She flickers in the shadows, emanating a powerful sadness. "I want revenge, Malin. I...need...revenge..."

Her words echo as her body dissolves into nothingness, leaving me in the haunting silence.

It's an odd night; a prickly sensation humming in the air. Everything is dreamlike, yet simultaneously weighty with tension. Chilled by the encounter, I scramble out of the nest and sneak outside, where I barge into my brother who looks just as startled as I feel. "Lei!"

"Malin? I heard you talking. Never thought you were one for chatting in your sleep." Slightly amused, he sweeps the hair hanging by my eyes behind my ear. "Are you all right?"

"Did I wake you?"

"I'm a night owl. I was already walking around when I heard you. No need to deflect. Are you all right?"

I pull my lower lip into my mouth, unsure how to address the question. *No, I'm not all right. I haven't been all right for a long time.* However, I presume he isn't asking for my biography. "I saw someone in my room."

"I see," he says slowly. "What color was she wearing?"

"No, it wasn't one of the pregnant girls," I dismiss, avoiding eye contact. He'll think I've lost the plot. "She's been following me. The dead immortal; except she's not dead, because she speaks to me. She only appears sometimes."

I anxiously await his response, his face relatively neutral. There's a small frown, but my brother isn't a judgmental person. If he is, he hides it well.

"Would you say this woman is transparent?" Lei asks carefully, speaking as if he were diffusing a sensitive bomb.

An image of the woman appears in my mind. "Yes."

"So you have a ghost."

The concept eludes me. Ghosts are a work of fiction. Through the darkness, I try to discern his somewhat lax tone. "A what?"

"A ghost. The energy of a person who dies. It's interesting she hasn't converted to the shadows yet."

"Right." I snort indignantly. "Immortals don't have afterlives."

He shrugs, his nonchalance irksome. "Nobody knows nothing. I'm interested in looking into her, though. Inform me when she visits you next, please."

"What do you want to study?"

"How she has avoided the shadow world. Is she a northerner?"

"No."

His nonchalance switches to genuine confusion. "Then how did she die? Only our corner can give up immortality."

"A god killed her."

"Oh." He throws his head back, smiling. "Of course."

He doesn't offer anymore to the conversation, and we're left staring at one another in silence for a moment. "I suppose I'll get back to bed."

"Are you sleepy?"

I consider the question. "Not anymore, no."

"Fancy a training preview? I'm alight with energy. Seeing my little sister safe and sound has me excited for our future."

What future is that? I want to ask. The mention of possession triggered my suspicion. "Sure. Show me."

With an eager grin, he slips his fingers into mine and leads me through a small opening in the mountain wall, down a winding cave which is dimly lit with candles. It's much cooler here, our steps echoing.

"Will we wake anyone?" I ask, cringing at the sound of my voice.

"Not a soul will hear us," he assures, speaking at a normal level. "I get the impression you'll do very well. Wylin has struggled. He can't seem to grasp the basics. But we've got good genetics, don't we sis?"

"I don't know."

"The answer is yes! You're a survivor!"

The cave ceiling gets higher as we continue, tiny droplets of water dripping onto our heads and shoulders. Lei comes to a halt in a circular room, where white circles have been drawn on the ground. I flick a curious glance at them. "What are those?"

"All part of the training. Go stand in the large one in the middle."

"It's not a sacrifice, is it?"

Lei lets out a hearty laugh. It's a shame he doesn't realize I'm serious. "I'm so proud that you managed to track your friend. It took me some time to discover that ability. You are definitely ready for telepathy." He waits for me to awkwardly shift into the circle. "Good. Imagine that circle is your barrier. Build the wall up around your mind. You may feel a tickle itching at your skull. Don't let me penetrate your thoughts."

I await more instruction, but that's it. Building an imaginary wall around me, I falter as an electric buzz tingles at my temples. Distracted, I hear my brother speak, but the words aren't coming from his mouth.

"Fight it, Malin. Fight me."

Tensing, I will my brother away as he invades my mind, clawing at my memories and thoughts. It's a bizarre sensation; like a rodent aimlessly searching through my mind, creating chaos and unease in its wake.

"Get out!" I grunt.

"Concentrate. Frustration won't get you anywhere. I'm almost in your mind. If you can hear me, then I'm knocking at the door. If you don't put up a fight, I'll have access to everything."

The concept horrifies me. I barely know how to manage my own thoughts, so I definitely don't need somebody else in there to muddy up my brain even more. Using the drawn circle as reference, I envision it building up around me, sturdy and impenetrable.

Something energetically flings out of my head, snapping back like a band. There's silence while I keep the wall up. Occasionally I fumble, like holding a sit-up or plank for too long, but I persevere. Even when my brother claps his hands and commends my efforts, I continue to imagine the wall. Just in case.

He notices.

"Well done, Malin! I knew you'd do well. You needn't keep that wall up now."

"It's good practice if I do, isn't it? Like working a muscle?"

"Very true. Would you like to attempt reading my thoughts?"

It's a loaded question. I can't believe how short-lived my happiness to see my brother was. I should be rejoicing and enjoying expanding my abilities with him. Instead, I'm sweating from the paranoia, solely based on two women's suspicions. How can I fault him? He's always been generous. A nomad, sure. But worldly and considerate. And look how smart he is, having figured out revolutionary ways to enhance the way we live. He's nonjudgmental and opting to stay away from the combat, unlike my psychopathic sister.

I've nothing to worry about.

Lei is a good man. He's the best man. He's my brother. Now and always.

Having calmed myself somewhat, I nod in response.

"Great!" Lei exhales slowly. "I'll leave my wall down a little to make it easier. If you ever want a telepathic conversation with someone, you'll need to leave your wall down, but generally it's good to always have it up. You never know who might slip into your thoughts one day. All right, sis. You will have a lot of fun with this. Let your mind go blank. Easier said than done, right? You can't be lost in your own head if you want to go into someone else's. As your mind goes blank, like those moments before slumber, grasp onto any thought that slips into your mind and ride it into mine. I'll think of one color. Let me know if you hear or see it."

His explanation isn't great, but it's worth a shot. Letting my mind go blank is a challenge in itself. The more I force it, the more I think.

"Take your time," he whispers hypnotically. It's that voice of his. That calming, rhythmic tone. As he soothes me, I find myself closing my eyes and reveling in the darkness.

Nothingness. Deep. Dark. Nothingness.

Distance. Layer upon layer of black. Ease. Peace. *Nothingness.*

Through the nothingness I'm tugged into a tight tunnel. Squeezing through, I weave aimlessly into a spiraling abyss. Sometimes I stick to towering walls. Other times I hurdle over every barrier. It's a mess. A deep, dark mess with no end and no beginning.

But there's something behind me. A voice? Or a light? No. A *thought.*

Ocean. Big, endless ocean.

Blue. Blue. Crashing waves. Sky. Blue.

"Blue," I croak, not recognizing my own voice.

My eyes fling open and I see Lei standing a little closer to me, nodding.

"I'm impressed. Did you see it or hear it?"

"I *felt* it."

His mouth parts a little. "That's...*very* good."

There's not one moment of celebration. I jolt like I've been psychically hit.

War. War. Control. Power. Leading. She's a good soldier. Take over. Together she'll help.

Something snaps shut in my mind and I fall backwards onto my behind, my mind reeling over the powerful words.

Lei stands over me, brow furrowed, his voice even. "A novice's error. I forgot to put my wall back up."

I scramble to my feet, simultaneously scared and heavily disappointed. "Lei...what did I just hear?"

"I don't know. What *did* you hear?"

War. War. Control. Power. Leading. She's a good soldier. Take over. Together she'll help.

The words repeat, verbatim, on a loop over and over in my mind. He's no different from my sister. He might not necessarily be a killer —that's not his style. But he has power unlike the north has ever seen. If he can possess people and manipulate them through thought, goodness knows what he's capable of on a larger scale. And he is under the wrong impression that I'll support him.

"Nothing." I swallow hard. "It was too muddled."

"Mmm." I don't know if he believes me or not, so I quickly build my protective mental wall. No way will he penetrate my thoughts. "That can happen."

In this moment, I'd much prefer the starvation and abuse in the Immortal Cells compared to the guilt I'm experiencing now.

One day. I couldn't have *one* lousy day to enjoy Lei? To reminisce? To feel safe for the first time? I had to jump straight to paranoid and suspicion?

"Well then!" Lei disrupts my thoughts. "You might be ready to attempt possession. Word to the wise: it's extremely unpleasant. Perhaps you could practice telepathy on your friends first. Don't tell them what you're doing until you want more of a challenge."

"That sounds like the ultimate invasion of privacy," I respond with little tact. "Why can't I keep practicing on you?"

"Because I've grown weary." He forces a yawn. "It'd be unfair for both of us. Why not see if you can hear your friend's dream? That's always interesting. Somewhat off-putting too, as you're listening to the subconscious. What you hear, see and feel will make little sense."

"I'm not going to invade their dreams without their consent." I puff out my chest, as if that will somehow give my statement more conviction.

"Suit yourself." His nonchalance is enviable. "I admire such a pure quality. It reminds me of the grace and etiquette our kind possessed. I hold such a resentment for our past that it's easy for me to dismiss their good traits. Thank you, Malin."

"Lei, wait. If I'm mortal right now, how can I utlize this ability? Is it tied to immortality?"

"It's part of the northern charm. You can give up your immortality but it doesn't change your right to power. A runner may retire, but they will still be a good runner. Now come on."

He leads me out of the strange space, his pace much quicker than before. We don't speak on the way back. Careful not to disrupt the others, he hangs by our guest entrance until I've snuggled into the large nest. He bows slightly and disappears.

Head spinning, I don't think I sleep a wink.

CHAPTER IX

When I was a child in the north, I often had trouble sleeping. It was especially troubling when I'd hear birds chirping outside, despite the darkness. It was that grim reminder that night had come and gone, and my chance to heal and recover had slipped away. There's something nauseating about everyone else having the chance to rest; feeling complete and ready to take on a new day, while you were still somehow caught in the past.

It wasn't a bird that sent a sickly sensation throughout my body this time, but more of a crowing cry. There were no windows in the rocky mountain, yet I imagined it wasn't quite dawn yet.

Slinking out of the nest for the second time, I pull my tunic back on and walk outside. A cold breeze tickles at my arms, goosebumps popping up against my skin. The ground is icy against my bare feet—something I've grown used to after living in the cells.

I return to the edge of the mountains, far away from the mossy, serenity caves. The sun teases the horizon, barely glowing against the dark purple blanket above. Hunching over, I sit on a rock and stare. My eyes are puffy. My blinks are slow. And I can see the air leaving my body when I sigh, reminding me just how cold it is.

I am at a loss. What am I to do? Can I trust my own brother? Is he just as bad as my murderous sister? Could I run away from them now? Fashion a boat and leave everything behind? It's beginning to feel like my only option.

"Aren't you cold?"

I turn to look at what I've come to learn is the ghost, who keeps close to the wall of the mountain.

"You look cold," she adds when I don't respond. "Not that I can judge for myself."

"You're much nicer than you used to be," I say, keeping my eye on the sunrise. "When we first met you were angry at me."

"After following you, I'm learning you're not the one I should be angry at. You may have inadvertently been the reason for my death, but you weren't the cause of my death." She pauses. "Your brother says I'm a ghost."

"You heard that?" I peer at her from the corner of my eye as she steps closer to me.

"I feel safer around you. It's like I'm real if you're nearby."

"What happens when you're not near me?"

"It goes dark," she says. "Really dark. And I'm hit with a bout of amnesia. In the pitch black, I listen for your voice and I can fight my way through to find you again. It takes a lot of energy to project myself to you, but I'm still around even when I'm concealed."

My lips curve into a small smile. It's a selfish concept, but I like not being the only lost one. "What is your name?"

"I can't remember." Her tone is sad, but her face appears angry. "It gets harder each day to recall my physical life. It's much worse when the darkness comes."

I contemplate my response, staring at the sky as the cool colors fade and a warm hue stretches out to replace the night. "My brother said to inform him when you speak with me next. I'm not entirely sure how I feel about him at the moment, but he might help you. Would you like me to ask?"

When she doesn't answer, I turn to find her.

She's gone; but apparently not *really* gone; merely unable to continue projecting herself to me, at least for now.

"Let me know," I whisper. "Tell me what to do."

Alone, but apparently not truly alone, I gaze at the sunset, its warmth only numbing me more. It moves swiftly, hanging high in the sky before I know it. Perhaps I should return to the others before they think I've absconded into the night.

I go to pull myself up, stopping when a stout man below in the fields merrily whistles. It's a bizarre sight to behold. You don't see many roaming alone outside of a village, and they certainly aren't as chipper as he seems to be. It's a dangerous land—for mortals and immortals alike. You only travel solo if you're on the run.

I flinch when he spots me, as he waves his arm high above his head.

"Hello!" he yells, teeth showing. He chuckles to himself as he ascends the mountain with ease, blowing his dark hair out of his eyes. He doesn't appear to be deterred by the weighty pack on his back, climbing towards me without a care in the world.

Fight or flight? Fight or flight? I can only seem to freeze.

"A mighty northerner!" He doesn't adjust his volume as he approaches. "How wonderful to see one out in the wild!"

I can't work out which part of the land he's from. His skin is bronze, hair dark, body short and wide. It's as if he's gathered attributes from various corners.

"Needn't look so troubled," he says, accurately reading my expression. "'Tis my scheduled monthly visit organized by your kin."

"Lei?" I ask, working up the courage to stand upright as he nears.

"A nickname, I presume? Yes. The northerner who pretends not to be a northerner. Are you Malin or Adalin?"

"Malin," I respond carefully.

"Ah, the good one!" He wipes his brow. "That's a relief. We foresaw two outcomes during my last visit."

His demeanor is suspiciously pleasant, but I dislike the way he acts as if he is an old friend. I know nothing about this man, and now he's talking about me appearing in a prophecy? My fear shifts to frustration.

"Who are you?" My tone is forced and comes across more aggressive than I intended, however this doesn't seem to upset him.

"A wanderer. I change my name dependent on where I travel, but your brother knows me as Detri. Ensure to roll the 'r', otherwise it can cause offense as the name closely resembles a profanity in some dialects. It doesn't concern me, though. I personally am fond of a curse here and there. A curse of the obscenity variety, not of evil incantations. Have I digressed? Did I answer your original question?"

I'm not sure. He has a clever way of changing the topic. Carefully, I repeat his name. "Detri. What is your purpose?"

Attempting to multitask, I mentally creep into his thoughts to get a better gauge on him.

"In life or in regard to my visit?" A cheeky glint sparkles. "I sell dreams to people."

"What sort?" I probe, sneaking into his mind.

"Good, bad, predictions, visitations to other worlds. Whatever you need. Whatever you want."

Good, bad, predictions, visitations to other worlds. Whatever you need. Whatever you want.

"Uh-huh," I reply absentmindedly, confused by the echo. He is thinking precisely what he is saying.

"Needn't read my mind, Malin."

Needn't read my mind, Malin.

"I hold no secrets," he continues. "I say it how it is. That's why your brother trusts me."

I say it how it is. That's why your brother trusts me.

He shoots a smug expression, seemingly proud to have trumped my doubts. I release some tension in my shoulders and relax. But only a little. Is it wise to trust someone when they trust someone you're unsure of?

"Tell me more of your occupation," I demand, then cringe. What an odd way to word that question.

Amused, Detri shifts the pack on his back. "I'm paid to create dreams. You'd be surprised how many suffer from nightmares."

"How do you do that?"

"It's a gift. Can't say how, can't say why, but I've possessed it for centuries."

I blink. "You're immortal?"

"Oh, yes. Guards leave me alone when I offer free dream predictions. Turns out I've got the one ability they find useful."

"How are you paid?"

"Through accommodation, food, secrets." He smiles. "Jewels, company, whatever is readily available. I enjoy a nomadic lifestyle. When you're immortal, it's tricky staying in the same place. Would you agree?"

"Yes. Mostly because guards spend their lives tracking me down."

The lack of sympathy he shows is painfully obvious. "I wager you lust after a life where you can stay in one place, surrounded by those you love. Would you be interested in purchasing a dream to see if this is a viable wish?"

"No," I reply after a short pause. "Those who live in the past are depressed, those who live in the future are anxious. I'm already feeling both of those living in the present, so I don't need to add to it."

"A noble answer." He claps his hands together. "Right. It's almost time to break my fast. Is your brother up and about?"

Before I respond, I backtrack. "Can you theoretically locate others in a prophecy dream?"

"Absolutely. Who did you have in mind?"

I think of Nellabix. It's not like I can zone in on her location like I did Taylin—I never shared immorality with her. On the other hand, I have nothing to give Detri. No jewels, no accommodation, no secrets. I get the feeling that his nice-guy attitude wouldn't go as far as charity work.

"Nothing," I mumble.

He nods and taps his nose. "Got you. Let me know when you're ready to do some business. Don't mull over it for too long though—I only stay for a day." And with that, he brushes past me and leads himself up the mountain towards the others.

"Excuse me?" I yell before he disappears into the rock. He turns before I even finish the sentence, seemingly pre-empting the query. "My brother. Is it breaking confidentiality if I ask what dreams he is buying?"

"Breaking confidentiality? Absolutely. But I'm aware my visit coincided with you learning how to unlock the barriers of anybody's mind, so it would be redundant if I tried to keep the secret from you." He waits, continuing when I don't answer. "Your brother is a good man. A little sly, a little strategic, but overall a good man. He has confided that his dreams involve him ruling the land...as a god."

My stomach turns over. This doesn't sound good.

"That's not possible," I say through gritted teeth, unsure whether it's a question or a statement.

"Anything is possible. Dreams are fickle though," he dismisses, turning his back on me. I suppose he doesn't want to waste time on somebody who isn't a client.

I sit down on a slanted rock, my knees pressed against my chest. Lei mentioned his theory on gods being nothing more than powerful immortals. Considering the intense mental training he's been practicing, it could very well be the path he's chosen. But ruling the land? He never showed much interest before. Or was that because he was never in line to rule the north? What if he's far more power hungry than I ever realized?

Unable to summon the willpower to stand, I remain seated; nothing more than between rocks and a hard place.

When my stomach grumbles, I allow hunger to overcome anxiety. As I stand, I smile when Greta appears, hand in hand with a young girl similar in looks.

Greta has a strained look on her face, her steps slow and calculated.

"Are you all right?" I ask as she nears.

She doesn't respond straight away. Her whole face tightens, her free hand pressed into her lower back. "My body is readying itself for birth."

My heart skips a beat. Birth is a dreadfully dangerous procedure from where I'm from and something only skilled northerners are equipped to handle. Many mortal northerners died giving birth, and many immortals suffered great discomfort and injury. Frantically, I search for something sharp.

"We mustn't panic," I say, *panicked*. "Um, do you have any knives? Sterilized? I've only heard of stories and not witnessed how it's done, but I can try."

Her eyebrow raises. "What are you talking about?"

The poor girl must be in a state of shock or denial. Firmly, I lock eyes with her and lower my voice to help execute the seriousness of what I'm about to say.

"We need to cut that thing out of you."

The little girl gasps and Greta chortles. "No. She will pass through naturally."

"Through where?" My eyes widen. "Surely you don't mean... Greta, it won't fit."

"Yes, yes she will. See my daughter? She's living proof of it. Don't tell me northerners can't have a child without intervention?" Her gazes drops to my hips. "Oh. The narrow pelvis. I see. Regardless, I have a few days left before delivery."

"Days?" I repeat. What an odd process. "That sounds awful."

She shrugs and smiles lovingly at the little girl. "The gain is worth the pain. Are you joining us for breakfast? Everybody is wondering where you are. Detri is showboating as usual, talking nonsense about dreams. Always out to make a sale."

"You don't believe in what he does?"

"I believe what he does is valid, it's the ethics behind it. Prophecies are for fools and cowards. We make our own path, period."

Something about Greta's words settle my nerves. Swiftly, I stand, reminding myself that no matter what path I carve out for myself, the choice is in my own hands.

CHAPTER X

A glorious feast of fruit lays across the table. There's a quiet chatter as everyone reaches for their meal of choice.

I note Taylin sitting slumped over next to Lei, who is murmuring something in her ear. She looks sickly, pale, defeated. It's only when she sees me that her eyes brighten and she sits up straight.

"There you are!" she almost shouts. "We thought you'd left!" Her excitement is out of character. Lei slowly glances at me, and if it weren't for the knowledge of the mental barrier protecting his inner thoughts, I'd attempt to invade them now—not that I could do it without more training and Lei's guidance.

Detri is doing precisely what Greta forewarned—detailing embellished tales about dreams his clients recently purchased, confidentiality be damned, using sweeping arm gestures as he speaks. Wylin and the pregnant women are enamored, hanging off his every word.

"It astounds me the amount of upper-class civilians who request lustful dreams. It's so monotonous! Whatever happened to scaling mountains made of cocoa or soaring through the atmosphere?" He takes a bite out of a thrandy—a lavender citrus fruit which makes my eyes water—and continues speaking with his mouth full, chewed pieces of fruit flying everywhere. "They're usually adulterous dreams, too."

Sierra is enthralled, leaning forward to hear more. "Tell us who!"

Lei notices us lingering near the table. He waves and indicates at spare seats across from him. We squeeze in, shoulder to shoulder. Taylin stares at me, as if attempting her own telepathy to communicate with me. I consider entering her mind, but decide against it. She'd kill me for breaking her trust like that.

The inside of my skull itches, my skin tingling. Instinctively, I imagine an energetic barrier and the sensation subsides. I'm unsure whether Lei did it deliberately to get my attention or whether he was sneakily attempting to read my thoughts.

"Had a chance to practice much?" Lei asks nonchalantly amidst the chatter.

Taylin darts her eyes back and forth, trying to make sense of the question.

"No," I reply carefully, hovering my hands above a selection of fruit. "Although I notice you practice regularly."

"Once you're aware of the feeling, you'll always notice when a visitor knocks. Most never realize."

Taylin frowns. "Is this some weird sibling code?"

"Yes," Lei and I say in unison

"Well, it's rude." She tosses her short hair and focuses on breakfast, sneering at the selection. She has confided that she is more of a meat lover, despite the stigma.

Greta grunts, her eyelids pressed tightly together.

"Are you all right, mamma?" The little girl places a tender hand on her mother's, her round eyes softening with each word.

"I'm fine, sweetheart," Greta responds through strained gasps.

Lei, annoyingly a little too laidback given Greta's condition, picks at his fruit. "If I recall, you had a silent labor with your last one." He motions at the little girl. "Are you feeling the onset of contractions?"

"A silent labor?" Utterly disgusted, I turn to my brother. "Did you *force* her to give birth in *silence*?"

He doesn't get a chance to respond, but the corner of his mouth twitches.

"No!" Greta almost laughs. "It means I didn't feel any pain. This labor is certainly different, but there is no cause for panic."

"A vast distinction compared to the north, eh?" Lei redirects his attention to me, his gaze cool. "Apparently birth can be extremely calm and even beautiful in various corners. It's nothing but gore and distress in the north. Goes against our elegant reputation, but it's our dirty little secret."

"One of many secrets, I'm sure," Greta says under her breath. "I'm tempted to purchase a dream from Detri to reassure myself that it'll be a healthy birth, but now I'm unsure if I'll last the night before she arrives. It's been quickening."

"You know it's a girl?" I ask.

"It's always a girl," she says, gently patting her daughter's head. "The last child I birth will most likely take over my role. When they reach my age, I will die and theoretically be reborn as her first child."

"You know for certain you'll be reborn?"

"Nothing is certain," she says with a hint of doubt. "But it is what we tend to believe. Belief staves off fear."

A truer sentence couldn't have been uttered. I feel as if I live in constant fear, which only hinders my ability to do anything. Fear of failure, fear of loneliness, fear of pain...a life lived in fear is barely a life lived.

Rune stumbles out from our assigned guest room, hair rustled and arms stretched over his head. Yawning, he plops himself next to Taylin and reaches for the fruit.

"I'm starving," he announces, blithely unaware of the newcomer. "How did everyone sleep?"

"What's sleep?" I attempt to show my mirth, but it only comes across as bitter. "I suppose it'd be useless purchasing a dream if I don't sleep."

"I wonder if I can heal insomnia?" Rune queries almost to himself, stuffing his face with fruit. "Lei; is that a thing?"

"Anything is possible," Lei responds, the words almost becoming a catchphrase. "Healing is a tremendous ability, so we can certainly explore the many avenues."

Excited by the concept, Rune nods eagerly and nudges an awkward Taylin. "Can born mortals learn these abilities? I feel bad about this one. Surely she might learn something?"

Lei blinks slowly, his eyes focused on his slender fingers that are entwined with one another. "Born mortals have no ability. That said; Taylin is an interesting case."

"Is that because I keep sharing my immortality with her?" I ask.

Taylin flinches, keeping her eyes down, and hands in her lap. It's as if someone absorbed all the sassiness out of her personality.

"Sharing certainly adds to the equation," Lei finally says. Seemingly bored, he twists in his seat and joins the conversation between Detri and the other women, leaving Rune, Taylin, Greta, her daughter, and me in our own bubble at the end of the table.

Desperate to find an excuse to leave the table, I dramatically clear my throat. "Excuse me. I have reflux from all the citrus. I'll need to walk around."

"I'll keep you company!" Taylin swiftly jumps up, knocking the table with her long legs, disrupting the conversation.

Lei smiles somewhat smugly, but doesn't object. I hurry towards our guest room, Taylin's breath in my ear. When we're out of earshot, I turn to face her. "What is going on with you?"

"We're related!" she splutters.

I half laugh, half snort. I suppose all northerners are related in the same way all southerners are related. She preempts my rebuttal, sucking in her lips as she shakes her head.

"That's not possible," I finally say. "My siblings and I never had children. My mother was an only child. The rest of my family died in the battle. If they happened to escape, I feel confident they didn't reproduce. Besides, you're mortal."

"Your brother said he slept with a mortal northerner! He's my great-great-great... I'm unsure how many generations there are exactly, but he's my grandfather! He didn't specify *when* he defiled a mortal. I was too perplexed to ask. Maybe he's my grandfather. Oh mercy, what if he's my father? I never met mine!"

"No," I gasp. "That was strictly forbidden. Mortals and immortals were encouraged to not reproduce."

"Since when have rules ever impacted your brother?" She rolls her eyes then checks over her shoulder. "I get the impression it wasn't a pre-conceived conception. I'm just worried he thinks he has some entitlement over me now."

"I don't think so," I say unconvincingly. "Besides, there's no way to prove it. Nothing but conjecture at this point."

Taylin hesitates. "The dream man confirmed it, apparently."

"Conjecture," I repeat. "Trust me, Taylin. Nothing will come of this. As lovely as the thought is to have a great-great-something-great niece, I can't make sense of it. Don't waste too much time overthinking it."

Slightly mollified, Taylin exhales shakily and pulls herself together. "You're right. It means nothing. Just interesting history. Or interesting fiction."

"Exactly." I smile, glancing over Taylin's shoulder as Lei approaches. "This reflux certainly is bothersome."

"Huh?" She checks my gaze. "Oh, right. I heard those pregnant ladies suffer from it a lot."

Lei stands between us, the picture of grace. Not a strand of hair out of place, not a crinkle in his clothes. He would have made a perfect king.

"Am I interrupting anything?" He doesn't wait for a reply. "Malin, I'd like to invite you to additional training. It could distract from your reflux."

It was a lousy excuse, and he reminds me by making note of it. Never have I met any northerner who suffers from reflux; it was a condition I'd picked up on over the years in hiding. Caught out on a pathetic lie, I shield my embarrassment with a cough and another fib.

"All that new fruit I've not come across before. I must be having a reaction to it." I clear my throat again to make the lie semi-believable but his expression tells me he isn't buying it. Sighing, I nod. "I'd love to train and spend time with you."

"Marvelous!" He claps his hands together and rubs them. "Taylin, enjoy the feast! We will catch up with you again momentarily!"

Politely waving her off, he throws his arm over my shoulder and leads me back into the depths of the mountain wall and towards the cramped training arena.

"What a busy morning!" He energetically twirls in the circle. "I do thrive off guests. Detri is a tremendous individual. Knows how to put a smile on my face."

"He mentioned he visits regularly." I reluctantly step into the circle opposite Lei.

"Absolutely. I'd be lost without his prophecies. I bought a few dreams today. I sense I'm going to need them."

"What did you buy?" I give him ample time to respond, but when he doesn't, I chime in. "A dream to confirm Taylin is your descendant?"

"Ha!" The boisterous laugh doesn't suit him. "Didn't take her long to share that news. You two are thick as thieves! But yes, it's true. It seems our immortality trait didn't trickle down the line. Congratulations though—you are officially an aunt, as old as you are!"

As cliche as it sounds, a shiver runs down my spine. Why doesn't the news sit well with me? Is it the airiness of its delivery? Is it because no matter how hard I try to escape my past, I'm always faced with an aspect of it? Is *that* why I saved Taylin when she was faced with certain death? Did I feel an unknowing desire to protect my own flesh and blood?

"It was confirmed months ago," Lei continues when I choose to remain silent. "In the dream, I mean. I saw you coming. It was inevitable." His shoulders rise. "It's a little chilly down here, wouldn't you say? Mind if I light a fire?"

He turns on his heel towards a dark corner. There's a wide, uneven gap chiseled into the wall that I hadn't noticed earlier. There are a few branches and flint inside. Lei quickly scrapes the flint with his pocket knife, causing a spark. A bright blaze soon follows. The fire is green with a violet haze—an odd mix.

"Always important to feed the fire," he says, throwing another branch into the blaze, which gulps it down immediately.

I stare at the fire, flashbacks of my time in the tower in the Immortal Cells.

Always feed the fire...feed the fire...

I'd throw blankets, food, rugs...any resource I had to ensure it never went out. It was apparently a life source to the god Sharnique, who had tremendous power, but drew on the elements of our land to wield it.

"What's that fire for?" I gulp.

Genuinely confused, Lei's eyebrows rise. "To...keep us warm?"

"And that's it?" I ensure. "Why is it a strange color?"

Lei shrugs. "Not my area of expertise but probably something to do with the level of oxygen down here. Why are you so concerned?"

"I'm not," I deflect. This is awful. I shouldn't distrust my brother like this. How did we even get to this place? "Lei, I'm so sorry. I think the whole Adalin situation has tainted my feelings towards you. I can't trust my own family. I'm paranoid you're secretly in on some absurd plan with her. You couldn't begin to understand. I'll never get that image out of my head. She tried to kill me, and she would've succeeded had Taylin not slyly swapped out her immortality with me. There was *nothing* in her eyes when she stabbed me. Pure venom...perhaps even pleasure."

"I'm sure there wasn't plea—"

"—it was," I interrupt, reliving that moment. "I can't believe it. I never stopped to think about it. She was *enjoying* it. Adalin covered it with noble sorrow, as if she was doing the *right* thing...but it was a game. How could she resent me that much?"

"She resents everybody," Lei reassures. "I'm sure that doesn't particularly help your situation, but take comfort in the fact that it's nothing personal. She's a maniac. I caught wind of her thoughts about me; attempts to permanently trap me in an abyss of sorts. Who would've thought she yearned for power that much? Sickens me. Our own flesh and blood. It hurts. I'm so sorry you went through that, sis. Truly, genuinely sorry. It's been a tough road for all of us, but especially you. I wish we could've found each other sooner. I had no idea about the exile until the north had already collapsed."

I hesitate, taking a brief moment to appreciate how raw Lei sounds. There's no showmanship, no charisma. He sounds like the brother I remember.

Shrugging off the mention of exile—and feeling far too vulnerable to delve into *that* painful subject—I motion at the fire. "Help me trust you again, Lei. Something isn't clicking with us and you need to help me. Tell me why you have that fire down here."

His face suddenly doesn't look so chiseled, so confident. Shoulders rolling forward, he gazes into the fire, the light reflecting in his dark pupils.

"It *does* help me." His voice is barely above a whisper. "I researched it, Malin. The fires feed into our abilities if we nurture it correctly. Now it's part of me." A dark shadow forms over his eyes momentarily. "I need it to live and it needs me."

I can't control my brows as they knit together. "What does that mean?"

He speaks with such precision, as if it's the first time he's thought about it. "It's like making a dutiful deal with a deity. I don't believe that immortals have souls, but if we did, it'd be akin to splitting our soul."

My legs ache from standing for so long, so I kneel in the circle, weakened by the revelation. "Why? Why would you do such a thing?"

"Power." He laughs without humor. "Maybe I'm more like Adalin than I care to admit. I've obsessed over various techniques to enhance our abilities in the event of a war. Nobody tells you how addictive it is. No wonder they wiped it from the history books. It must've caused more trouble than it was worth. And you know what has been driving me crazy? How quickly you took to it. No doubt I'm a great teacher, but within the hour, you learned how to tap into a mental vault."

"Not really," I humbly dismiss. "It's hard, *really* hard and I don't have the desire to do it again."

He draws his gaze away from the fire and finally sets his sight on me. "See? That's another thing. You don't crave it. You don't yearn for it. Maybe you will eventually. Or maybe you're just different. You never fit in with us. I didn't either, but I could pretend if I needed to. You could never pretend."

"Life's too long to pretend," I say, considering standing again. "What is your role in the uprising? Wylin said you wanted to hide away, but I suspect that's not true."

"It's true sometimes." He pulls something out of his pocket and tosses it in the fire which blazes happily. "I've been accused of being a liar, but I'm not. My story and opinions simply change when I'm presented with new information. That's why I ask Detri to help me so often. A revolution is happening whether we want it or not. The last three months have depicted the exact same prophecy which won't be changing anytime soon. Wylin's siblings will find the water people and use their power to free the beings trapped in stone, controlling them and using them as ammunition against their enemies. Adalin and Zain will join forces, releasing the immortals and torturing the mortals. They will marry, not for love, but for convenience to bring the north and the east together, building a large and powerful empire. Mortals will be slaves and we'll be back where we started." He sighs. "This is why I need to get involved. It's why I need you and Rune and Taylin. I don't want to live in a world like that again and I'm sure you don't either. With these mental techniques, we can foresee and prevent their attacks, their strikes."

"And what about possession?" I ask stiffly.

"It's the easiest way to ensure victory, is it not?"

"It is. But ethically..."

"How can we discuss ethics in war? What *they're* doing is unethical. We're simply fighting fire with fire." He glances at the flames licking against the wall. "You can hide away, Malin and I won't judge you. This doesn't have to be your fight, but we need you.

You're the rightful heir to the throne. Seeing you stand for the mortals could bring peace to the land which it so sorely needs. If an immortal princess fought for mortal rights—"

"—I fought for their rights lifetimes ago, and look where it got me," I interrupt.

"It was a different era. I promise it'd be different now."

"Then *you* rule!" I flick my hand petulantly and fold my arms.

"What? A man? You know how they'd feel about that." Glum, he runs his fingers across the mountain wall. "I can't force you into anything, and I wouldn't want to. You've always run your own race."

It's difficult to discern whether his remark was a compliment or an insult. Lost for words, I reluctantly stand and brush my tunic off, desperate for him to say *anything* to fill the silence.

My wish is granted when he clears his throat. "Has your ghost friend been about?"

I consider the question. She never had the chance to say if she felt comfortable with me telling him more information. Careful to respect her, I shake my head. "Haven't seen her since. Maybe it was a dream afte—"

Something slams into my body, a cold sensation worming through my insides until I'm numb. Paralyzed, my vision tunnels while my brother stares at me, deep in concentration. His mouth moves, but I hear my voice.

"You forgot your mental barrier, sis," I say.

In horror, my hand lifts and wags a disapproving finger. I fight as hard as I can, envisioning a mental barrier but it's too late. He's already in.

"Once you're possessed, there's little you can do about it," I say as panic sets in. He makes me march on the spot like a soldier.

Violated, I try to swing my arms towards him to fight. I attempt to shout, scream and yell obscenities. But nothing can be done. My body belongs to him.

I gasp for air as his thoughts are vacuumed from my body, allowing me to voluntarily collapse to the ground and regain control of my now heightened senses. He approaches me and I scrambled backwards as he throws his head back and laughs.

"See, sis? It's that easy! To your feet. You'll block me this time. Then you'll enter me. Come on."

Cautious, I stand with my hands at the ready. I'll strangle him if I need to. He only rolls his eyes.

"I'm not out to get you. Get your wall up. Now."

I obey, feeling a heavy gust of wind pulse by my forehead. My brain feels as if it's throbbing against my skull as I use every ounce of willpower to push him away. There's no way I want to be his puppet again.

"Well done, Malin! Such a fast learner! Take a breather...and when you're ready...I'm coming once more."

CHAPTER XI

The sun has almost set by the time we exit the training room. It's remarkable how quickly the time passes. We hadn't eaten or drunk anything since breakfast. I feel mentally shattered, every emotion suppressed and every humanly desire diminished. I just want to sleep.

Lei, on the other hand, seems as energetic as ever. "I best spend time with Detri before he settles in for the night. He tends to leave early in the morning. Do you need me to escort you to your room?"

"No, thank you," I manage to croak. To the naked eye, I more or less stood in one position all day, but I may as well have run several marathons.

He gives me an affectionate kiss on the cheek, a gesture which feels unnatural, to say the least. Turning a corner, he pulls back vines and mysteriously vanishes to his cave.

I blindly find the way back to our guest room, stopping when I almost run into Detri who is leaning against the mountain wall.

"Evening," he greets. "It's nice to see you and your brother spending so much time together."

"Not by choice," I reply bitterly. "Should I be concerned that you're waiting outside of my room? Er, I mean, cave? I don't know what to call these things."

"You're the only individual here who didn't purchase a dream."

My eyes flutter in disbelief, thinking of Rune and Taylin. What could they have possibly given him in return?

"I'm broke," I say seriously.

"You're stubborn," he retorts with a smirk. "As fate would have it, I had a dream of my own." It's only now I realize I'm holding my breath as he reaches into his satchel and pulls out a small, jagged crystal. "It was a prophecy detailing the importance of giving you your own dream. I couldn't piece all the details together, but I've handed fate to you."

He places it in my reluctant palm, watching as I turn it over and over. "How does it work?"

"Place it under your pillow while you sleep."

"That's it?"

"That's it. Be aware that it only works once. The crystal merely becomes a souvenir or memento after use."

Suspicious, I attempt to hand it back, but Detri doesn't budge. "What's the catch?"

"My fate is tied to yours. *That's* the catch." Voice uncharacteristically stern, he meets my gaze. "Don't run away from destiny. We all serve a purpose. Some more than others."

He doesn't wait for a response before he turns on his heel and whistles a familiar tune to himself. Immortals, I've discovered, are either extremely patient or incredibly impatient. There is very rarely a middle ground.

I tuck the crystal into my tunic for safe keeping, reluctant about using it. I've no idea what kind of power it draws on to induce prophecy dreams, and I don't know if I trust it. It could very well be a manipulation tool.

Inside our guest room, Taylin and Rune are cross-legged and speaking in low tones.

"Malin! You've been gone all day!" Rune speaks the obvious, but he seems happy to see me.

"Not by choice," I say. "There's been a lot of talk and a lot of training."

"And I noticed Detri gifted you a crystal," Taylin says slowly, scrutinizing my body language. "Did you give him anything?"

"No, it was a gift." I wait. "What did you give him?"

She shrugs. "I told him Lei is my great-grandfather. He laughed and said he knew that secret. Then he said he was privy to a secret I was yet to discover, so he gave me this. He said he'll add it to Lei's tab, whatever that means."

Rune reveals a transparent, round crystal in his hand. "I offered produce when I return to a farm one day. He was very pleased with that. Said he'll definitely make good on that. I like him."

"You like everyone," Taylin mutters and I snort back a laugh. "Malin. Tell us about your brother. Where do we stand with him?"

I inhale shakily, sitting down beside them on the leafy bed. "Neutral, for now. Leaning slightly towards ally again."

It's only as I speak that Lei's sentiment echoes in my mind.

My story and opinions simply change when I'm presented with new information.

The excuse comforts me, reminding me I'm not a liar or a fraud. It's simply a wait and see.

Taylin says something but I don't hear her. I'm already drifting into a deep slumber...

It's BEEN a lifetime or two, a memory long forgotten.

Surrounded by impressive marble structures, I marvel at the complexity of the architecture. Tall statues of my family tower over the northerners in the courtyard, accessible through the jeweled maze.

The majority of dwellings are two to three floors tall, with open balconies designed to overlook the view of the distant mountains and the coastline. The sea breeze cools my flushed face. Despite the peaceful, idealistic atmosphere, my blood is boiling.

I loathe my pristine robes, my bedazzled tiara, my *everything* as I watch my father speak from the throne. The commoners have gathered to listen.

Masculine despite our kind's androgynous look, his golden eyes match his locks. Wearing royal blue robes, he exaggerates his troubled expression.

"Dearest northerners, you understand this time of year is never my favorite. To sacrifice a mortal, albeit a noble deed, is still a tragedy. As always, we accept volunteers before selecting a civilian at random."

I shudder at the thought, keeping far away from the crowd. I don't want to listen, but I can't seem to escape his booming voice, no matter where I am.

"As our daughter, Malin, is next in line for the throne, she will perform the upcoming sacrifice. Perhaps that knowledge will guide reluctant mortals into their choice. Imagine going down in history as the first sacrifice for our next ruler!"

I swallow the bile rising in my throat and curl my fists. My father has another thing coming if he thinks for a *second* I'm going to kill an innocent being. Desperately trying to suppress my rage, I climb the marble stairs that lead to the crystal road outside of the city, ignoring the commoners' hateful stares.

"I thought you were one of us, Princess Malin," a mortal child says meekly as I pass her. Chagrined, she wipes the tears from her big eyes.

"I am," I say through gritted teeth. "I will not sacrifice any of you. I don't believe in it."

Before the little girl can respond, her mother furiously shields her with her body, as if under the impression I would kill her then and there. Rolling my eyes, I continue down the road until I'm free of the scrutinizing stares. Inhaling deeply, I stand in the middle of the road and consider my options. I don't want to make a public display but I won't let my father speak for me. He will go ballistic when I confront him, but it might be the only way. Unless I run away like my brother...but where would I go? I know nothing of the outside world.

No, that's not an option. There's nothing outside of the north for me. I simply have to stand my ground.

"Princess! What are you doing on the crystal road?"

Lost in my thoughts, I realize how odd of a sight it must be for me to be standing in the middle of a road predominately used for trade.

Standing before me are two men from the east, a feature I've come to recognize by darker complexion. They aren't carrying bags or pulling a cart, but their sandals are worn and covered in dirt. They must be messengers.

"Two of you?" I ask, surprised. "Do messengers usually travel together?"

"Treacherous roads of late," the one with intense eyes says, his voice silky. "Mating season. The animals are particularly predatory and territorial. We've been advised to travel in pairs to ensure the messages arrive safely."

I've never heard of such a thing, but it must be true. I wouldn't know what was going on beyond this road if it weren't for messengers. "How awful. Can I pass the message on? My family are somewhat busy."

"Yes please. There is a rumor regarding mortal leaders; talk of an uprising against immortals, or even imprisonment. Nothing substantial yet, but the mortals need to be kept in line. *Perhaps more sacrifices*, is what they're suggesting."

"A lot more," the intense one adds. "Mortals are irrational and wild. With shorter lifespans, they make decisions based on emotion. We can't let this rumor come to fruition. They're foolish little oxygen thieves."

The other immortal does well to contain his displeased grimace. He isn't on the same page as his passionate colleague. "We are simply the messengers. Will you pass this onto your father please?"

I pause, presented with an interesting opportunity. The messengers should know better than to entrust someone else to deliver their message. It is quite insulting to be asked to do their job for them. On the other hand...it is rather flattering to help them with such a big favor.

"You want to deliver the message, don't you?" The intense easterner repeats, his charismatic tone difficult to ignore. I feel like I don't want to let him down.

"Of course," I blurt. "I would be delighted."

For some reason, the reserved immortal looks somewhat repelled by the intense messenger and I can't understand why. Perhaps there is an underlying issue between them.

"Would you be so inclined to rest in our traveler's quarters?" I continue. "We provide beds made from the softest fabrics and water from the finest streams."

"Yes please!"

"No, thank you."

Their words overlap one another as they exchange firm glances.

"We have many messages to deliver," the serious one finally explains. "We appreciate the gesture, but we must leave. Many thanks to you, Princess Malin. We wish you all the best. See to it."

Turning on their heels, they leave, squabbling with one another in hushed tones down the crystal road.

What an odd exchange. Regardless, I feel compelled to keep my word and share their message with my father. Striking up a light jog, I turn and run back towards the city. It's only as I reach the crowd once more that the haze of the easterner's instruction begins to clear.

No. I'm not going to tell my father that other corners are thinking of increasing mortal sacrifices! He doesn't need that validation!

"Father," I shout from atop the stairs. The commoners all turn to look at me, my father's confused face mistaking my anger for eagerness.

"Malin! Wonderful, would you like to address the crowd?"

"Ideally I would like to speak to you in private, but the people have a right to know that I do not support or stand by mortal sacrifices. It is not something I will be taking part of, so please stop misinforming the public."

Audible gasps and intrigued whispers. I watch my father from afar, his face glowing with rage. If he were mortal, I'd fear a fatal heart attack.

"You are all dismissed," my father demands. He is known for his temper, but only within the family. To most, he is stern, but calm.

The commoners would never suspect him to raise a hand to anyone... but I know better.

Standing my ground, I watch the crowd disperse, shielding my face from those who bow at me. Most seem skeptical of my stance and merely frown instead, avoiding my presence.

When the throne room has cleared, my father motions at me to join him. Reluctantly, I stride towards him, determined. I will *not* surrender.

"Yes?" I ask, with a sense of rebellion.

"*How dare you*," he spits, his low voice trembling. "You have humiliated me. Shamed me. Disobeyed me."

"How dare *you!*" I correct, my own voice quivering. "I've told you I don't want to kill anybody, and you refused to listen. You have no right to throw your beliefs onto me."

"It is not a belief, it is a way of life! You are a princess and future ruler! If you do not continue the tradition, there will be pandemonium! Absolute chaos! The mortals will band together and there will be an uprising! The time of immortals will come to an end! There are more mortals. Their genes are recessive, dominant. Ours are not! We are an endangered, albeit superior species. We must see to it that our kind continues to rule. We know better."

"I'm not disputing any of that," I argue. "I'm disputing the need to kill mortals to maintain power."

"Cease with the verb 'kill'. It is a degrading, vulgar term. Sacrifices must be made."

"I will use the word kill, because that is what you are doing."

My father doesn't respond immediately. He inhales after remaining perfectly still for an eerily long time. "If you will not abide by our lifestyle, then you must leave."

Frowning, I scope the throne room, decorated in gold. "As in, I leave the palace?"

"The north," my father says. "I have spoken to your mother about this. You have been relentless in your ongoing attempt to defy your family. We can no longer have you representing us, *endangering* us."

I roll my eyes at his dramatic perspective. "I just want peace."

"We *have* peace *because* of the sacrifices! The instant we pretend to be equal is when we welcome war. Everybody wants power. Everybody thinks *their* way is the right way. We know better. I had *hoped* you knew better. Perhaps it is youth. Perhaps you aren't ready for the throne."

"That is one thing we agree on; I don't *want* the throne—not if this is what is expected of me. And if you sincerely wish for me to leave the north based on my beliefs, then so be it." Part of me is bluffing. I have no idea what to expect out there. I can't survive on my own. I don't know how to cook. I don't know how to find shelter. I don't know a single thing. I've never even accurately read a map. So why does an even larger part of me want to leave this prison for good?

"Go." My father remains expressionless, emotionless. An outsider would conclude that we were nothing more than strangers conversing.

My eyes flutter. "Pardon? To my chambers?"

"No. Go. Leave. Get out of my sight and leave the north this instant."

I can't bring myself to move. The direction is so incomprehensibly cold that I fail to do anything beyond stare vacantly.

"Now!" My father's shouts, snapping me out of my trance.

Lightheaded from anxiety, I don't think to pack belongings. No map, no food, no blankets. I'm too distraught to think clearly, under the assumption I'll be back soon. There's no way my father would cut me off like this. No farewell, no negotiation. It's nothing more than a scare tactic.

With this in mind, I remind myself to breathe. I'll play into this ridiculous game. It won't be long before he sends the help out to retrieve me and apologize for his actions.

Emboldened by this prophecy, I storm out of the palace, through the courtyard and down the crystal road. I continue until it transitions to dirt and find a large tree to relax beneath. The city is about a twenty-minute walk away, but I can see the taller buildings from here.

This will do nicely. I'm safely in the confines of the north, even if I'm near the outskirts. The weather is quite nice and I could do with the alone time. My absence will certainly cause concern within the palace walls. Adjusting my position, I use the opportunity to meditate and watch the sky.

When twilight hits and I find myself still sitting alone, my stomach flips. Why hasn't my sister come looking for me? Or my mother? Do they know what just transpired? Has my father lied to them? Or do they not care?

Thirsty, hungry, and caught in a web of despair, I brush myself off and stand. It's late at night now. Nobody is coming for me. My attempt at bluffing didn't work. When I return, I'll apologize for my puerile actions.

Walking sheepishly towards the city, I frown at the red glow growing betwixt the buildings. What could *that* be? The glow spreads across the city, as a thick, dark cloud rises. As I watch from afar, I gape at the fire smothering my home as muffled screams sound.

A mortal family sprints towards me; a mother and her two young children covered in blood and ash as they escape the disaster.

"What happened?" I shriek.

The mother glares at me and without warning, she spits at my feet. "Dirty immortal! We're sick of your kind controlling us!"

Suppressing my contempt for her revolting gesture, I speak calmly. "Please, miss. The fire. What is happening in the north?"

She snorts. "A war. My husband hung back to fight. There were rumors of it coming, but it happened suddenly. Mortals ambushing immortals. Trapping them. Putting an end to these sacrifices once and for all. Now back off, heathen, and perish with the rest of them!"

Pushing past me, she disappears into the night.

This is my fault. I should've warned my father after the messengers warned me. And the way I spoke up in front of everyone...was that small action enough to encourage enraged mortals? Staring at the flames engulfing the city, I consider hurrying back to help, but at what cost? I can't fight. I can't kill the mortals out of self-defense after declaring I wouldn't sacrifice them.

My...my family will be fine. We're immortal, after all. This will all blow over. It has to.

And yet I feel physically ill, unable to purge an empty stomach.

But it'll be all right...it'll be all right...

Hardly believing my own ignorant lies, I turn my back on my home, too guilt-ridden to mourn the loss of everything I've ever known.

There's nothing here for me anymore...

CHAPTER
XII

An animalistic grunt startles me awake.

Sandwiched between Taylin and Rune, I shake off the vivid dream and drag myself out of bed to follow the sound.

It doesn't happen again. Instead, controlled breathing reverberates outside. Following the mountain wall, I peer through a veil of vines into the bathing room. Sitting alone in the hot spring, gripping the edge with her eyes closed, is Greta.

My chest tightens at the mortifying scene. I've stumbled into a tragedy.

Her eyes spring open, glassy and tired. "Malin?"

"You best get out of there," I say, unable to cover my distress. "The baby will drown."

She's too tired to laugh, a breezy sound coming out instead. "It's a water birth, Malin. Babies don't breathe until they're exposed to air."

The thought confounds me, so I push it aside. "Do you need help? Should I get somebody?"

"No, I'll be fine. The babies shoot out pretty quickly and the water keeps us clean." Her eyes squeeze shut, her breathing slow and forced. "*This. Hurts. More. Than. Before.*"

Awkward, I linger by the entrance, unable to assist, but unable to leave. It seems immoral to wish her luck only to head straight back to bed. Perhaps I could find one of the others. I'm beginning to understand that their kind (amazingly) don't require medical intervention, but it'd be nice to have a support person.

"Can I fetch any pain relief?" I blurt. "The north used a flower. Or an herb. What was it? Maybe it was honey berries? It was definitely something to do with honey."

"No intervention, it disorients the baby," she grunts, another wave of pain hitting her. "Ugh. *Ugh.* She's closer. She's coming."

"Rune!" I shout. "Rune can help with your pain!"

"It's nearly over. It's nearly over," she repeats, her face twisting into controlled concentration. "Two pushes. Two pushes. Wait for the wave. Wait for the surge."

I'm freaking out. What am I supposed to do? I don't want to *see* anything, yet I'm morbidly curious.

Clenching, she groans as she loses her grip in the bath for a moment and slips backwards. I rush over to help from behind, holding her still in the water so that she doesn't float up awkwardly. My long body remains out of the water while I lean in to keep her steady. I can't believe I'm doing this. At least my view from this angle is hindered for the most part. Curse my sensitive ears and light sleeping—why did nobody else wake up?

"You can do this," I cheer nervously. "Just keep breathing. You're doing so well."

"I'm glad you're here," she confesses. "Thank you for holding me."

"Are you sure you don't want me to find anyone else?"

As if by magic, Lei slips inside, hair ruffled and with one eye open. Light sleeping must be a genetic trait of ours.

Surprised by my presence, he opens both eyes. "Oh, goodie. I haven't missed it. Way to go, nurse Malin. Greta, are you coping?"

"Peachy," she says between deep breaths. "This is the one. She'll be out with this push. Lei, come catch her."

She may as well have asked him to pass the salt. I've never witnessed a northerner so nonchalant about birth. Calmly, he rolls up his sleeves and joins us, bending over to dip his arms into the water. She loses control for a moment, her legs floating to the surface as she bears down, so I use all my strength to hold her.

With one rather elegant grunt, Greta's prediction proves accurate. A tiny baby shoots out like an arrow, straight into Lei's arms who tenderly gathers it up and out of the water. He instinctively passes the baby to a relieved Greta, holding the newborn close to her chest.

I'm in awe. This was nothing like the horror stories from the north. It was peaceful, it was magical, it was...beautiful. No herbs to relieve pain that caused severe intoxication and at times, poisonous side effects. No cutting, no fear, no nothing. I envy such a vision, and in a brief moment of weakness, long for one of my own.

"She's perfect," I whisper, gaping at the newborn's face. I mean, she's ugly. The crying face is puffy, scrunched up and covered in mucous—or whatever that substance is—but she is still stunning. Life was formed right before my eyes and it gave me a bizarre sense of hope for the future. "What are you going to call her?"

"Maybe I should name her after you! Thank you for being here for me." Greta's voice is breathy, but full of gratitude. "I would've—"

She trails off. Face frozen, she pulls the baby from her chest and stares in horror.

"What?" I ask. "Is everything all right? What? *What?*"

Greta swallows. "It's a boy."

Relief floods my system. "Oh, phew! I thought it was something bad! How exciting; a boy!"

"No." Her tone darkens, leering at Lei. "You son of a bitch. What have you *done?*"

The accusation seems a little unjust. Sure, it's normal for a woman to resent a man during such a painful process, but this was a little left field. I consider jumping to his defense, but decide to wait for his response. When he doesn't say anything, I step in.

"What happened?" I ask. "What's wrong with a boy? Why are you blaming Lei?"

She's shaking and refusing to so much as look at her baby. She aggressively hands the slimy boy to me, who begins to sob once he's away from his mother's touch. I've never held an infant before, and I'm convinced I'll break him, but I keep him close as Greta stands in the water, towering over Lei.

"You promised nothing would happen!"

"Nothing did happen," he responds coolly. "I don't understand what the problem is."

"The *problem* is I birthed a boy! A *boy*! Sleeping with you tainted the bloodline! We create our own children without a male's contribution! We birth girls and that's *that*. Males are not made! You've selfishly, singlehandedly destroyed our kind!"

"I think you're being overly dramatic..."

"I'M NOT BEING DRAMATIC!"

The baby screams and I gently cup my hand around the back of his head, keeping him close.

Prickled by the hysterical scream, Lei lowers his voice. "If that's the case, allow me to hold my son."

"No! You're not going anywhere near him! He's a threat! We'll need to dispose of him!"

"What?" I ask, cuddling the newborn. "Are you insane? He's an innocent child."

She turns to me, teeth bared. "Don't speak of things you know nothing of! I'm responsible for creating new life to ensure the continuation of our kind. What are we supposed to do with a male? Who knows what kind of threat he will be?"

"Men aren't evil," I say through gritted teeth. Alongside mortals, men have fought for many years in the north to have equal rights. Women were always chosen for the important roles and were revered. Men in the past have been second-class citizens and I won't stand for history to repeat itself. "He's your son!"

"That *thing* is not my son," she hisses, pointing at Lei. "He ruined everything! He knew what he was doing!"

"No I didn't," he counters calmly, exchanging a concerned glance with me. "I didn't know this was possible."

Using the little mental energy I have left, I knock on Lei's barrier.

"*What do we do?*" I ask telepathically, lowering my own mental gate. "*We must protect the baby.*"

"*I dreamed this. I'm afraid there's no happy ending here.*"

Greta climbs over the rocks, searching for a loose one. "I'll let you decide what is more humane, Lei. Smash the rock over his head or toss him over the mountain. I don't care either way, but if you don't do it, I will." She finds a smooth rock and shoves it into Lei's hand. Turning over her shoulder, she stares at me holding the baby. "Don't get attached, Malin. That thing is a crime against nature."

With a threatening glare, she leaves us alone as the baby sobs into my chest. I desperately try to console him, tearing off part of my tunic to wrap him. The poor darling is soaked.

I instinctively bounce up and down, gently patting his bottom. "Gee, Lei. Are you trying to be everybody's father or what?"

In a state of shock, he stares at his son. "I genuinely thought it was impossible. They've always grown their own children."

"How about we just assume anything is possible? That's your philosophy, right?" I breathe a sigh of relief as the baby settles, nuzzling in close. "What do we do? We're protecting him, right?"

Lei doesn't answer.

"*Right?*" I repeat shrilly.

"He *could* be a threat."

My jaw drops. "Are you kidding me? How could this baby be a threat?"

"I don't know!" Lei's arms flail above his head in a distressed huff. "We don't know what this kid has inherited! He's an unknown anomaly!"

"No. You know something. What did your precious dream reveal?"

Paler than usual, he cracks his knuckles. "So much power, Malin. It was a little blurry, but I believe I witnessed him killing immortals. He's dangerous."

"Power doesn't automatically equate to danger. Lei, this is your son and my nephew. Why aren't you protecting him? You're punishing him for something he hasn't done yet—or may never do! They're just dreams!"

"These dreams haven't led me astray yet." I hate that he is more protective of those stupid purchased dreams than his own son. "We spoke about this, Malin. There's a war coming."

"We never spoke about killing your child!"

"Don't say it like that..."

"Then how should I say it? That's what you're proposing, is it not?"

"I'm not proposing anything."

"But you're not objecting, either! What will it take to save this baby?"

And that's when it hits me. The only person willing to free this poor child is me. Lei comes to this conclusion at the same time.

"You've always championed the underdog," Lei mumbles, defeat spread across his worn face. "If you're going to take that child from here, I can suggest a place where he is less likely to abuse his abilities."

"I won't take him anywhere you'll be privy to."

He shrugs. "So be it. Be prepared for some hardships. This child was a mistake, and he could mean the end of us all. If you want to be the cause of the downfall of another corner, or *all* of the corners, then that's up to you."

He may as well have thrust a knife into my side, his words more painful than anything physical I've endured. "I did the right thing, even if the outcome was wrong."

"And you're doing it again. That's just you, Malin. That's just you. Don't say I never warned you." He slowly follows after Greta, leaving me with a sleeping baby nuzzled in my chest. What am I thinking? I don't have the capacity to care for a newborn. How can I feed him? Maybe I can convince one of the others to help. Theoretically, he should age relatively quickly before settling into a youthful, immortal body—but as Lei said, we just don't know what he will inherit. He might be mortal. He might take years before aging into a toddler. It's a genetic gamble.

I need to get out of here.

Ensuring the baby is bundled up, I sprint to my room, concerned that if I don't hurry, someone might take him away from me.

"Rune! Taylin!" I hiss. "Wake up! We need to leave!"

"Dreaming," Taylin mumbles, eyes squeezed shut. "Let me finish my dream."

"It's an emergency!"

Rune springs up, one eye closed and the other squinting. "Who needs healing?"

I hadn't thought of that. I glance down at the baby, who seems fine, but I figure a courtesy heal couldn't do any harm. Without wasting another second, I turn the baby around in my hands, fumbling awkwardly.

Rune frowns. "What's that?"

"A baby," I say.

"Where'd that come from?"

"Greta. The baby is my nephew."

"Greta's your sister?"

"No, Lei's my brother."

"So how is that your nephew?"

"OH FOR CRYING OUT LOUD!" Taylin springs up, daggers in her eyes. "What is with this man? He gets around! *And* you've ruined my dream!" She composes herself. "Why are you sneaking around with a baby?"

I bring the baby closer and allow Rune to quickly heal him, just in case. Whatever he does, it settles the newborn. "They want to kill him because they suspect he's a danger to immortals. I can't let them. We need to leave."

It's only now, in the safety of my friends that I allow the tears to stream down my cheeks, my speech peppered with sobs and gasps.

A softness comes over Taylin. "Oh, Malin. What do you need? Do we need milk? When are we leaving?"

Grateful for her eagerness, I wipe away the tears. "Yes, we need milk. And we need to leave straight away."

"On it!" Taylin leaps up and runs out. I have no clue how she plans to source milk, but if anyone can do it, it's Taylin.

When I spot the reluctance on Rune's face, my heart sinks. "Rune? You're coming, right? You promised me in the Immortal Cells you'd always be here for me. Remember? Tell me you remember!"

His lips suck in as if he's tasted something sour. Very timidly, he shakes his head. "I'm learning so much here. My healing ability is only growing. Imagine what I could do with another week. Another month. I could heal anyone with any injury. Think of the mortals I could save, especially if there are casualties in this revolution. Your brother knows how to teach extraordinarily well."

"Family first," I say through gritted teeth. "We *need* you, Rune."

"I know, but I can heal you from afar."

"How will you know if we need it? Besides, how far is far?"

"I don't know," he says after a pause. "That's what I want to learn. My goal is to heal multiple people at one time and to heal proactively. Wylin says it's possible, and that your brother is constantly discovering new techniques to tap into our abilities."

The image of the fire flashes in my mind's eye, causing my stomach to churn. "Don't merge with the fire, Rune. I don't fully understand it, but my instinct tells me to stay away. It strengthens your abilities, but it seems to be a weakness, too. It's not worth it."

He cocks his head to the side, not grasping the concept. "Do you have to leave this instant? I'm positive we can talk it over."

Remembering both Greta and Lei's insistence, I shake my head. "This boy needs to be far away from them. Rune, can't I convince you? We may never see each other again if you stay."

"You know how you need to protect that baby?" He smiles sadly. "I know I need to do this. For the greater good."

"I'm tired of the greater good," I say, pressing my cheek into the baby's head. "There's no such thing."

Rune shrugs, outwardly disagreeing. "What's his name?"

Startled by the question, I glance down at the baby and examine his features. With a full head of hair streaked in blonde and black, his chubby face matures before my eyes. Love sweeps through my bloodstream as I hold my tiny nephew. I'm partially scared to name him anything in the event I'm unsuccessful in our rescue. I tell myself it'll be easier to mourn someone with no name, but as he yawns, I conclude it's far too late for that. I'm hooked. I'm devoted. I'm already perishing the very thought.

"Diarmuid."

"That's interesting..."

"I'm not naming him after any corner's tradition. He's unique and deserves a unique name." My stomach flips. "I can't believe I'm doing this."

Rune places a tender hand on my shoulder. "I believe in you. I'm going to heal you from afar, all right? I'll become the best healer I can be and find you. Then we can live together as a happy family!" His smile isn't sad this time. "I saw it in my dream. This is the best decision I can make. Promise. And I remember that first night in the cells with you. I am *always* here for you. Even when it's not physically, I am with you always."

Taylin bursts in, a bottle of milk miraculously in hand. "Got it. Let's go."

"How..."

"Sierra. Between ranting about how much she hates pregnancy and its unpredictable side effects, she filled this bad boy up in no time. Should last a few days. Come on." A tiny, uncharacteristic smile spreads across her hard face as she locks eyes with Diarmuid. "That's cute. Is he hungry?"

"Probably, but let's get out of here first." I hesitate. "Sierra? Did you tell her why you needed milk?"

"She already suspected. Greta told her about Lei, so Sierra had concerns about the implications. She agrees we should protect the kid, though."

The words of encouragement validate my decision, even if I feel nauseated by it. Why does the right thing feel so wrong?

I catch a glimpse of my transparent friend, standing by the

doorway. She nods once before fading once more, and I hold back tears as Taylin takes me by the hand and pulls me away from a somber Rune, who waves longingly. Despite his promise, I can't help but get the nagging feeling it's the last time I'll ever see his enthusiastic face again.

It's only now I notice Taylin carrying a woven satchel over her shoulder, a woolen blanket peering over the top.

"I grabbed leftovers, too," Taylin says. "I've been thinking about leaving this place since the minute we arrived. We'll have food to keep us going for a little while, and blankets for the night. No more huddling into one another clutching at our growling stomachs."

I've never been more appreciative of the grumpy mortal.

As I'm dragged through the darkness, our feet slap against the ground which has cooled to the point of freezing overnight. Doubting my choice, I consider reasoning with Lei and Greta once more, and glance back.

"Don't even think about it," Taylin warns, sensing my reluctance as we run. "Come on."

"I don't know where we're meant to go," I whisper, my throat tightening as I hold back hysterical tears.

"I do."

Her confident words come as a surprise, but they're enough to keep me powering through. Leaving the weaving, tiny sanctuary and exiting onto the mountaintop, we waste no time scaling down. The poor baby's head bobbles as I slide down the rocks. It hasn't been a great introduction to life.

Once we reach the bottom of the mountain, reunited with the expansive, open field, I regret absolutely everything. Maybe it's not too late to go back. I can give the baby to Taylin and run back to Rune and Lei. But what would that do? There was nothing left for me there. I always considered Rune and Taylin my adoptive family, but it turns out that Taylin and Diarmuid are my literal family. We must stick together now, no matter what.

"All right," I begin, covering the quiver in my voice with a cough. "Where are we supposed to go?"

"To Nellabix," Taylin says, the warm words lighting the abyss I feel I'm drowning in. "That's what I dreamt about. She was my responsibility, and I lost her. Now, we're going to find her."

CHAPTER XIII

Between intensive training, internal conflict, rescuing a newborn, and absconding into the night, I haven't taken the time to truly appreciate the revelation of Taylin being my distant relative.

As we navigate through sharp blades of grass that reach our hips, and wildflowers that tickle my fingertips, I'm filled with a gratitude and love I've not felt before. Together, we are a real family protecting one another through thick and thin.

Taylin is marvelous with the baby. She constantly checks to see if he's warm or if I need a break carrying him. Every two hours on the dot she makes us stop so that he can drink the tiniest of portions from the bottle, but he seems bigger by the minute. Maybe my arms are just tired, but I struggle to hold him after each feed.

"Do you think Rune is practicing healing us?" I ask. "I cut my thumb on a thorn an hour ago. There's no mark now."

"He's dead to me," she dismisses. "Staying in that cult? I'm livid."

Stunned, I replay our last encounter with him. "You never said goodbye."

"Nope. When I heard him say he was remaining with the psychopaths, I cut off. Selfish jerk."

I go to defend him, but it's redundant. Taylin is pretty adamant about her feelings. "I've been trying to work out if the baby is your brother or not."

"Nephew, I think. It's been annoying me too. The family tree for immortals must get messy." She looks over her shoulder. "Speaking of messes, how's the little man?"

"Asleep. Smiling, so he's happy."

"Smiling at that age means wind."

Mildly disappointed by that news, I choose to ignore it and decide he's happy instead. "Did you have much to do with babies?"

"Yes." A fond smile curls on her lips, her tone lightening. "Women always brought their babies into the seamstress. I hid out the back as you know, due to the whole northern stigma, but whenever a client was either ignorant or unfazed by our history, they'd allow me to babysit while they shopped. Or I'd do the measuring for the baby's clothes, so I could cuddle and play with them. I loved every single one of them. Wanted seven of my own but I've long suppressed that dream. What man or woman would want a tall, grumpy outcast like me?"

I instinctively extend Diarmuid to Taylin. "Please, have a cuddle!"

"Keep walking," she says, her sternness returning twofold. "I will give my all to that gorgeous little man when we are safe. For now, we're sitting pluckles out here. I'm being as vigilant as possible. If you can manage, you should keep a mental ear out for enemies."

I hadn't considered that, but she's right. By tuning in to any passerby from a distance, I can decide if they're friend or foe. Drained but determined, I push out my mental reach, scouring the land for any sign of life. Over time, I tend to lose the will, but I push it back out again.

As days pass, we take turns resting in the field and feeding the little one. Milk is running low as he grows at an alarming rate; squirming and crying more regularly for a bigger feed.

"What do we do about food?" I ask. "I don't even know if he's immortal or not. What if he dies from starvation?"

Taylin scoffs, motioning at his chubby arm rolls. "I'm more concerned that his cranky growls will alert enemies. I can almost guarantee that kid is immortal. No mortal child grows a couple of months' worth in a couple of days. I mean, I wish they did. They're more fun as they get older."

Warmth radiates through my body, giving me a burst of renewed energy. I know not to mention Rune in front of Taylin, but I thank him, even if he can't hear me. He may not be with us, but he's definitely looking out for us.

"Does this mean he'll be on solids soon?" I ask hopefully, concerned about our milk supply.

"Solids that are mashed, yes. We can try that tomorrow."

Taylin continues to discuss the game plan, but I've blocked her out, too invested in the mental voice...*voices*...tickling my mind.

"*...searched every skerrick of water...maybe they don't exist after all...maybe this is a distraction...ugh. Does he have to breathe so loudly?*"

"*...she is so bossy...cynical...has to be around here somewhere...I saw the tracks...*"

I pull on Taylin's hand and she drops into the grass with me. I let the baby suckle on my knuckles, keeping him oblivious to the danger while he's in a placid mood.

"Enemies?" Taylin mouths.

I nod. "Wylin's siblings."

I can't discern how near or far they are, but the implication is they've been spending time near water. There's a small lake about an hour's walk from our current location, so they could be anywhere in that radius.

"What are they saying?" Taylin mouths again, a hint of fear in her eyes. She's currently mortal, having swapped with me last night when I opted to skip dinner so she could eat more of the limited rations.

I relay the information as it comes to me, wincing every time Diarmuid slurps loudly on my hand.

"What do you think?" Taylin asks. "The water folk? Are they here? Can we find them first? Is it even worth it?"

"I think so. They have the power to release anything from stone. That massive rock elephantano. Sharnique. Even if we don't participate in the war, we can't let anyone else have that sort of power." I inhale. "I'm going to go. If you can stay here with Diarmuid, maybe I'll find the water folk and state our case. Or at least convince them to not fall victim to anybody else's wishes."

She nods in agreement. "It feels like the right thing to do. Can you keep in touch with my inner thoughts to ensure I'm all right?"

"That's a given. Don't forget that Rune is consistently sending healing ener—"

She raises a dismissive hand. "I don't want to talk about him."

"I'm just saying, you'll both be safe out here. I won't be long."

"Take as long as you need. Just make sure you come back."

The statement startles me. I daren't ask why she thinks I *wouldn't* return.

I stare longingly at my baby nephew, already guilty about leaving him, even if I know he's in safe hands. An irrational part of me thinks of Taylin losing Nellabix when she was left alone, but those circumstances were out of her hands. It won't happen again. She'd die before she'd allow anything to happen to Diarmuid.

"I'll be back before nightfall," I promise. "No matter what. If you need to move from here, just keep projecting loud thoughts. I'll find you."

We hug, and I use every ounce of willpower to tear myself away from an oblivious Diarmuid. Turning my back, I deliberately don't look over my shoulder to check on them because if I do, I won't be able to leave.

It's an uncomfortable stealth pose, but I keep low to the grass, my back throbbing and my face itchy. But like any immortal discomfort, I remind myself that this is only temporary. Everything is. Everything except for my disturbingly never-ending life.

Approaching the water, I'm met with nothing but the quietness of the still lake. The siblings must be gone. I reach the shore and tickle the water with my toes. It's a slight chill, but nothing uncomfortable. Closing my eyes, I focus.

Nothing, of course.

I step further into the water so that my ankles are submerged.

No voices.

I go further until I'm up to my waist, flinching at the cold. What is it about the stomach that takes the hardest hit when it comes to cold water?

When nothing happens, I consider giving up. The water folk clearly aren't here. As I turn to leave, an inner voice stops me.

What if I can't hear underwater thoughts if I'm *above* the water?

It's worth a shot. Building up the willpower, I bounce up and down and force myself to submerge. The cold is jolting at first, but I'm quick to adjust.

"It's another one of them. Must be a war or a trend or a treasure hunt. Been a while since anyone's come looking for us."

"Shh. This one's different. Feel that tickle at your head? It's trying to read minds."

"Oh frebble, what? Not a god, is it?"

"A god-wannabe more like it. Ugh, it's in. Stop talking, stop thinking, stop doing! It'll find us."

"I'll alert the others!"

And as quickly as I found them, the voices cease. I remain underwater, a little stunned. Kicking off, I return to the surface to breathe and tread water. The good news is they were *definitely* nearby. The bad news is I probably *won't* be able to speak with them.

I consider turning back to inform Taylin, but I know exactly what she'd say. She'd say get back in the water and finish what you started. And she was right.

Inhaling a big gulp of air, I submerge again. I'm dreading it. Sure, I'm not going to die, but I'll definitely drown. Returning to land will be painful as I bring up copious amounts of water. The burn will last for days. So will the cough. But hopefully Rune's distant healing with negate most of the negative side effects.

I swim as quickly as I can to the bottom of the lake. It's already eerily dark and getting colder by the second, but I persevere. There's nothing immediate in my line of sight, even as I reach the sand at the depths. They're hiding, I know that, but I expected to find some fancy sunken city. Wouldn't there be somethi—

—through darkness and blurry vision, I spot a statue of someone likely from the south. I swim closer, dizzy from the lack of oxygen. I try everything to keep from breathing in water, as the distraction will be too much.

The statue wears a surprised expression and I get the distinct impression this isn't a statue at all. I don't want to join him.

"Hello? I'm Princess Malin from the North. I come with a message of peace to inform you of a war we are trying to prevent," I mentally project the message as far as I can, telepathically shouting. *"I can leave if you wish but I wanted to warn you of others who wish to use your stone casting ability."*

No response. I don't intend to wait for long, the growing discomfort in my lungs too much to handle. Hopefully somebody heard me, even if they're too rude to acknowledge me.

Kicking off from the sand, I begin the ascent upwards when I hear a mental voice.

"Grab your breath, princess. When you're ready, come back. We wish to discuss."

I'm too focused on reaching the surface to appreciate the response. When I'm greeted with the sweet taste of oxygen, I gasp and spit up remnants of water I inhaled. It's unpleasant, but I'm coping, no doubt attributing it to Rune.

When I'm ready, I dive and kick as fast as I can until I've returned to the surprised statue. Only there's something different now. Next to the well-defined stone is a tiny opening in the sand. It would only just be wide enough for my shoulders. I'm not one for tight spaces at the best of times, but underwater? In the dark? I'm tempted to see if Taylin would be willing to trade places.

"We won't turn you to stone unless you give us reason to. Enter through the tunnel. You will be greeted by our guards."

I don't respond. I squeeze through the hole, wriggling all the way. I certainly hope this isn't a trap. I can't imagine a worse way to spend an eternity.

A couple of times I bang my forehead against a wall, panicking.

"You're close. Keep swimming."

The calm but firm voice reassures me. At the end of the tunnel is a dull, blue light. Two blurry figures wait, holding tridents.

When I squirm out of the tunnel, they assist me out before bringing the trident up as a warning to my throat. I can't make out their faces with my blurred vision. Their bodies are smaller than I imagined. Dull in color, too. They're about half my size, their tail twice the length of their height. I can't work out if they don't have eyes or if I simply can't see them, but they seem to be covered in scales from bald head to toe.

"It's rude to stare."

"I'm sorry," I apologize. "I can't see well." That's when I realize something. "You're still speaking telepathically?"

"Of course. We can't speak with our mouths underwater, can we? Never fear, we have learned to separate private thoughts from projected ones. Our history is neither here nor there, though. You said you're here for a purpose. Etiquette would have us take you to our dwelling, but we would prefer to keep our kind safe from the above. You could be rife with disease for all we know."

They raise a fair point. I glance down at various 'statues', or more likely curious immortals cast to stone over the years and keep from wringing my hands. One wrong word and I might slip to the eternal abyss with them.

"I understand," I say—well, I mentally project—with as much respect as I can garner. "Who am I speaking with now? I need to discuss this with your leader."

The guard flits around me, trident still skillfully in place. "I am. Leaders protect their kin at all costs."

Guarded by their leader? How courageous and...risky. It feels incredibly informal to be speaking in the open waters like this, but I'm beyond caring. My lungs feel like they're about to explode, even with Rune's distant healing take effect.

"I'm honored to meet you. We've been told for years that your kind were nothing more than a myth."

"That's what we tell our young about your kind," the leader says with a swish of its tail. I cannot for the life of me distinguish its gender, if it has one at all.

"Probably for the best," I say. "I won't take up too much of your time, especially as I have a newborn waiting for me. There are other northerners looking for you. And an easterner."

"We know."

"They want you to side with them. There's a revolution happening. Mortals against immortals. Immortals against gods. It's all over the place and it's all completely unnecessary, as far as I can see. The easterner and the two northerners aren't working together as far as I can tell, but they both want your kind on their side. We have grave concerns they may want your stone casting ability as an intimidation tool. I can only humbly plead that you won't get involved."

A pause which lasts so long that it has me screaming internally. I want to *breathe*. My body is already involuntarily writhing, *pleading* for air.

"And your part in all this?"

"Nothing," I say adamantly. "I want to go into hiding with my family and have another attempt at happiness."

"Noble."

I frown. "I understand your sarcasm but—"

"—there's no sarcasm intended. To put your family first and avoid war is indeed a noble choice. Don't let others convince you otherwise." The voice paused. "We appreciate your honesty, and no doubt, your intense discomfort coming here. There is no need to prolong your visit. You can rest with the knowledge that we will not partake in this revolution. It brings no benefit to us. We are from different worlds and we are at peace. There's no shame in keeping out of something that doesn't concern you."

They have a point, but the sentiment also brings me tremendous guilt. How can I simultaneously want to help *and* run away?

"Thank you," I project. "My friend will be very jealous of our meeting. He has always believed in tales of the water folk."

"As will my daughter in regard to the tall, land folk," they say, projecting a laugh. Lowering the trident, I feel one of them place a rock in my hand. It glows gold in the murkiness, dimming as I stroke it. "We give this to those who do not need it. It is a sign of our desire to be allies. This extends to you and you alone; not necessarily your corner."

"What is it?"

"Our pride. Our protection. You can uncast those lost to stone. This will not, however, cast anyone *to* stone. We're not entirely foolish enough to give you that ability. Think of this as a thanks for your cooperation and your like-mindedness. We ask that you do not undo the past, such as those cast below you. They're like that because they were curious. Naïve. *Dangerous.* This is to be used as a last resort if your near and dear are inflicted. Do you understand?"

I attempt to nod, but I'm already thrashing as my body pleads for air. "I'm sorry for my body. I'm exceptionally grateful; I just can't breathe."

"We see that. Your heart is pure. We value you. Flee with your family and be well. We shall retreat with ours and remain concealed. It was wonderful to have met you, Princess Malin from the North. Be gone."

"Thank you, thank you, thank you," I say, pleased to see that my royal diplomatic skills, albeit rusty, are still intact. I give a lousy underwater bow, then squirm through the tunnel, gulping water involuntarily. The sensation forces my body to behave erratically, stopping me in my tracks.

No. *No no no no.* I need to return to the surface.

I exit the tunnel and catapult myself upwards, the surface seemingly further and further away. Part of me dreads reaching the top. Recovery is going to be unpleasant.

My face is met by a gentle breeze and I can't even gasp for air, choking on the water filling my lungs. I splash towards land, collapsing on the shoreline, spluttering. I should be dead. I think I am. I'm confident my heart has stopped beating, because I'm cold and heavy in a manner unlike an ordinary dip in the lake.

I vomit... I vomit some more... I take a raspy, distressed breath... then everything goes black.

I WAKE up on my back with my arms sprawled. How long have I been out? It doesn't seem like too long. The sun hasn't moved much. Unless it's been a day.

Oh, surely it hasn't been a day!

Skin sizzling from the rays, I pull my nauseated self into a sitting position, instantly craving Rune's distant healing. Either I need more, or he hasn't timed this one particularly well. My chest ironically feels like it's on fire, each rattling breath disturbingly loud and shredding at my vocal cords. The aftermath is infinitely worse than I imagined.

My rib cracks when I breathe in, and a weak heartbeat pulses. I'm not dead, then. At least not anymore. I've miraculously revived myself.

I cradle my side and force myself to my feet, tilting to the side as I do so. Water trickles out of my ears which I only just realize have perforated. It would explain my muffled hearing.

Please Rune...*please* send me *something*.

I shuffle forward, gripping onto the stone the water folk gave me. My vision is still a little fuzzy, but I'm captivated by the unnaturally smooth texture. There's a symbol etched into it, presumedly something from their language. It's beautiful; the vertical strokes angled diagonally and the horizontal strokes curved. I cannot believe they entrusted me with such a gift. Had I not been drowning, I would've questioned it more.

At least the meeting was successful. Short of intense manipulation, the siblings and Zain won't win the water folk over. We reached them first, which is a huge step in stopping the revolution. To have the power to uncast those turned to stone would've surely meant the end to any enemy. Now that *that* option is off the table, it's an even playing field. I can rest easy knowing I've helped. It might be enough to bring the revolution to a grinding halt.

Now that I can breathe, literally, there's so much I realize I wanted to ask them.

How do they cast things to stone?

What do they eat?

Are they blind?

Do they reproduce like us?

Do they live in that lake or do all watery roads connect?

What do they *really* look like?

Their kind are immortal riddles of the deep; forever mysterious given that few seem to return from the depths, which seems to be the way the water folk like it. Part of me is indebted to such a meeting... but mostly I find myself craving another encounter to learn more about the elusive species. This must be what my brother felt when stumbling upon various kinds.

My brother.

The reminder washes away my curious thoughts and transmutes to my baby nephew. Is he all right? Surely he is wondering where I am!

Fighting through the giddiness and breathlessness, I jog forward, too exhausted to hide deep in the grass. I just want to get to my family.

I reach the place where I'm certain I left them, but there is barely a trace. There's an imprint where Taylin was sitting, but it's not terribly distinct. I attempt to follow a trail, simultaneously relieved and disturbed to find Diarmuid sitting betwixt the long grass all on his own. I can't believe my eyes. He's grown so much already! A cheeky smile spreads across his chubby face. I've never seen a baby so cute in my life. I wish he didn't have to grow so quickly.

How is he sitting up on his own in just a few short hours? His head still bobbles a little, but I can't help but feel a tremendous sense of pride.

The pride is abruptly swallowed by fear.

"Diarmuid?" I whisper. "Where's Taylin?"

The image of my baby boy sitting alone in an open field fills me with dread. I was so taken by his very presence that I never stopped to consider the implications.

He gurgles, the smile uninterrupted. He's already so much bigger than when I left him. He's sitting on his own, his massive bobble-head no longer bobbling. His neck is strong, sturdy. He's growing at a rapid rate, just like his mother's species tends to do.

I take a careful step closer. "Sweetheart? Where's Taylin? Are you hurt?"

I don't know why I'm asking when I know he can't speak. At least, I don't *think* he can. I haven't worked out how speedy or how steady his development is yet.

"Me? Hurt? *Never*. This gangly sidekick of yours? She's gonna be."

I let out a horrified shriek as Taylin rises from the long grass with blood smeared across her throat. Her eyes are rolled to the back of her head, but she's alive. *Just.*

"A bit of pageantry never goes astray."

A different voice. A feminine voice. I'm half relieved that it doesn't belong to Diarmuid, yet equally mortified by its invisible owner.

Dalin and Cheralin appear from the concealed position, their slender, pale bodies standing out in the sunlight. Cheralin holds Taylin close, a wicked smile imprinted on her cold face as she revels in someone's pain.

"Feels good to be here," she says dramatically. "It's a chance for redemption after how we left things. I thought after my traitorous brother sabotaged our last encounter, I'd never mend my wounded pride. Yet, here we are! The upper hand. The higher ground. It's mine."

Dalin approaches Diarmuid and picks him up.

"Don't touch him!" I growl as Diarmuid bursts into tears. "Put. Him. Down."

Dalin shrugs. "Leverage is a beautiful word."

"What do you want?" I demand. "You've come all this way and tracked us down, so out with it." I carefully watch Taylin, mentally willing Rune to send a burst of healing energy. There's a lot of blood...

"Your head, originally," Cheralin says, her cheery tone contrasting with the dire scene. "Then this one's head. Now your sister suggests we don't *need* your head after all. Especially if you're leaving the picture, we can make some story up about you. We're after power. We'd like to get advice from Sharnique, so uncasting her from stone is a priority, obviously. Then winning over the lower species so we can create alliances to successfully rebuild the north. Your death is just a perk, now. At least that's what your sister said. Two birds with one stone and all that. Now Miss Soaking Wet. Hand over what those slippery water folk gave you."

My heart leaps and I instinctively tighten my grasp on the stone. Processing the information, I frown. "What water folk?"

Dalin snorts and Cheralin chortles. "Malin, you're funny! If you're going to lie, lie well! Your friend is dying! Just pass it over so you can spend whatever few moments you have left with her. Otherwise we will just kill the baby as incentive!"

I shriek as Dalin pinches Diarmuid's arm who screams, stretching out his little arms to reach me. "M-m-mum!"

Time stops. My jaw drops. That little boy called me his mum. It's not a word we use in the north for birthing mother, but I've heard other corners use it. I recognize the association and the *power* behind the word. He must genetically know it from his real mother. Not that it matters. What matters is he used it to describe *me*.

My brain no longer listens to reason, acting only on raw emotion. I lunge at Dalin and swing a punch at his face, catching a wailing Diarmuid as Dalin drops him.

In that moment I spy Taylin from my peripheral elbowing Cheralin in the abdomen.

"I forgive you, Rune!" Taylin shouts in the wind, weaving as Cheralin comes at her with her knife. Seemingly enjoying the conflict, she laughs in the face of her enemy, a renewed energy from the distant healing.

While she successfully combats her counterpart, I'm left in a much more vulnerable state, weaponless and with a hysterical baby in my arms.

Dalin recovers from the shock and charges towards me with a vicious, manic gaze. "Give us the stone, Malin and we won't kill the child."

I don't have any reason to believe him.

"You're a healer?" I hear Cheralin shout. "Northerners can't heal like that! Especially mortals!"

"Never judge a talent by its skin!" Taylin doesn't explain—and she shouldn't. The less they know, the better.

I ignore Cheralin's response, reaching down to throw mud in Dalin's face, but it proves useless. It barely stains his cheek. I'm overwhelmed by the baby's cries and the terror coursing through my veins. I can't cope. What do I do? There's nobody here to help.

"Possess him," a firm voice directs.

I look over Dalin's shoulder to find my transparent stalker.

"I can't," I choke. "I don't know how! The baby..."

Her lips tighten and as if she were diving into water, she charges at Dalin and leaps into his back, vanishing completely.

Dalin halts in place, eyes wide and limbs periodically flailing. He stands perfectly still, staring at me.

Mouth dry, I struggle to formulate words. "Is that..."

"I don't know how long I am in control. I can feel he's...stunned. Temporarily." Dalin is speaking, but his voice is higher and on the verge of cracking. "I learned by watching your brother. I can trap this body somewhere. Or at the very least hurt it." Dalin's arm lifts to punch himself. "Ow. All right, it seems I can feel that. Not worth it. I'm just going to run away from you and tie myself up. I'll catch up."

"Don't go too far. You said it's dark when you're not near me."

"I know." Dalin smiles, but his eyes glisten sadly. "Don't worry about me. Go."

It's strange to take instruction from your enemy, when you know they're not the one relaying the message. What's more bizarre is my relationship with this entity possessing Dalin—I don't know if we're friend or foe or somewhere in between. And I never found out what my brother wanted from her...

Dalin awkwardly scuttles away, sometimes stopping to thrash before running even faster. Whatever she plans to do with him is on borrowed time.

"Shh, Diarmuid," I rouse on the baby, unable to tend to his cries. Taylin needs help. Not because she's a weak fighter, but because she's ultimately a mortal up against an immortal and because of that, she'll never win. Unless...

With a quick incantation and exhale, I switch our immortality, bequeathing it to her. I regret it instantly, having not fully healed from drowning. Rune is a phenomenal healer, but he isn't a miracle worker; especially not from a distance. Not yet. All good things take time.

I drop to my knees, even more irked by the baby's wails as I struggle to catch my breath. I find myself occasionally choking on air as I bring up more water, my insides bruised and battered. I'm coping, but it's physically harder as a mortal.

Diarmuid picks up on my sudden fragility, garbling instead of crying, staring at me with wide, concerned eyes.

"I'm fine," I assure breathlessly. "I'm all right."

Taylin is thriving with her sudden burst of invincibility, clawing her way towards a deflecting Cheralin to strangle her. It's a pointless battle; Cheralin has no leverage now. They can literally fight forever.

"Hey Cheralin," I rasp, repeating the name several times before she pushes Taylin off to look at me. "Your brother is trapped in a watery ditch somewhere. A watery grave. Why? I possessed him. That's what you get when you mess with us and try to hurt my family. You can either back off or join him."

She shifts uneasily, quickly scanning the area to disprove my warning. "You...you can't possess people."

"You have no idea what we are capable of," Taylin grunts, puffing out her chest as she speaks. "Go tell your evil boss that nobody wants to see her on the throne. Nobody cares about the north, and nobody wants it rebuilt. It's dead, and it's not coming back."

"Adalin is not my boss!" Cheralin snaps, a little too defensively. "She is the north's royal leader. You're selfish cowards if you don't want to see your own home revived."

"It'll never be revived," I say. "And it never should be. It was the pinnacle of division. This is a new age and a new land with new people. There might be a revolution coming, but mortals and immortals should not be pitted against one another. Species should not be left out of history books because they don't have any noteworthy abilities."

"Bleh, bleh, bleh!" Cheralin rolls her eyes. "Like all of you oxygen thieves, I bet you're not in the thick of doing anything to help; instead you're running away to save your own behinds."

The statement cuts deep, so I pull Diarmuid in close, as if his tiny body will shield me from emotional pain.

"You're running *towards* something to save *your* behinds," Taylin retorts when I don't. "I'm not wasting another breath on you. Stay away from us or we'll possess you and toss your body into the closest volcano. There you can choose to suffer for eternity or give up your immortality. Trust me, I'm satisfied either way."

I can tell the last thing Cheralin wants to do is listen to us, but she's left with a lousy choice. Eventually, she snarls and runs in the direction I motion towards, chasing after Dalin's poor possessed body.

Relieved, Taylin wipes the sweat from her eyes and rejoins us with a wide grin. She tickles Diarmuid under the chin and returns my immortality, just in time for me to choke and splutter on more water that graphically spurts from my mouth.

"Well, we're never boring," Taylin jokes. "This little man has grown a lot since you've been gone. I know they say babies grow fast, but this is something else. He'll be walking by tomorrow, easily. It's a little sad, really. Anyway. I'm beginning to sound like...like..." She closes her eyes tightly before they fling open once more. "How did it all go? What was it like down there?"

I fill Taylin in as we continue through the open field, checking over my shoulder every so often. I allow her to lead the way forward as I speak, somewhat distracted by the strange image I had of Diarmuid sitting in the field.

It sounds irrational, but that image of him sitting alone with a smile on his face...and for a moment thinking he was the one speaking and making that threat...has me fearing, if only for a minute, that maybe this innocent baby isn't so innocent after all.

CHAPTER XIV

"**U**nihorn!"

"That's right!" I laugh and clap as Diarmuid correctly identifies the shadow Taylin makes against the cave wall. "That's Nellabix. It's who we are going to find."

"She smart unihorn," he says, his diction good, but not great. Certainly not bad for an infant who is technically only a couple of weeks old.

We're nearing the mountains. Our trek has been rather uneventful since the run-in with Dalin and Cheralin. I've been on edge ever since, but they haven't caused us any problems in the interim. Rune seems to have slowed down on healing us, too. It's been maybe four days since we've felt anything from him, and I can't help but wonder if we're out of range now. It's the lie I continue to tell myself, rather than consider something bad has happened to him. He's safe with my brother. He *has* to be.

Taylin transforms and maneuvers her hands to look like various trees; a subject Diarmuid is not as well-versed in. After a few wrong guesses and confusing trees with shrubs and mountains, he loses interest and makes his own shadow puppets.

"He's so cute," I gush.

"He's all right," Taylin says with a coy smile. "Now, you're not going to want to hear this, but we're low on food supplies. If we don't find something to forage soon, we'll need to hunt."

I grimace. "I'd rather starve."

"I knew you'd say that, but you need to think of Diarmuid. There's not much left to mash up for him. Plus, he has most of his teeth now. A growing boy needs meat."

"He still feels so little to me."

"From a time perspective, he is. Biologically though, he'll be out of the toddler age group within a few days. My dream indicated that Nellabix isn't too far away from here, but I never saw what happened after that. We might still need to scavenge, even if we find her."

"But at least our travels will be quicker. We can get to the nearest village and barter."

"With what money?"

I hate that Taylin's logic is right, but it doesn't stop me from trying to swing alternate paths. My life feels so remarkably different in such a short time. Diarmuid's hair has grown into curling locks, Taylin has a newfound softness, and I have a sense of confidence within myself which I didn't have before. Despite being homeless and amidst plenty of horrors and uncertainties, I feel free. I feel fulfilled. For once, I feel like there's hope.

"As always, your silence is very reassuring." Taylin rolls her eyes. "I can hunt if you're too squeamish."

I nod. "I won't eat any of it. Is there any possibility of holding off hunting until it's an absolute last resort?"

Taylin purses her lips. "One more day and that's it. I can wait one more day, but I need the energy to hunt."

That's the extent of the negotiation. "All right. Then where do we go next? The sooner we can go, the less chance of meat being on the table, right?"

"We continue our ascent. Feel that chill in the air? We're on the mountain path. I'm positive it's where I saw Nellabix in my dreams. Any reason why she'd go towards the mountains?"

I consider the question. "She's smart. Mountains are high and therefore statistically more likely to be safe from predators. A better vantage point so that she could look for us. I'm just speculating."

"Would she know that this trail leads to the ogres? I'm not too sure what their dinner menu is, and whether she'd be on it."

I try to shrug nonchalantly, but my heart leaps at the thought. I can't even formulate a coherent answer. Reading the fear on my face, Taylin changes the topic.

"Then let's gather our things and keep heading forward."

I scoop a lively Diarmuid up while Taylin kicks out the fire and picks up the bag. My upper body strength hasn't had time to grow accustomed to Diarmuid's rapid growth. He's beginning to feel like a little boulder. A snuggly boulder, but a boulder nonetheless.

Without the shelter of the cave, we are exposed to the chill of the twilight air. It isn't the season for snow, but there are small patches of white scattered along the ground as we ascend. The mountains are different here. The ones where my brother has set up camp are jagged, rocky and dead. These are full of life and rounded, tricking you into thinking you're not actually in the mountains at all.

Diarmuid hates the wind. He gasps dramatically whenever the breeze catches his breath, which alarmed me at first, but now I find it amusing.

We try to conserve our energy by not talking, the trek alone exhausting. Even Diarmuid seems fatigued as the oxygen level drops with each stride. I feel like any connection we had with Rune is long lost. From this moment on, we're on our own.

"Getting harder to see," Taylin says, her voice carried in the wind. She's right. As the sun sets, a strange haze sets in, making it difficult to navigate. "There's nothing out here. No villages. No people. We should find another place to stay until morning or retreat back to the cave."

I dread the thought of retreating. What a waste of time that would be. Civilization might be nonexistent along this trail, and I'm hoping the same applies to any wildlife.

"Five more minutes," I suggest, too tired to elaborate. I don't even have the energy to mentally project to hear the thoughts of nearby beings. If Nellabix were nearby, she'd hear us first; that unihorn has uncanny hearing.

I'm startled by the sound of snow shifting in the trees behind us.

Consumed by thoughts of Nellabix, I get ahead of myself and turn around with a triumphant smile.

But, as with most of my life recently, what I'm actually facing is full of disappointment.

An ogre. Six of them. Upsettingly tall and made of pure muscles and overstretched flesh. Despite the cold, they're clad in the thinnest of cloths, a homemade club in one hand and a dead man's bones in the other.

Bald on top, they sport only a few teeth the size of my fist. Their eyesight doesn't look to be terribly great, as they seem to have trouble honing in on my location, glancing over me, then settling, then staring at my shadow, then back to me.

I'm unsure whether to move or not.

"I can hear them," one says, his voice gravelly.

"I can smell them," the other says in more of a whisper.

"I can sense them," another says, his voice much richer than the others.

I don't know much about ogres. Their level of intelligence or friendliness is but a mere mystery, and judging by Taylin's pale face, she's thinking the same.

Right on cue, Diarmuid uses this moment to garble, causing the startled ogres to flinch and settle their gaze on us.

"Bit taller than your average crystal folk." One bends over until we are face to face, his nostrils flaring as he sniffs. "State your reason. Lost, traveler? Or a hunter?"

My teeth chatter, but not due to the snow. I hug Diarmuid close, who furrows his brow at the ogre. I consider an aggressive tone, but choose the diplomatic path instead. "Neither. We are only searching for our pet, who answers to the name Nellabix."

"Pet?" The ogre stands upright and snorts. He bends over again, squinting his eyes at the golden band around my neck. Using his club, he pokes at it. "Prison folk. Must be an immortal. Interesting. Never seen one out in the wild before. What corner are you, then? If you're from the east, we want nothing to do with you. Forced our kind to learn their filthy language and forget our ancestor's tongue. Wanted to enslave us, but we overcame it. My grandfather was a champion of the ogres. Your vile mouth cannot taint us again. Our generation is immune. So *are* you from the east? Eh?"

"No sir. We don't much fancy the east ourselves," I reply truthfully, unsurprised by the revelation. Say all you want about the north, but the east has a sneaky way of controlling others. It's amazing they haven't had their own civil war. Touching my necklace, I am reminded of our conversation deep in the woods weeks ago. "Do you know what these bands are for?"

His lips tighten, an ogre behind him grunting. "Looks like one of Torg's."

"Yeah, but was it an inside job? Is he 'elpin' them or 'inderin' them?"

A few more grunts. Indistinguishable mumbles. Then finally: "You ever meet Torg?"

"The half ogre? The functionalist?" I clarify. "Yes. He isn't like the rest of you."

"Parents mixed about. Hard for him to thrive in the snow up here without our tough skin but he has bigger brains. Very bold of him to find a life away from the mountains. We worry. Not many places would accept him, I imagine. That's why he's basically locked himself up in those cells. No different from working there to actually being imprisoned, I say." A wave of sorrow clouds over the ogres. "He needs to come back. It's not safe for him down there. If you escaped, you can retrieve him."

"Extenuating circumstances," Taylin says under her breath. "No side quests, Malin."

"He'd remove that band for you," one ogre says, a glimmer of hope in his dull eyes. "The tracking devices used to be made from titanium. It's interesting he made them from gold this time...unless he actually intended to make you all stronger for some reason. I can't fathom it. Can't tell you what's in this."

The tallest ogre pushes the others out of the way, towering over me. He stares at Diarmuid, who I shield. "What are you doing bringing an infant out here dressed like that? Your flesh can't withstand the bite! Give him to me."

My eyes almost bug out of their sockets. "You can't have him."

"The little one must be protected! He will freeze! Give him to me!"

"He's fine. My body warmth is enough."

"Your body is not warm! Your lip coloring matches the sky! Our skin is coarse but we have sacks we use to forage." He opens a hessian bag packed to the brim with mountain shrooms. "Place him in here."

I squirm at the ferocious demand, unable to believe a hessian bag could possibly compare to my nurturing embrace. "No."

"Our mountshrooms are warm! Feel them!"

The other ogres nod. Succumbing to the peer pressure, I keep tight hold of Diarmuid as I lean over to touch one of the mountshrooms. To give credit where credit's due, they are delightfully warm. Like a toasty bed in the middle of winter, I wouldn't mind squeezing into the sack myself. "All right. But he can only go in there if I carry the bag."

"You?" The ogre scoffs. "Be our guest. It's heavier than it looks." He rudely drops the bag at my feet, motioning for me to proceed.

I soothe Diarmuid as I maneuver him betwixt the mountshrooms. He giggles at the soft, toasty touch, nestling into the bag as he keeps an intense eye on me. I go to lift the bag, only to be laughed at by the ogres when I groan and go weak at the knees.

"Quick, you better lift him up before we eat your child!" The one with the husky voice taunts. "All ogres gobble up children for supper, didn't you know?"

I don't appreciate the sarcasm and assume the quip must be something to do with being wrongly stereotyped. It of course flies over my head, so I don't respond. I only allow them to carefully lift the bag with Diarmuid in it, as I maintain eye contact and force a smile so that he knows he's safe. I don't trust the ogres—only because

I don't trust anybody—but he isn't in immediate danger. I could take control of the situation if I needed to.

"Cute little fellow," one of the ogres says when Diarmuid flashes a wide grin. "It's settled my nerves popping him in here. He wouldn't have lasted the night! What were you two thinking?"

"We weren't going to spend the night out here!" Taylin objects before I do, already mortally offended by their accusation. "I foresaw our unihorn and already said we should retreat!"

"She did," I say, cold without Diarmuid's snuggly touch. "I suppose we've arrived full circle. You haven't happened to see a unihorn around?"

"We don't see real well," an ogre says with a hint of resentment. "Colorblind, one corner called it. It's not that. It's like it's all shadow. The two of you standing there look like four murky beings that are only shorter than the other murky trees."

"For all intents and purposes, we haven't come across your unihorn," another softens. "We can keep an ear out."

"What even is a unihorn?" The one with the husky voice asks. They all look remarkably similar so it's easier to distinguish them by voice.

"You know. The four-legged creature with a horn on its head that we have locked up in our cavern." The largest ogre grins. "Gotta have some sort of leverage, 'aven't we?"

Taylin strides forward, ready to fight, but I restrain her. They have Diarmuid—and I'd rather risk an empty threat of my pet than a physical demonstration of my...my...he *isn't* my son. He's my *nephew*.

"Who are we supposed to believe?" I ask, scratching at their mental projections, but it's like white noise for all of them. Maybe their kind isn't prone to inner monologues.

"Bring Torg home," the largest ogre demands, finally thinking ahead and pointing at Diarmuid in the hessian bag. "Or we'll hold on to this little fellow! Or we'll kill your pet! Or we won't remove your neck bands!"

"Or all of the above!"

"Or all of the above, yes!"

"Give me the baby," I say firmly, "and we will retreat from the mountain."

Taylin tugs on my shirt, whispering harshly into my ear. "But Nellabix is here! I saw her in the dream! She was here!"

"I'm not risking Diarmuid," I respond in a low voice then redirect my attention to the ogres. "We can't rescue your friend. It was a miracle we escaped."

"If it's a tracking device, then you'll certainly want those bands off. You'll never be safe with those on," the large ogre taunts, a glint in his dull eyes. "Torg for freedom. Torg for your pet. It's a reasonable request. In return, we won't eat your baby."

I don't believe they would really eat Diarmuid, even if part of me is worried they're only keeping him warm so he'll taste better. Their thoughts are nonsensical and their words are inconsistent—but they're offering something I know we need. No matter where we run, no matter where we hide, if these wretched bands are truly secret tracking devices, then we will never be free.

Glancing over at Taylin, I nod. Tense, she nods back in return. "I never finished my dream. You woke me up. All I know was Nellabix was in the mountains."

"We need to get these off." I stroke the neckbands, a constant source of annoyance and anxiety. "We can use the 'p' word to get him out if he won't come voluntarily. It won't be fun, but it'll be manageable."

"Agreed. I just need to get that unihorn back. I have so much guilt, Malin."

"Then we have an accord," I say with conviction, walking forward to grab Diarmuid from the hessian bag. He stretches out his little arms in anticipation of me collecting him. "We will see you all soon."

The ogres almost seem disappointed. "You can stay the night if you'd like."

"No thank you, we won't impose," I say politely, eager to leave their presence. "It's much too cold. We will return with Torg. Please take care of my pet in the meantime."

I hope they're not lying about Nellabix, but it's redundant eavesdropping on thoughts they do not possess. I'm putting all of my faith in them—I just hope they don't make me regret it.

It's a skill of mine; trusting the wrong kinds.

A shivering Taylin tugs on my arm as we descend the mountain at a rapid pace. We don't need to communicate our desire to return to the little cave. It'll be a miserable night, but it'll be tolerable.

"I can't believe this!" Taylin says once we're out of earshot—well, what we assume is out of earshot.

"What?" I ask, stroking Diarmuid's hair. He's overdue for a haircut.

"I saw the tracks. I saw the mountain. We were so close to getting Nellabix! If I'd only seen how that stupid dream ended—"

"—then you might've been disappointed when your expectations were not met," I say calmly, not wanting to upset Diarmuid. "This could all be a blessing in disguise. I've been wanting to get these awful things off."

"But now we have to return to the Immortal Cells! How do you feel about that?" When I don't respond, she snorts, albeit strangely due to her chattering teeth. "Why don't you just use your dream? I don't understand why you won't. Aren't you the least bit curious?"

"No," I reply honestly. "Dreams are changeable. Sometimes life makes decisions for you, just like it has now."

Rolling her eyes, we continue down the mountain in silence, stopping at our cave. The wind is less icy, the snow is scarce, and the cave seems inviting compared to what we've just endured.

As Taylin pulls the blankets from her pack and entertains Diarmuid, I light the fire, basking in its instant warmth. My teeth involuntarily grind together as I contemplate the severe implications of returning to the Immortal Cells. Is it worth it? Surely there's an easier way to find Nellabix. Just because I couldn't penetrate the ogre's thoughts doesn't necessarily mean I couldn't possess them—

does it? And the neckbands—do they *really* need to come off? We've done all right thus far. Sure, they're itchy and they could be a tracking device, but they could also be a stylish, permanent fixture that aids in our strength.

I curse under my breath. There's no use trying to treasle out of this one. I know what we must do.

It's a miracle we managed to escape the Immortal Cells once.

I doubt they'll make the same mistake twice.

CHAPTER XV

I haven't moved from my spot, as I stare grimly at the distant tower. There's no purple haze drifting from the window this time.

The prison looks just as intimidating and just as soul-crushing as ever. Memories—even those I've suppressed—resurface, threatening to drag me deep into an emotional pit of despair.

Diarmuid rests on my hip, playing with my hair, while Taylin holds my free hand. Our little family of outcasts gaze at our fate ahead. The cells represent what brought us together and what could also tear us apart.

"I don't want to go," I say, my quiet voice lost in the breeze.

"Why?" Diarmuid asks, his little voice mature beyond his age. I'm not ready for him to grow up, but the hours are seemingly akin to months of progress.

"We have to," Taylin says. "Nellabix needs us. And once we get these things off, then the revolution is no longer our issue, is it? We leave. We leave this land. We have a semblance of a life as a family elsewhere. That's the plan, isn't it?"

Swallowing, I shrug half-heartedly. "I've never really had much of a plan."

"Maybe that's been your problem." Taylin blinks away a tear. "Although, I've always had a plan, and look how that turned out. I planned to marry. Planned for children. Planned to open my own store and expand into cobbling. Plans are merely unfinished dreams."

"Ever planned to travel?"

"I wanted to, but never thought I would."

"Look at you then." I squeeze her hand encouragingly. "We've seen and met so many in the past month alone. And look—we have a child. The plan is coming along nicely."

She raises a sardonic eyebrow but I can tell that deep down, she appreciates the sentiment.

Arms heavy from holding a constantly growing Diarmuid, I carefully place him down, in awe of how strong his legs are. He's standing and walking, having completely skipped the crawling stage. The black strands of hair are even darker than before, complete contrast to his blonde hair which is so fair it can at times be mistaken for baldness.

"A few weeks ago we were trying to work out where to go and what to do," I say.

"A few months ago I was a sheltered mortal," Taylin says. "It's certainly been...*unpredictable*."

"I hear that's what life is."

"How exciting!" Diarmuid throws his arms over his head, his cheeks rosy and his eyes full of wonder. I have no clue whether he was replying to our somber conversation or whether he coincidentally threw a couple of random words together, but it's enough to lighten the mood.

"We may not come back," Taylin says once she settles.

"Of course we will. Possession," I remind, the word dirty coming from my mouth. "I promise we won't be prisoners again."

"I'm not scared of being a prisoner. I'm scared of the unknown. Zain could have transformed that whole place by now, or infiltrated it somehow."

"Impossible," I assure. "The water folk would not partake in the revolution. The doggans also said they didn't want to get involved. The ogres are only interested in retrieving Torg. No doubt there are other species we know little about, but it sounds like he doesn't have a leg to stand on."

"He has the immortals. He has his corner. That's all he needs. Imagine convincing warriors from his corner, or even the prisoners who escaped with him. Once he releases all the prisoners, it's going to be a bloodbath." She glances at Diarmuid who is listening a little too intensely, his wide eyes narrowed. "Allies or not, it's mortals against immortals, and we know who will win that battle. The gods are weak from the land's divide."

"It isn't our problem," I say, my throat tight as the words slip through my lips. "We get Torg. We get Nellabix. That's the extent of our journey. We find our happily ever after."

"I thought you wanted to save the prisoners?"

"I have a new destiny," I say, glancing at Diarmuid and squeezing Taylin's hand. "Family first. I can only save those who want to be saved. If there are prisoners who won't partake in the uprising, then that is a different story. If they choose Zain, then..." I needn't finish my train of thought. Taylin understands what I mean.

Diarmuid nears the edge of the mountain a little too confidently, so I call out to him. Pouty, he returns to my side, arms folded. "I can't die. It's not a big deal."

That is certainly news to me. Is that a genetic memory or has he overheard our conversations? "You can be hurt, *forever*. Arguably, it is a fate worse than death."

"Nah-uh," he says, his diction improving with each and every word. "Uncle Rune can heal us."

Flabbergasted, Taylin and I are speechless. He has picked up on everything we've said since his birth. I knew children had a tendency to learn things quickly, but this was somewhat unprecedented and a little troubling. Should he be privy to so much information at such a young age?

"At least he won't be young for long," Taylin utters, seemingly reading my mind. "It's unnatural hearing a toddler speak like this, but he will be fully grown soon enough."

"He hasn't...he won't have a childhood," I lament.

"He was never supposed to," she says. "It's not in his species to do that. They grow up quickly to ensure the continuation of their kind. He just happens to be a boy and luckily for him, he won't be pregnant for his entire existence."

I cringe at the memory of Sierra's incessant complaining, relieved that pregnancy isn't a card I've been dealt with. "You make a good point. All right, then. Onwards?"

Inhaling sharply—then coughing on the cool breeze—Taylin nods. "Onwards."

THE PRISON DOUBLES in size visually as we approach. I'd forgotten just how horrifically large and morbid it was. That's a lie. I remembered it well—I'd simply chosen to delete as much of it from my conscious mind as possible. Eternity is a long time to remember the negative parts of life.

Seeking shelter from the rain, we build a makeshift roof over a cluster of trees and huddle together, using the blankets to keep the mud off our legs.

We're now officially in hybrid territory, this time without Nellabix to aid in a quick escape. We take turns keeping guard, but it's difficult in the rain. We can hear the growls nearby circling us, but they haven't made a move yet. They seem to be waiting, watching. They're close, but they won't strike. What they're waiting for, I can't be sure of.

"Is there anywhere potentially safer?" Taylin asks. She peers up at the branchless trees, her mind working overtime to find an alternative.

"They're keeping their distance for whatever reason," I say, locking eyes with a hybrid who sits amongst the cluster of boulders up on the hill, peering down at us. "They would have attacked by now. Something has changed."

"It's me," Diarmuid says nonchalantly, the equivalent of a five-year-old mortal. My baby is all grown up. "They can sense my power."

"Power?" I ask, unable to control my eyebrows from raising. "What power?"

"I don't know yet," he says, drawing circles in the mud with his finger. He looks young, but he speaks at a far more advanced level. "I can feel a surge bubbling within but I can't work out what it does yet. It itches at my skin, though. Do you ever feel that?"

"No," I say dismissively, hoping this sensation will just go away. My memories flash to my brother standing stiffly across from me, fear in his otherwise calm eyes. He wouldn't hold his own child, adamant something was wrong with him. I refused to believe it at the time and I refuse to believe it now. Diarmuid is kind. He giggles at the wildlife. He enjoys touching the flora, but will never pick at it because he knows it will die once he does. He offers to find water for us. He always asks if we feel all right whenever we begin to puff after an arduous hike. There isn't an evil bone in this boy's body. I *know* it.

"You mentioned you'll possess a prisoner so you don't have to go inside," Taylin says, her eyes fixated on the hybrids. "How does that work? Do you stay here and we protect your body while you do this?"

"It's a bit of trial and error," I confess. "I don't even know if I can do it well enough. It's our plan A."

"What's our plan B?"

"Attempt plan A again and again?" I say with a bit of a smile, unwilling to so much as imagine failure. I will do *everything* I can to avoid physically entering the premises. While morally I am uncomfortable with possession, it's the only viable option. If I can get in undetected, then I can keep my family safe. "You should be immortal while I go in, just in case you need to protect yourself."

"Is your body going to go all limp or something while you're driving somebody else's mind?"

I blink. I think. And I shrug. "I'm not too sure. Possibly."

"Ugh." Taylin massages a knot in her neck. "We are so out of our element."

"Have faith, Aunty Taylin!" Diarmuid says, his eyes alight with passion. It still doesn't seem like he should be old enough to walking, talking or motivating us. They say time flies when you're raising kids, but I never envisioned this. "I can help. Mum is going to be amazing and we will support her!"

Oh. My heart melts. I still can't believe he refers to me as his mother. It's a surreal moment, and I certainly don't feel worthy of the title. He assigned the roles himself, as neither Taylin nor myself have referred to her as an aunt. It's confusing, and I wonder if on some level, Taylin resents me for it. She was the one who always wanted children of her own. I'd love to find out more about Diarmuid's kind works, marveling at the abrupt manner in which they grow and develop a personality.

"Go on," Taylin whispers. "The sooner you do this, the better. I don't want to be a sitting pluckle with those hybrids watching us."

I nod. Breathing out the nerves, I focus. "I love you. Both of you."

"Love you, Mum."

Taylin doesn't reciprocate, but as I scratch at any nearby mental barrier, I hear her inner thoughts.

"I love her more than she'll know."

I extend the projection, stretching past the hybrids who appear to be too animalistic to have cohesive thought. I pass through them, searching...searching...searching.

"...so boring. All this excitement upstairs and gossip and hub-bub and I'm stuck patrolling a damn door. A door nobody even uses. At least it's fresh air. I better get paid this week. So many redundancies. SO BORED."

My mind's eye sees the plump mortal, his blonde sideburns mismatching the hints of red in his unkempt beard. His guard's uniform is grey—like the rest of the prison—and smells of sauce. I feel myself merging with his body, the sensation hideously overwhelming. It's like I'm losing myself within his being, as our consciousness become one. I can feel the dull ache in his right knee, the indigestion, the itchy ear. I can hear his inner thoughts question why he feels dizzy, as my thoughts take over. I see everything through his surprisingly alert eyes and I think I am officially in control.

I'm careful not to arouse suspicion, despite this guard appearing alone. I scope the immediate area, and he's inexplicably the only one patrolling the side entrance. Through his body, I clear his throat and enter through the side door, wincing at what awaits me inside.

Within moments, I am greeted by the hostile atmosphere, the pungent stench, and the chilled air, the unpleasant memories smacking me in the face.

And just like that, I'm back in the Immortal Cells.

CHAPTER

XVI

I'm safe. I'm safe. I'm *safe*. I can cut this tether at any moment if I need to, and nobody would be none the wiser.

So why am I sweating? Why am I convinced that now I'm in here, there's no way out?

Tense, I feel as if I float through the narrow corridor, painfully aware of the deafening shrieks of tortured inmates. I wander aimlessly, my breaths sharp and fast, the mortal's suppressed thoughts panicking deep inside as he wonders why he has lost control of his body.

Pushing aside the guilt and paranoia, I rifle through scrambled memories in an attempt to locate the functionalist's quarters.

Get in. Get Torg. Get out.

The premise sounds simplistic enough. Forcing a huge male with ogre genetics to do something he may not want to do, however, may prove difficult.

I swing a left, grimacing awkwardly at another guard. Do guards smile at one another? Frown? Roll their eyes? Am I outside of my assigned area? Will he chip me for it? Tell an official? No, surely not. Nobody seems to care about anything around here. Morale was low when I was a prisoner not so long ago and I doubt much has changed in the brief interval I've been free.

The corridor is familiar. I mean, it smells like sweat, urine, and defecation like everything else in here, but the wall with the jagged stain rings a particular bell.

The functionlist's quarters are up ahead.

Chest tight, I walk with feigned authority and stop at the foot-thick door.

"Open up," I bellow, unaccustomed to the low voice coming from my body. There's a strange vibe in the air. A prickle. A buzz. The prisoners are unsettled and the guards are on edge.

I have no clue where Garu is or whether Sharnique is still frozen in place. I don't even know if my sister is still in the tower or not.

Frantic, shuffled footsteps sound on the other side of the door, when it is nearly ripped off its hinges to reveal a tall, panicked Torg. I remember him being shorter, but I suppose I'm in a smaller body. I have to crane my neck to look at him and can finally appreciate how it must feel not to tower over everybody. It's a strange sensation. I actually feel intimidated by those who are larger than me in this form. Usually, I feel like I stand out and am embarrassed by the stares. Now, I fit in. I blend. For better or for worse.

"What is it?" The red-headed half-ogre asks. He doesn't seem to recognize the body I'm in, which makes sense if it's usually on guard outside.

Taking control, I barge past and into the room, motioning for Torg to close the heavy door behind him. Fumbling for words, I clear my throat and push out the guard's increasingly frenzied thoughts.

"You tell me," I reply vaguely. "Seems to be a strange stir out there."

Torg snorts. "You coming to chip me? I have nothing to do with escaped prisoners. Where do you get the audacity to speak to me like this? You're just a guard."

"You assigned them their neck bands," I reply, hoping he can't hear the quiver in my voice. "Rumor has it they're tracking devices. Rumor has it they're gold, thus giving prisoners strength. What is it? Can't be both."

Torg's expression is difficult to read, but there's a glimmer of pride in his round eyes. "I was unaware I was part of so many rumors. Why would I confide in you? New kid on the block trying to assert authority you don't even possess?"

His use of the word 'possess' alarms me and I almost lose enough focus to leave this poor body. There's no way I can convince Torg to come with me unless I tell him the truth.

"I'll level with you, Torg. I'm not who you think I am. Your mountain family wants you home. A war is coming, and the prison isn't safe."

He flinches at the mention of family. Voice tight, he speaks. "What do you know of my kind?"

"I know that they're concerned."

He curls his ginormous hand into a fist and slams it against the steel slab, his eyes manic. "Don't lie! You know nothing! My kind aren't welcome amongst mortals and immortals! They'd never contact the likes of you! It's only that I could pass as human that I came here to find a semblance of an education and a life."

"Life in a prison barely constitutes as a life," I mumble, forgetting who I'm possessing. "I mean, you can do more. You just need to leave."

Breathing heavily, he calms down just enough to clench his jaw and grind. "Tell me, *guard*. Who are the real enemies? Who are the antagonists? Immortals or mortals?"

There is no easy answer. There never is.

"Neither," I finally say. "And both. They've both done awful things to one another. They've both done awful things to other species. And they're both victims of horrendous violence they didn't deserve. The revolution is petty and useless."

Silence. Stillness. And then...a smile.

Mollified, Torg vanishes behind another steel door for a moment, reappearing with a golden neck band. "That's the smartest answer I've heard in a long time."

Staring at the piece, I stroke the guard's short, sweaty neck, relishing the freedom. It's incredible to swallow without the pressure of the band against my esophagus.

"Before I came along, these were made of titanium," Torg explains, his tone softening. "They infused it with tracking elements in the unlikely event a prisoner escaped."

I can feel the guard's blood pressure rise. "And now?"

"And now?" Torg grins. "Pure gold to give innocent immortals the fighting strength to persevere."

I want to drop to my knees and worship Torg, relief flooding my system. However, I'm taken by his choice of words. "Innocent immortals?"

"My question has no easy answer. The truth is, some immortals deserve to be in here and they're given titanium. The others are given gold."

"How can you define who deserves it?"

"Usually based on their corner. The northerners for example." Spluttering for words, I go to ask whether northerners are deserving of gold or not, but he interrupts me. "I'm leaving the prison tonight. I don't care what you tell the others about me, but if you're wrong about my family, I will personally return with a vengeance and throw you into one of these cursed cells myself."

"You're returning to the mountains?" I ask a little too eagerly. His safe return means we get Nellabix back.

"That is none of your concern. So long as I have distance between myself and revolting prisoners, that's all I care about. I may not be the enemy, but the prisoners are up to something. You can practically smell it. There will be riots. Violence. An uprising. The escaped immortals gave them hope. The dead immortals gave them clarity. The new owners and better food gave them a renewed lease on life. It's a recipe for something magic or something tragic. I don't want to be around to find out. If you're smart, you'll get a move on yourself. You won't stand a chance, mortal boy."

I go to smile, but the body begins to twitch instead. Gasping, a cold breeze washes over me as I'm flung out of the conscious mind, snapping back from the prison and hurtling through the fields until I crash into my own body which is inexplicably sprawled on the ground. My throat feels tight against the neckband, my ancient body aching with pains in comparison to the spritely mortal body I was in.

Torg's revelation must've shocked the guard enough to evict me from his state.

Catching my breath, I'm met by Taylin and Diarmuid who hold on to my hands.

"Are you all right?" Taylin asks.

"Are you?" I reply frantically, checking for hybrids.

"We are fine," she says, rolling her eyes. "Your body was spasming the whole time you were gone. Wasn't a pretty sight. Did you speak to Torg?"

"I did." I'm oddly thirsty, my voice raspy from the sudden shift from body to body. "I think he was already planning on leaving. He said there's a riot coming. Rumblings from prisoners. Taylin, I know I shouldn't do this, but I think I should go back in. Maybe as a prisoner and find out what's going on."

"Malin..." Taylin admonishes. "Come on. You said this wasn't our fight."

"It isn't. It is. But it isn't. But shouldn't we at least have some understanding? There was a strange vibe inside. I can't explain it, but something is happening, and it's happening soon. Won't it serve us well having intel?"

Taylin hates to admit when anybody—other than herself—is right, so she acknowledges my proposal with a begrudging wave of her hand. "Don't be gone too long. Diarmuid has already aged another year or so."

"This is true," he says, a cheeky glimmer in his eyes. "She owes me several birthday cakes."

Oh. The realization hits me. Even in the short interval I've been away, he seems older somehow. It's almost enough to convince me to stay when I stare at that loving gaze. He is perfect in every way, at least from my perspective. His deep chuckle. His contrasting hair color. The little freckle underneath his right eye. I wish he'd stay young for a little longer. *Give me a year.* One puny little year *surely* isn't asking for the world? Or perhaps it is when we're caught in the middle of a historic uprising.

"Mum," Diarmuid says, highly intuitive. "I can read it all over your face. Go."

"I hate that you're growing up without me," I confess. "It's bad enough sleeping, only to awaken to a new era in your life. You already speak like a teenager. It's difficult to comprehend when I held you in my arms not so long ago."

He shrugs unsympathetically. "Welcome to parenthood. I was never destined to be a baby or child, but my age will never impact our love for one another. It only strengthens our relationship. Luckily you don't have to suffer the resentment most parents secretly harbor. Sleep regressions, toilet training...you missed all of that! Great, right?"

Wrong. A flicker of jealousy for the normality. He definitely has the gift of the gab like his father, but I wouldn't have minded any of the unpleasant events he listed. They don't sound so unpleasant when you miss them entirely. In hindsight though, given our arduous journey amongst the elements, his brief childhood has served us well. Still...

I pull him close so that he falls into my lap, and I cradle him like a newborn. He giggles, so I ruffle his hair before smothering him with kisses. "Just try to stop me."

"I don't mind," he says, cuddling into me. "You saved me. Eternal kisses are a fair price to pay."

I saved him? He saved *me*.

I am in no rush to possess another. I use the remaining twilight to laugh and swap stories with my family until my son yawns and falls asleep on my lap. We don't light a fire in the hopes of preventing attention, optioning to huddle together for warmth. The sliver moon offers little light, and I think back to my childhood when a second moon briefly orbited our world. It was smaller, bluer and drifted away after only a year or so, but I recall it vividly. Those were bright nights and strange weather patterns. I can't help but wonder if it impacted the feuds between mortals and immortals. The moon seems to have a strange effect on people.

Taylin wakes me for my night shift watch. It's a gentle shake as opposed to her usual shove. As she settles in, I ensure that a sleeping and ever growing Diarmuid is comfortable by my side, his appearance now that of a ten-year-old.

As I lament his fading youth, I glance towards the horizon, squinting at daybreak. In the distance is Torg, bags on his broad, slumped shoulders and a triumphant grin on his face, striding towards the mountains.

He's going home.

CHAPTER XVII

"Do it now, or not at all," Taylin, ever grouchy in the morning, instructs. "I don't want to spend another second here, so if you feel strongly about this, it's now or never."

I wring my hands together, conflicted. My heart tells me to leave, but my gut tugs at me to stay. Which internal organ am I supposed to listen to?

"All right," I choke, locking eyes with a hybrid licking its snout while watching from the boulders. "I'm going in."

Diarmuid takes my hand and squeezes. "I'll hold on until you're back. That way you'll know you're safe."

My little sweetheart. I squeeze back and focus on my goal, searching for a rogue thought inside of the prison; something to latch onto.

It isn't easy. Concentrating is always the hardest part, as my mind wanders back to Diarmuid and Taylin, and the daydream that is life beyond the current conflict. But I persevere, knowing that the daydream could become a reality if I focus solely on the task at hand.

Floating through a sea of pained thoughts, I cling to one of a nearby female. Her inner monologue is quiet, more resigned to her fate. She will be easier to possess because she won't fight me as much. Zoning in on her consciousness, I glide in a little easier than the guard. Within moments, it's as if I fade away and into her body; my long fingers shrinking down to fit hers, my chin elongating into what feels like a loose, potentially broken jaw. It doesn't take long for the cold concrete to press into my malnourished body, my tattered clothes offering little protection against the urine-soaked floor. Depression floods my body, each breath only adding to the pain in my shattered ribs. I don't know what happened to this poor immortal, but my heart bleeds for her. She is too tired to even be surprised by my invasion.

"*Is this death?*" I hear her ask.

"Just a break," I whisper. "I'll respect what's yours."

The cell doors are open, the prisoners mindlessly wandering around. Some are in better shape than others, having taken advantage of the better food. I still don't know why this body isn't healing. Maybe it already has, and this is as good as it gets for her.

I groan involuntarily as I pull myself up, my roommate curled up in the corner. Dizzy from what I assume is dehydration, I struggle to find the energy to move. It's made me grateful for the far more bearable limitations my own body has endured.

Keeping close to the cell, I pay close attention to the small groups of prisoners. There are a few easterners who have had their tongues cut out, using a sign language I don't understand to excitedly express something.

I go to walk, only to realize how twisted these vessel's ankles are. Gripping to the bars, I limp forward, keeping an ear out for any useful information.

A lot of the prisoners are tired, injured or disinterested. The select few, the ones who perhaps haven't been imprisoned for as long, share quiet gossip. A group of central landers, their skin the familiar pale blue from a recent blood drain, gather in a cell at the end of the corridor. Inattentive guards tend to linger in the mid-section of the corridor, too bored by the monotony of the job to take it seriously.

"—happened when they carted me here. I swear it's true. The revolution is finally happening."

"I knew something was going on. The new owners. The dead immortals. The escaped prisoners. It was only a matter of time. So what does this mean for us? Do we kill the guards when it all goes down?"

"Probably. It's mortals versus immortals. Payback is inbound, at last."

Uncomfortable at the thought of eavesdropping, I clear my throat so they know I'm there. I haven't spotted my reflection, but this body looks worse for wear. They no doubt assumed I was a walking corpse. "Excuse me?"

They stare at me, pity in their eyes. The one with a healthier glow, plumper lips and cleaner clothes must be new here and a relatively young immortal. "Hi. Are you all right?"

"I couldn't help but overhear," I wheeze, suppressing a tight cough. "You mentioned a revolution."

"Yes. Word reached the mortal cities about the escaped immortals. It's pandemonium out there. They're gathering the mortal armies and preparing to take down the escapees and the Immortal Cells. They're blabbering on about the prison being too risky, and that we should all be permanently buried or thrown into one of the active volcanoes. Seems like an overreaction, but the armies are coming. This prison will be nothing but dust in a matter of days. It's us or them." She glances at the state of the others. "Most of them are already half-dead, but I'll fight for my rights. I don't care how many mortals I need to kill out of self-defense."

I shudder at the thought, processing what's to come. It's on a much larger scale than I anticipated. "What about the immortals? I heard about the escaped ones; Zain, I believe his name was. He was the leader of the immortal revolution?"

"Yes, I wasn't sure if he was nothing more than a myth. Word is he is gathering up the forgotten species of the land. I didn't know there was such a thing. I only recently discovered the northerners existed. I thought they were a fairy tale to warn others about the dangers of greed and control. If he can gather enough of the species, then we see the rise of a new land. One without mortals. One where we have rights and control."

The concept never sat well with me. Immortals had their time to get it right, and they failed. Nobody can ever be in charge, because it *always* goes to their head. The mortals were treated poorly, so they fought for their rights and punished the immortals. Now the cycle is repeating itself in reverse. The other species will no doubt realize they've been forgotten by history, pushed to the side, and will inevitably overtake the immortals as their form of revenge. And so on and so forth. It's a never-ending cycle. Why can nobody else see that?

Uncomfortable in this body, I thank them for their time and hobble away, feeling the onset of a panic attack. The stench of sweat suffocates me as I feel caught between worlds.

I can't seem to leave this body. I'm too grounded in its pain and suffering. My thoughts and emotions crash into one another, leaving my reality scattered. I can't untie myself from this being. I think of Taylin. I think of Diarmuid. I think of Rune. They need me... I need them...

"Malin?"

I don't expect to hear my name. For a moment I assume I'm back in my body, but I'm still very much trapped in this hellhole, struggling to catch my breath.

My jaw cracks as it drops at the sight of a very surprised Garu—a god whose face usually wears either a stern expression or no expression at all. This vulnerable look doesn't suit him. He seems so much bigger and intimidating while I'm in this smaller form, but his eyes are softer than I remember. I wonder what has happened since I've been gone.

"How can you tell?" I croak.

"I see beyond the body," he says, his tone reflecting my own. Eyes flitting from my head to my toe, he swallows. "The soul is evicted. You evicted the soul..."

I frown, unable to comprehend the statement. Mentally, I search for a sign of the body's owner but it's eerily silent. My thoughts are the only inhabitant of this vessel.

"Impossible," I rasp. "She's just...she's just..."

"What happened to you, Malin?" *Fear.* Is that *fear* in Garui's eyes? "How did you become a god?"

"What?" I attempt to shriek, but the vessel I'm in has damaged vocal chords. Garu raises his palm and rather violently shoots my subconscious out of the body like a cannonball. I pass through a floating voice that echoes on the wind.

"Sweet relief. I'd never return to that broken shell."

Slamming back into my own body, I'm not met with relief and comfort like last time. Instead, the scent of blood lingers in the air, with Diarmuid shouting at Taylin who rocks back and forth on the ground, strands of hair clinging to her sweaty, flushed face.

Groggy, I attempt and fail to sit up. "What happened?"

Diarmuid's bottom lip drops as he points to a slaughtered humanoid a few feet from Taylin. I stumble towards it, unable to recognize the species amidst all the blood. Upon closer inspection, I realize the throat has been aggressively slashed. The sight makes me dry heave.

"Taylin," I say through gritted teeth. "Why would you do this? They were our allies! The truce is off!"

"I didn't know," she cries, face scrunched up. "It was only as she was dying she explained she had a message that the rogue immortals were coming to fight. She looked like the things that attacked Nellabix and me!"

Speechless, I stare at the dead doggan. The timing couldn't have been worse. I should've stayed behind. This could've been avoided entirely.

The doggans will side with Zain for sure, now.

We've just lost the fight.

CHAPTER XVIII

"We need a service," I say, mourning the loss of the life in front of me. "We need to bury the remains."

"I'm not so sure we have time for that," Diarmuid replies, gazing at the hybrids who are inching closer, their hackles raised. "I don't think my presence will fend them off now. They're royally furious. They'd rather risk a fight on principle."

"Can you read their thoughts?" I ask, confused by how specific he's being.

"I can see it in their eyes." His tone is dark, far too mature for the young boy who stands before me. For a moment I mistake him for my brother, a man plagued by torment and troubles, who successfully plays it off with an abundance of charm and charisma. "How does one kill a hybrid?"

"With great difficulty," I recall. "If at all."

"I didn't mean to..." Taylin stares at the corpse, out of touch with reality. Her eyes are glazed over, seemingly lost in the moment she stole the doggan's life.

I don't have a chance to metaphorically talk her off the edge. A large hybrid leaps from the boulders and latches onto Taylin's ankle, thrashing her body about as it shakes its head. About six other hybrids follow suit.

Instinctively, I leap in front of Diarmuid and take the brunt of the attack, my back slamming into the hard ground. I hear my spine pop in protest as the weight of the hybrid crushes my lungs. Diarmuid screams something incoherent, but I can't hear him over the insidious growls. The hybrid's breath is warm against my skin, and I feel encompassed entirely by its large body, as if I were already in the belly of the beast.

There's no escape. Not this time.

A sharp current surges through my body, and the hybrid collapses on top of me, knocking the wind out of me. There's silence. Diarmuid says something. There are other voices. Some I don't recognize. Others I recognize all too well.

Two hands reach underneath my shoulders, dragging me out from the corpse. When they lift me to my feet, relatively unscathed, I gasp at the sight of the easterner, practically glowing with energy.

"Zain?" I say, unable to wrap my head around his presence. He looks so healthy compared to his time in the prison. "What are you doing here?"

"Good to see you've escaped, Malin!" If there's any resentful undertones in his statement, I don't notice them. He even appears more muscular than before. Maybe it's because he just rescued me, but it's the first time I could willingly call him handsome—attractive, even. I push the thought aside and force myself to remember that he chose to leave me behind in the cells, and is about to start a war to end the lives of all mortals. This man has evil intentions.

Mitty, the mortal guard who has been completely brainwashed by Zain's sweet talk, doesn't look as thrilled to see me. He definitely looks worse for wear. While Zain's health has vastly improved after leaving the cells, it appears the harsh life on the outside has only taken its toll on the much more fragile mortal body. Where Zain has regenerated, Mitty has lost a significant amount of weight and looks exhausted.

I smile politely, then quickly search for Taylin and Diarmuid.

My son is crouching next to Taylin who nurses her leg, which is covered in blood. We seem to be out of reach of Rune's healing abilities, so we'll need to tend to her before risk of infection.

The hybrids lay scattered around our tiny campsite, some dead, others too injured to move.

Behind Zain and Mitty is a small army of about thirty immortals, most with neckbands and the infinite tattoo imprinted on their wrists.

"Why are you here?" I ask Zain as I rush to Taylin's side to examine her wound. Two gaping holes left by the incisors have penetrated her skin, close to the bone. She won't be walking any time soon.

"To build up the remainder of our army and release the innocent beings from the prison," Zain says. "I told you a revolution was coming. And now it's here. I wanted more time, but the mortal armies are coming here first. I have to protect my kind. I assume that's why you're here?"

I'm too flustered to respond. Taylin is biting down on her wrist to keep from screaming, while Diarmuid tears off his makeshift robe of spare blankets and woven grass to apply pressure.

"It's fate we found one another," Zain continues, unsympathetic to the graphic scene before him. "A destiny we can't outrun. Immortals will rule the land!"

"And what's the plan?" I finally blurt, silently ensuring Taylin has our shared immortality. Unfortunately, it won't take away her pain.

"We infiltrate the prison. Storm it, actually. We can kill all the guards; cause a stir. Take down the smaller mortal villages. Burn them to the ground, recruit allies like Mitty. Work our way up. We are unstoppable, and our time is now."

I refuse to believe he is unstoppable. The fact he was searching for a bigger army says it all. Thirty immortals against trained guards and nasty weapons won't bode well. I wonder if he knows what I've been sneakily doing behind his back.

Releasing prisoners is idealistic, but converting them into soldiers is cruel. Sharnique, for better or for worse, might be the only one who can stop Zain. She was the god who literally killed an immortal. She might be our only answer.

As I tend to Taylin, I shudder at the memory of Garu's accusation. Why would he call me a god? Clearly he was misinformed. I didn't evict a soul. Her consciousness simply chose not to hang on to her crumbling body.

Unless...that's what Sharnique did to my transparent ally...

I push aside the thought. It's not serving me in the present. "Sounds like a great plan, Zain. I'll join you. We can infiltrate the top floor of the towers. Ensure there's no mortals up there who might send out a signal for help."

Zain pauses. "Good thinking. Mitty can go with you."

My heart flutters at the sight of a malnourished Mitty, the dark circles beneath his eyes now permanent fixtures. He's almost unrecognizable beneath the ratty beard, but he looks just as displeased with the idea as I do. I *almost* pity him. It wasn't necessarily his fault that he fell for the allure of Zain's charisma. Most easterners have their tongues cut out due to their ability to convince most people to do what they want, but the particularly intelligent ones can talk their way out of a tongue cut before it happens.

"Mitty?" I repeat, unsure of what Zain's angle is.

"Yes. It'll be safer for him to go into the tower. A potential bloodbath is on the horizon. Mortal guards and a mortal army attacking immortal prisoners. He'll die, and I don't want that to happen."

He *sounds* sincere but my gut says otherwise. I consider listening to his thoughts to check, but the exercise seems redundant. Besides, I'm a little put off after my last experience. I'll check in with him when he least expects it and when I'm not as jittery.

Zain nudges Mitty to the front and I take note of the immortals awaiting instruction from behind. They all share the same intense gaze, the same locked jaw. Nothing more than angry copies, fixated on their leader and buzzing impatiently beneath the surface, they crave mortal blood on their hands. I don't need to read their savage minds to know they want to see Mitty dead. It makes me wonder how much bullying and torment Mitty has endured since journeying with them.

"Hi Mitty," I whisper, but we both avoid eye contact. He's

ashamed, and I've yet to forgive him. It makes for an awkward exchange.

"Hi," he mouths, undoubtedly too physically weak and too emotionally drained to say much more.

"No time like the present," Zain announces. "Crew, you know what to do. We strike clean. We hold no prisoners. We are better than them."

We're as bad as one another, I think, throwing myself into the mix. I'm not above any immortal, mortal or god. We all have something to learn from one another, and I can't understand why I'm the only one with that mentality.

As Zain gathers his immortal army, they stoically stride forward, while I stay behind with Taylin, Mitty and Diarmuid.

"Zain," I shout, knowing that this could be the last time I see him. Although my intentions are to stop him, I'm still grateful. "Thank you for killing the hybrids just now. That would've been very messy for us."

He stares at me with an eyebrow raised. "They were dead just as I got to you. Dropped like they'd had a heart attack. I thought you must've had something to do with it."

I don't respond and he's too distracted with his army to interrogate me further. They continue towards the prison. Taylin is still cursing with her eyes squeezed shut, nursing her injury. Mitty folds his arms, swaying back and forth like he's nauseated by the stench of death. And Diarmuid looks at me sheepishly, his lips pursed.

All I can do is gape at him.

CHAPTER XIX

"You can't leave me behind!" Taylin shouts in between strained gasps. "Besides, you're mortal! It's suicide going inside!"

"We're going to the tower," I say dismissively.

"Exactly! You don't know if Adalin is still in there! She'll kill you on the spot!"

"You're forgetting I have a new little talent." My tone is somewhat arrogant, but I certainly don't feel confident using it. Now that Garu knows I'm around only adds to my paranoia, but I'm in too deep with Mitty by my side. I need to free Sharnique and stop Zain. Now that Taylin killed a doggan who was most likely only warning us of his arrival, I can't be sure the hybrids and doggans won't switch sides on principle.

"What? Diarmuid? Did you see what he did? It was like Garu the way he shocked the hybrids. This kid might be something more. Maybe your brother was right."

Diarmuid and I widen our eyes.

"*Stop talking so freely in front of Mitty*," I project into Taylin's mind.

"Oh, he's a dead man walking," she dismisses. "His eyes are all glassy. Barely knows he's alive."

"Don't underestimate him," I say, and Mitty only looks at me with an appreciative, albeit weak grin. What has Zain done to his spirit?

Taylin is in too much agony to argue, and instead flinches when Diarmuid gently tries to sweep the hair out of her eyes. "Aunt Taylin?"

"Thanks, but no thanks," she says, breathing through a wave of pain. "You're scary. Those eyes were like lightning when you shot them. You are not staying here with me."

I watch as Diarmuid's face drops and my heart breaks. I hurry towards him and wrap a supportive arm around his shoulders. "You don't trust him?"

"He's powerful, Malin. You didn't see it. I know his kind age quickly, and we've witnessed it firsthand, but he's only a month or so old. He hasn't harnessed his ability. There's no control. He could accidentally kill us all."

"That's not true!" he protests. "I knew what I was doing! I trusted the sensation and focused only on the hybrids! Mum, you believe me, don't you?"

"Of course I do," I say, stroking his hair. "Thank you, Diarmuid. You saved us."

"There's a reason why your brother and his birth mother feared him, Malin. I didn't understand until I witnessed what they most likely foresaw in their dreams. That boy has extreme power. More than your puny little mental abilities. He might be on par with Garu. He could be even mightier. I don't know, and I don't want to know."

I'm too blinded by rage to form a coherent sentence. "Taylin, I, you...you fought for...we...he only..."

"Save it!" Taylin grunts. "I'm done for, anyway. Go to the tower. I'll hold the fort here, and if we all survive what's to come, then we can revisit our bleak future. I'd rather chance a war than an ever changing, almighty boy." She inhales shakily. "Although I doubt you'll want to return to me now that I've said that. I'm sorry, Malin. I'm sorry, kid. The truth is, you freaked me out."

"I was only protecting my family," Diarmuid utters, using my body as a shield. "I never meant to scare anyone."

Taylin is only overreacting because of the pain—that *has* to be the excuse. I relay this to Diarmuid, but his little heart is already broken. He can no longer suppress the sobs, which only makes me more emotional. In his short life, he's been rejected for reasons that he can't control and that don't make logical sense.

"We have to go," I decide. "We don't have time for a family feud. If you're here when we return then we'll take it from there."

I'm not interested in a reply. Taking Diarmuid by the hand, I charge towards the prison with Mitty close on my heels.

"Ah, what is wrong with the child?" His breath is pungent, his voice much raspier than I remember.

"Nothing," I practically spit. "He is a gift."

He wheezes uphill, but I don't slow down to accommodate him. It's like he wants to engage in a deep and meaningful conversation, taking a breath as if about to begin talking before thinking better of it.

"Why does Aunt Taylin hate me?" Diarmuid finally asks as we approach the prison.

"Stop it," I admonish. "She doesn't. Delirium caused by pain, coupled by the surprise of the attack means she isn't thinking straight. When she is healed and this war is over, everything will be fine. Just you watch. I imagine she is already feeling guilty for how she reacted."

He reaches out and squeezes my hand. As I squeeze back, I feel his hand grow ever so slightly in my palm. Loosening my grip to make room for his longer fingers, I glance at his face. No matter how chiseled he becomes or tall he grows, he will always be that beautiful baby I rescued from certain death. He will always be the uncertain boy who was neglected by his own family. He will always be my child that I'll love unconditionally.

"There are no guards outside," Mitty says, redirecting my attention back to the prison.

"The prisoners were on edge. The guards might be preparing for a riot." As we take a turn towards the tower entrance, I watch as Zain's tiny army scales the walls. It is peculiar watching them break inside, when all we ever wanted was to break out.

"They're relentless." Mitty stares in awe as the immortals help one another climb the walls. "I've made a lot of mistakes in my life, Malin. I left behind a wife and a daughter. I chose to work in a job that offered security instead of a job that offered happiness. I helped slaughter a defenseless mortal to feed hungry immortals. I don't want those moments to define me, but they do. I'm a good person who has made bad decisions. That ends today. Malin, I'm twisted. I'm broken. I feel so confused to the point of being unable to tell the difference between good and bad. I am finished. Please, allow me to put my faith in your decisions."

"I'm awful at making decisions," I confess.

"I don't believe that." He motions at the unguarded doorway which leads to the tower. A cold shiver runs down my spine as I remember my last moments fleeing down those stairs, chased by Wylin and his siblings. Now that I'm standing face-to-face with my past, I'm terrified that Taylin might be right. What if Adalin is waiting upstairs? What if Mitty is in on it? What if I release Sharnique from stone and she kills me—just like she killed my transparent ally who has been disconcertingly quiet ever since she possessed Dalin.

I attempt to listen for rogue thoughts, but instead I'm inundated with mental anguished cries from mortals and prisoners alike. The attacks have begun. It's not too intense yet. There are sneaky hits. Strangulation. Those taken for leverage. I need to get to the top of the tower before too many lives are destroyed. It's what drives me forward.

Hand in hand, Diarmuid and I hurry up the stairs as Mitty pants heavily from behind.

He isn't well.

Bursting through the curtain and into the circular room, I'm both relieved and suspicious to find nothing but a stone Sharnique, exactly where I left her.

Oh, the guilt. The *guilt*. I never intended for this to happen to her, of course. It was self-defense, but I feel terrible all the same. At least I can atone for my sins by releasing her from such a horrific fate. I can only hope she's in a deep slumber. It'd be much worse if she was frozen in place and aware of each monotonous second passing her by.

"Oh, my..." Mitty marvels at the sight of the magnificent woman, picture perfect even cast in stone. She makes death look glamorous.

Diarmuid is less impressed, his attentive eyes taking in the image in all of its tragic glory. "This was a god?"

"And she will be again," I say, pulling the stone from my pocket.

"Why?" Mitty asks, glancing at the stone with a little too much intrigue. "Why would you release her?"

"She never wanted a revolution," I explain. "She can stop Zain."

Mitty visibly flinches at my words. "Stop Zain?"

"Don't have reservations on me now," I warn. "You just said you trust my judgment and my decisions. I have no time or patience for a traitor. Not again."

He wants to object. He *wants* to reason. But to his credit, he inhales sharply and nods once. He knows it isn't worth it. We're both mortal, so he could technically stop me in my tracks, however with Diarmuid by my side and Taylin's snap reaction, Mitty can only guess what he's capable of.

"I have no idea how to use this properly," I admit, tossing the stone over in my hand. There is no telling if I'm making the right decision or not. I could be unleashing something much worse than an angry immortal hellbent on destroying an inferior species. I just have to trust my instinct.

I blow on the stone, although I have no idea why, and place the pointy end on the tip of Sharnique's forehead. I feel like I'm violating her for some reason, so I apologize under my breath.

Electricity surges through the air, the fire is suddenly ablaze and hungry for sustenance. I step back, watching as the stone in my hand turns to black, completely fried of power.

Sharnique's cast trembles, the stone transitioning to a shiny marble before small lines appear all over her body. Unpleasant cracks sound as I step backwards, the cast smashing at her feet. Within moments, color is restored and Sharnique is reanimated. She stretches out, wriggles her fingers and greets me with a sly grin.

Mitty bows awkwardly at the sight, but Diarmuid holds his ground, a suspicious look on his round face.

"Hello, Sharnique," I greet.

She grunts delicately, the way a baby might when waking up from a refreshing nap. Taking in the environment, her expressionless gaze lands on Diarmuid. "Hello, Malin. First thing is first."

Before I have a chance to react, she aims her palm at Diarmuid and an invisible force shoots him out of the window, his little body thrown through the air and vanishing out of sight.

I scream. I drop to my knees. I vomit. I scream again. And I pass out.

CHAPTER XX

"Where is he?" I hear myself repeat over and over, but it's like I'm not in my body. It's as if I'm beside it, completely disassociated. I feel the cool, unhelpful breeze as Mitty fans my face, the stench of my own vomit only adding to my nausea.

The image of Diarmuid being flung out the window is on replay, fading with each re-run as my brain scrambles to destroy the traumatic scene. It knows my body can't cope.

"Please please please please," I hear myself plead, my chest compressing with each word. My body has forgotten how to breathe.

"The boy was a threat to immortals," Sharnique says calmly. I can't see her, and I'm not sure why. My eyes must be closed. Everything is a distant concept, a reality overlapping with a world I no longer feel I belong in. "An abomination. Mixed species never bode well. Why do you think the corners were always separated? Other entities tucked away and hidden from history books? Even the gods chose to leave this land. That child should not exist. I digress. How are you, Malin? My premonition of one sister living in the name of peace is unfortunately still an accurate depiction of the future. Have you managed to confront her yet? Did I miss the revolution? I certainly hope so. I do not enjoy confrontation."

"My son, he's my son, give me my son!" My words. My mouth. But I feel *nothing*. I control nothing.

"*Malin*. This is tiresome. Let him go. He wasn't yours to begin with and he is gone now. This is why you should resist naming entities. Attachment is a mortal error. Immortals know better than to bond with anything. We understand that nothing lasts forever."

I force my eyes open. Nothing has changed in this sinister,

luxurious tower. It remains untouched by the last few chaotic moments that have irrevocably altered my entire future, my entire being.

Sharnique is staring at the fire, running her perfect fingers through her perfect hair. Mitty is crouched beside me, his face blotchy and wet from tears. I want to charge at her and kill her, but the action would be useless.

"I know what you are thinking," Sharnique says. "And you would be correct in assuming the uselessness of such a choice. I can certainly stop this Zain character. By stop, I mean kill. You have recently discovered how easy it is to annihilate an immortal, yes? It takes the fun out of the mystery once you accidentally do it, doesn't it? He won't slip away as easily though. He is very much linked to his body. However, Zain is the least of your worries. I fear my abilities won't be much use soon. The land is poisoned by the uprising. My abilities are weakening. So are yours."

Dizzy with grief, I can't pay attention to anything she says. "Diarmuid. Where did you send him?"

"Nowhere." Sharnique glances over her shoulder and rolls her eyes. "I am anticipating his death will be caused by the impact of his landing. At least, I hope so. I didn't have time to foresee the event. That is a whole ritual which takes time I did not possess. Malin, I grow tired of the exposition. Surely I don't have to explain *every little thing*. You can't be a princess in this state. You can't overcome your sister like this. Pull yourself together."

"You took away the *one* thing that means anything to me!" My vocal chords shred as my shrill cry fills the small space. I can't kill a god—but I plan to hurt her as viciously as I can before I throw myself out of the window.

Mitty links his arms through mine and holds me back. "Breathe, Malin. Please, breathe. Your blood pressure looks like it's through the roof."

"For what purpose should I breathe?" I snap. "Each breath is agony! Each breath means nothing!"

"So dramatic," Sharnique laments. "What is done is done. You can join your 'son' afterwards if you so wish; I can even help you. However, the revolution is upon us. I can hear the thoughts below. The prisoners are attacking the guards. The mortal army is approaching. The doggans are coming, as is your sister. Choose the selfless path and aid in history."

"Aid in history?" I clench my jaw, shrugging off Mitty who is utterly unhelpful with his constant desire to rest his hand on my shoulder. "I don't owe anybody anything!"

"She might be able to bring your son back!" Mitty blurts, his eyes widening when we both turn to stare at him. "I mean, you're a god aren't you? You can do that? M-maybe you'll bring that boy back if Malin agrees to be the sister who survives?"

I shoot a hopeful look at Sharnique, who merely lifts a flippant hand in response. I'm unsure of the power the gods hold. She threw my son from the tower in a brash manner, not even utilizing her foresight to see if it was for the best. There is the possibility that she knows she acted irrationally. Could I trust her enough to bring him back?

The thought is enough to calm me. My heart still feels like it could burst through my rib cage, but I can think a little clearer. There's hope now. There's *hope*. She might bring him back. I just need to hold on...

"Fine," I relent. "So what do we do now?"

As Sharnique's eyes reflect the blazing fire, she curls her hand into a fist. "Curses. I thought as much." She speaks mostly to herself, before turning to address us. "I channeled Zain. I glanced into the near future. Malin, I cannot kill him. I cannot possess him. My powers have depleted significantly. It happened the second the riots began. We are extremely sensitive to the land in that manner. We need peace and we need it urgently. I trust you will feel your own abilities sinking into the abyss the longer they battle. You must throw yourself into the thick of it. Get the immortals who don't wish to fight away from the prison. Keep faith in the friendships you've made along the way. They are our only hope."

Friendship seems a rather loose term. I've made acquaintances, perhaps, but even that definition is pushing the boundaries.

Tugging on Mitty's arm, I am all too eager to face my destiny so that I can return to my son. "I'll be back, Sharnique. And if you don't return my son—"

"—then *what?*" She remains perfectly nonchalant. She knows I'm bluffing. "There is very little you can do to me, Malin. Why do you think gods gather together? We are stronger together than apart. We are our own worst enemy and our only advocates. Peace is a feast. War is a bore."

I ignore the panicked look in Mitty's eyes. "I assume you are not referring to me as a god."

"Of course I am. You are one of us."

I forget how to swallow, unable to cope with the continuous revelations. "I'm barely an immortal."

"What do you think gods are? Nothing more than immortals who have accessed greater abilities through genetics, training and intelligence. Welcome to the club, Malin. From one god to another; I wish you all the best."

I've stepped into a nightmare. Perhaps I stumbled upon a creature in the fields who distorts reality and makes you think you're awake. Or maybe I did use the dream crystal, and this is a vivid dream. Literally anything else would make sense.

Only, it wouldn't. Deep down, I had a feeling this was the case. I could feel something within me shift the moment my abilities grew. From tracking Taylin, to hearing thoughts, to possessing others, something on a cellular level altered. I just couldn't acknowledge it. And I still won't.

"Stop lying," I say flippantly, choosing those as my last words. It's not extravagant. It's not pithy. It is however, all I have to offer.

Mitty trips over himself as I pull him down the stairs with me. We run. I want to sprint for miles and find my son, but it would only be a disservice to all of us. I need to get to the prisoners.

Outside of the tower, alarms sound. The muffled explosion of guns firing and the warrior cries of guards and prisoners alike take place within the walls. I can't begin to imagine the horrific bloodshed. My imagination is creative, but even that can't prepare me for what I'm no doubt about to find.

"What's the quickest way into the prison?" I ask Mitty, who looks even paler than usual.

He pats his trouser pocket, pulling out a set of keys. He offers me a rusted, copper key that has seen better days. "There is an entrance from the yard; the one the carnivores tended to utilize the most. Follow me."

"You'll die," I dismiss. "Just give me the directions."

"If I die, so be it."

"No, Mitty. You said your father fought for immortal rights. You said you've left behind a wife and a daughter. Why would you choose to repeat history and allow your family to go on without you? You have played your part in history and have done your father proud. You don't have to die like him."

He blinks as if it's the first time it's occurred to him, or rather as if a misty veil has been lifted from his perspective. "Zain said I did."

"Zain says a lot of things. You do not owe anybody anything because you are mortal. You should never be sorry for who you are because of what your ancestors did. You are not responsible for their karmic debts. You must not feel guilt or shame. Their past is not your present. Do you understand?"

He nods, but he looks unconvinced. "Mortal guilt is legitimate. My kind should have never—"

"—did you ever hurt an immortal?" I interrupt and wait for him to say no. "So why should you be punished? It is an absurd notion to carry the blame of a previous generation."

Mitty doesn't argue, whether it be because he is far too brainwashed to think clearly, or because my opinion has finally shed some light, I can't be sure.

Snapping my fingers, I wait for Mitty to reluctantly place the key in my palm. With an enthusiastic pat on his shoulders, I push him away from the prison. "Find your family. This war is not yours to fight."

He can't meet my gaze. "I hurt you. You asked have I ever hurt an immortal and I hurt you."

"Doesn't count," I say. "Zain manipulated you. Besides, I am almost certain I was a mortal when that happened, so your conscience is cleared."

A forced smile curves on his lip. As much as I'd love to help him, I'm short on both time and patience. All I can think about is getting Diarmuid back.

"If it helps," I say, "I forgive you. Now go."

Mitty takes my hand, his sunken eyes watery. "I hope you find your happily ever after, Malin."

"Me too." I hug the ex-guard and urge him in the other direction. Like a lost child, he wanders away from the screams and over the mountains. I don't know how he plans to get home, or even where that might be, but just like Torg, he has taken the first step. He is free from his past, in more ways than one.

In a strange way, I feel like the shackles from my own past have been slightly loosened. Gripping a key which has no doubt seen its fair share of distressed prisoners and guards in turmoil, I bolt around the prison block until I find the door to the yard Mitty referenced.

The screams from inside make me want to shrivel up and hide, but I have a duty. As a princess, as a mother, as a mortal, as an immortal, as a *god*...I need to serve the land.

I lean against the door to open it, grunting at the weight. I'm overwhelmed by the stench, the shuddering screams and the weapons clanging.

Through the dull corridor, I persevere, knowing how unprotected I am without my shield of immortality. But I don't care. Fueled by anger and motivated by hope, I charge forward...

...before squealing like a young child as a guard is thrown mere feet in front of me, his spine cracking against the concrete. Across from him is a wide-eye immortal prisoner, frothing at the mouth.

Cautiously, I point at my branded tattoo and neckband to prove I'm one of them. They merely nod, their appearance difficult to discern through the mud, blood and goodness knows what else.

I doubt there is reasoning with this particular prisoner.

Navigating through the cells, I project my thoughts to find the thoughts of the reserved prisoners who don't want to battle. They're the ones I'll release first. Then the wounded mortals. Then negotiate with the embittered immortals. Another plan which only sounds simplistic in theory.

The thoughts are a mixed bag and I can't pinpoint whether it's the guards or the prisoners.

"ABOUT TIME. I'LL KILL THEM ALL."

"I've been wanting to use this for a while..."

"Just kill me. Just kill me."

"I saw this in a dream."

"Ouch, ouch, ouch, ouch."

"Play dead...play dead."

"Idiots. They think they can win?"

"No..."

"This is just like last time. What a waste of blood."

"How dare they! I'll show them!"

"What is the point?"

"Blood!"

The thoughts certainly contradict the barrage of screams and profanities echoing throughout the confined battle field.

I attempt to listen in again, but find my concentration struggling, as if in the throes of falling asleep. It's like I'm being pulled back into my own mind. Is it fatigue? Or is Sharnique's warning accurate? Are my abilities weakening with each passing second?

I'm fortunate enough to find an immortal cowering in the corner of her cell. She is pale blue from a recent blood draining, her once white gown now torn and covered in filth. Most immortals look relatively young, and I'm guessing she would only be in her sixties or so. A child, essentially.

Offering my hand, I pull her to her feet. Trembling, she screams when a nearby gun sounds.

"I don't want to fight," she says, her teeth chattering. "I don't know how, and I don't regenerate! I've always taken care of my body. I didn't even know I was an immortal until I survived being poisoned!"

"You don't need to reason with me," I say gently. "See where I came from? I left the door open. Escape. Run. Go back to wherever you call home. Despite the actions of a few, mortals are not your enemy. We can bring peace to the land again."

"How?"

"Just trust me. War does not bring peace. Find others like you along the way and do not get swept up in the propaganda."

There must be something about my eyes that allows the young immortal to trust me. Visibly terrified, she nods and looks at the direction I came from. Following my instruction, she runs through the corridor. I know it's the last time I'll probably ever see her—I just hope she makes it out safely.

My ears ring, and my left cheek stings from a graze. When a warm essence gushes from my flesh, I turn to find a wounded guard slumped over in a prison cell with a spear in his back. His eyes glazed over, he forces a smile and spits up blood, his revolver hanging loosely in his hand.

Heart racing, I realize how narrowly I avoided death. My emotional response would be to kill this man, but he can suffer in silence. I enter his cell and snatch the revolver from his hand and stuff it into my pocket.

"Hideous flesh wound," he mocks. "You may not die, but your body can live with that scar forever."

"Joke's on you," I taunt. "My best friend is a healer."

He doesn't hear me. He's already dead.

And I feel like a petty fool for sinking to his level.

I'm tempted to find out how ugly this mark is, but it's the least of my worries, especially considering I'm technically mortal. The pain is excruciating, but blood loss could kill me. Tearing the fabric from the guard's uniform, I wrap it around my face to support the structure and consider myself lucky that it serves as a disguise. It also helps cover the putrid smell.

As I turn into the next cell block, I'm inundated by immortals who have been hacked into, mostly cut from the waist down. Their torsos drag across the floor as they try to reassemble themselves and aid others. The sobs are genuinely heartbreaking and I wonder how many of them actually fought and how many were already resigned.

"Rune can heal them," I whisper to myself. "Rune can heal them. My brother will teach other healers. We will heal all of them."

There's nothing I can do for them. I try to communicate, but their anguish distracts them from my instructions. I can only hope Zain doesn't find this cell block. It will only enrage him to the point of absolute mortal annihilation.

My endless search proves to be a hopeless exercise. After covering three cell blocks, I only manage to release two prisoners and one guard. At least, I can hope as much. I have no confirmation whether they make it outside or not.

I did, however, come up with the idea that those who do not wish to participate in the uprising should have a signal to use with one another in the event they cross paths. If they run into one another on the outside, they are to flash their index fingers and thumbs held together, to symbolize the infinite sign. This signifies peace. I don't know if it's a good idea or not, but it might prevent any spontaneous attacks out of self-defense.

My mortal body feels the ache of my wound and the dehydration that accompanies it. Following the warrior cries, I take the circular stairs, sneering at the bodies that have been carelessly thrown down.

The other cell blocks were paradise compared to this one. I'm on the floor of the carnivores who have had a feast. Zain, shirtless and proud of the various bullet holes in his abdomen laughs wickedly as he impales a guard with a spear.

There is no sense of heroic duty here. No melancholy. Nothing. Only sheer delight.

I attempt to read his thoughts, thinking I might be able to possess him, but Sharnique is right. I'm weak. The more death this uprising brings, the less I can pull on the power of the land.

Loud horns play a triumphant melody from outside the walls of the prison. I recognize them; it's the warning call from the mortal army. They're smart enough not to fight against immortals, so they'll probably destroy the prison from the outside in. Explosives, fire, vicious hybrids—anything and everything.

"Hear that, boys?" Zain declares, and I take offense at his reference to his gender despite his fellow women. "The army is here. It'll be delightfully messy, but once we show them we are the boss, we will take back this land!"

"No it won't, Zain." My voice is muffled through the makeshift tourniquet, so I pull it down. "I'm begging you. Ruling using fear never works."

"Oh. It's you." He rolls his eyes, his loyal followers sneering at me. "Didn't recognize you. I see your precious mortals made artwork of your face."

I won't allow his snide comment to hurt me; not when it's already physically painful enough. Besides, my appearance doesn't matter. And Rune can heal me. Rune can heal me...

"If the army is here, they've already surrounded the prison," I say. "They'll burn us alive. Your existence won't be worth it. Surrender now and we can work this out another way."

"I don't understand you," he says disapprovingly. "Mortals put you here and you still deign to save them."

"I deign to be their equals," I correct. "I've lived through war before. I've lived through ruling mortals. I can't be clearer when I say it doesn't work. It never has and it never will."

"Says a *northerner*!" An immortal I don't recognize hisses, using my heritage as slander. It is impressive how they manage to make my geographical location sound like an obscenity.

"Yes. Says a *northerner*," I respond, finally taking ownership of my past. It isn't a glamorous past, but it's mine, and without it I wouldn't be here standing between worlds. "As a *northerner* I understand firsthand how greed and control divides all. I have witnessed the implications of living such a lifestyle. Who else can say they've watched their kind turn on one another? Because that's what happens. When there are no more mortals left, immortals will turn on one another because power attracts the desire for more power. It is never enough."

"We will not relinquish our rights!" Zain shouts and for a moment I'm convinced he is about to lunge at me.

"We shouldn't," I agree. "But killing mortals and imprisoning them isn't the solution."

"It's the only way they'll listen."

"It isn't! Believe it or not, most don't want to fight. Most don't hold resentment. It's fear. Look at us. Look at what we're doing. Of *course* they fear us. Of *course* they want us locked up."

Smoke seeps through the various cracks of the prison. I don't need to be told that the army has begun the process of setting the giant building aflame. Escape won't be pretty, regardless how we go about it.

Redirecting his attention, Zain snarls at the black mist as it snakes through the corridors. "A bit of fire never hurt anyone. They will pay for this."

He alerts his 'boys,' and as they gather together, they seemingly unite as one and channel all their hatred, all their tension onto me. I don't know what to do. In any given minute, they might spring at me, ending me once and for all. I can only hope it'll be quick and relatively painless.

As I brace for whatever is about to happen, we simultaneously freeze in our spots.

Frantic screams are heard outside. Frenzied shouts. Gunshots.

Snarls. And the howls of grief-stricken doggans hellbent on revenge after one of their own was betrayed by a tall northerner.

Zain merely turns to me and smirks.

CHAPTER XXI

I t's a race outside. Suddenly, the remaining guards are low on Zain's priority list. He doesn't even care to help the injured immortals or convince them to join his violent cause—he just wants to breathe fresh air and secure a premium view as the doggans tear into the mortal army.

I'm right behind him; struggling to keep up. My strides are longer, but he's so incomprehensibly fast. He powers through, despite his various flesh wounds and injuries, seemingly resilient. I'm not as fortunate. The pain in my jaw is beginning to hinder my grasp on reality. Light headed, each heavy step feels like it shakes my brain around, but I can't focus on the physical. Even though I understand the importance of living in the present, years of perpetual torment and pain have trained me to imagine my present state in a future without such ailments. Some say that's how they manifest their realities, but I mustn't be doing a very good job at it, because I'm still miserable despite envisioning a happier life.

We run towards both salvation and impending doom. Choking on the smoke that continues to waft through the prison, I change my direction. I don't know how Zain intends to leave, but if it's via athletically scaling a wall, then I don't have the energy. I retrace my steps, screaming at the wounded to leave, knowing full well there is nobody who can help them.

"Do you know a way out?"

Startled, I turn to find one of Zain's immortals close on my heel. He has a bruised eye and tear-stained cheeks. "What?"

"Is it close by? I'm strong. I might be able to drag a few of them out."

I glance at the broken immortals and take note of a couple guards who are barely breathing, slumped over in the cells. "Only if you save a mortal for each immortal."

I expect him to object, but he doesn't. Instead, he runs towards a petite guard and throws him over his shoulder. He then lifts a prisoner to her feet and encourages her to walk. "Show us the way."

We charge through the winding corridors, and I open the doors. Outside is just as chaotic, flames licking at the prison walls. Covering my face with the tourniquet, I watch as the immortal finds a safe place to lower the injured. Without missing a beat, he rushes back inside to help whoever he can. A nameless hero.

Sweat stings my eyes, the incessant heat worsening as I run towards the front of the prison. The Immortal Cells are so big that the army has yet to surround the entire perimeter, and by the sounds of the battle ahead, they won't find their way back here any time soon. Ahead are the vicious warrior doggans, magnificently beautiful in battle as they slay the clumsier mortals who will always be inexperienced with weapons and martial arts in comparison to any immortal counterpart.

Clearing the lump in my throat, I watch the slaughter in horror. The doggans are only doing this because Taylin killed their kind. I attempt to use my abilities to do something, *anything*, but I'm tapped out. I can't read a thought. I certainly can't possess a mind. There is literally nothing I can do.

Full of energy, Zain and his followers scale the walls at the front of the prison and leap from the top, rolling through the flames and into the bloodshed. Brutally, they join the doggans and attack the mortals, halting only when decapitated. The mortals seem to be using that as their only form of defense. It obviously doesn't kill their enemy; but it stops them.

So much gore. So much death. It's torturous and unnecessary. They're as bad as one another...both sides victims *and* perpetrators.

"Disgusting."

A familiar face, no matter how transparent or haunting.

"You've returned," I say, relieved. "Are you all right?"

"I told you. I never leave you. You are the light in the darkness. It just takes effort to project."

"What did you do with Dalin?"

"The obnoxious northerner? It will be an effort to retrieve him. Never mind about him."

Her flippancy would be cause for concern if I remotely cared for his wellbeing. For all I know, he deserves whatever horrors have befallen him.

"What do we do?" I ask, referring to the battle. "How do we stop this?"

She frowns, shimmering in the breeze. "I am not sure if the word *we* is the correct terminology. That Zain character needs to die, though. His death will be enough for his followers to stop. They're mostly brainwashed by his gift of the gab."

I snort. "How do you kill an immortal?"

"A god killed me," she says. "In hindsight, she possessed me. My soul, my consciousness, whatever you want to call it, didn't know how to reattach to my body."

The thought upsets me and I dispel the notion that I unintentionally did the same thing to an innocent being only hours earlier. "I can't do that."

"This isn't the time to be ethical."

"I mean I physically can't. The land is suffering from the battle. Abilities are drawn from the power of the land. I'm weakened."

"But I'm not. I no longer belong to the land. It doesn't affect me." She pauses. "Is this why I was killed? Was I chosen for a greater purpose?"

Being chosen implies a destiny handcrafted by the universe, or a protagonist with a story specifically carved and designed just for them. This isn't the case. She was selected at random, her destiny tethered only to mine.

"I can't guarantee it will work," she continues. "I possessed Dalin, and he had no intention of separating from his body. I am not quite sure how to evict Zain's consciousness entirely. He seems far too stubborn. What a revelation. Was I not strong enough to hold on when I was killed?"

"On the contrary," I say, "perhaps you were selected because you showcased utter determination. If Sharnique killed an immortal with little ambition or anger, then we wouldn't be having this conversation. In fact, there was a second immortal whose life she claimed. Maybe that's why she targeted you afterwards. Maybe the first immortal had no desire to fight back. Maybe Sharnique foresaw that." *Maybe* she was *chosen* after all. "You are the key to ending this. You possess the anger that I don't. If I get too aggravated, I break down and cry. I don't have the willpower to follow through on violence. You were sacrificed, but you're the answer. You are the only one who can evict Zain from his body."

Her expression is impossible to read. Stunned, perhaps. Chagrined? Whatever she's feeling, she needs to channel it. She needs to end the war.

"I wanted to kill Sharnique when you uncast her from the stone," she says, flickering in and out from this plane. "I thought about striking amidst your grief, but something stopped me. I don't like what's become of me, but I think you are right. Without me, the land has no chance. I don't want my daughter growing up in a place like this."

"You have a daughter?" I ask, bewildered.

"Somewhere," she smiles sadly. "Our connection was lost long ago when I was imprisoned. I'd love to see her again."

"I can find her," I say. "It's the least I can do. Travel with me and we will locate her when the war is over."

She shrugs. "Play it by ear. We do not know what the future holds. Not all of us, anyway."

There's something about the way she says it, like she is aware of something I'm not.

"Thank you for this," I say, the pair of us lost in an ethical conundrum as chaos unfolds around us, the prison collapsing and crumbling from fire and mortal catapults.

Deep down, she isn't a murderer. We are like two sides of the same coin. She, ferocious and me, too sensitive for my own good. Yet, we don't truly wish harm on anyone, especially not when we have to be the ones to inflict said harm.

"It is a cliche, but it is for the greater good." She stares at Zain from our safe vantage point, mustering up the emotional strength. "No use in delaying the inevitable. Each second wasted is another life that could've been spared."

"Thank you," I repeat. What else could I possibly say?

She vanishes into a wisp, floating towards Zain who narrowly avoids what would've been a clean decapitation served by a skilled mortal. Noticing the near miss, Zain lets out an animalistic cry and lunges towards the attacker. Weaponless and shieldless, he uses brute force to strike a blow, the sheer confidence alone enough to confuse the enemy.

As the wisp invades Zain, he seemingly malfunctions for a moment, trembling violently. He doesn't dodge the mortal as well as he could've and shouts a loud profanity as a sword strikes his shoulder. I can't help but wonder whether the curse came from Zain or the entity possessing him.

I crouch down as I watch, not wanting to draw attention to myself. Glancing over my shoulder, I notice the free prisoners and injured guards helping one another sneak away, fleeing into the mountains. A weak smile spreads across my face as I beg the skies to offer them protection. To see perpetual enemies—immortal versus mortal, prisoner versus guard—come together and aid one another in such a crisis gives me hope for the dark future ahead.

"RETREAT!" Zain yells, his voice tight. He drops to his knees, then leaps up suddenly. "ATTACK!"

His confused followers stumble over themselves, several of them losing their heads. The doggans aren't as distracted from Zain's random outburst. They don't work for him after all; so long as their ally isn't the northerner who killed one of their own.

"RE...TACK!" Zain cries, fighting not only the mortals but the invader in his mind.

"Come on," I urge, watching helplessly. "End this. *End* this."

I think of Diarmuid, but push the thoughts away, lest I begin sobbing uncontrollably. I can't break down now. There is no sense in entertaining the thought that he's gone forever. I won't allow it.

I want to help, but I also want to turn away and run. I don't want to kill Zain. An immortal's death is unknown. Do we truly cease to exist for all eternity? I may not be the one physically pushing him out, but his death is due to my instruction. There will be blood on my hands forever.

"Sir?" An immortal reaches over to Zain, who swings a mighty punch and knocks the follower out cold. It's impossible to tell who is in control of Zain's body.

After a moment, Zain drops to all fours and dry-heaves. He shouts something nonsensical, convulsing involuntarily. Despite the physical battle around him, the internal war is a fight he appears to be losing.

I watch on with a glimmer of hope. It's *working*.

With a petrified bellow, Zain collapses face first in the dirt. He doesn't move, which only arouses suspicion. What happened in there? Where is my transparent ally? Did she make it out?

It's only when a dark shadow steps out of Zain, hovering over his body that my heart sinks.

A *shadow person*.

There is no denying it. The silhouette is that of Zain, the body language both confused and on edge. My own body is filled with a hefty dose of despair once I piece the puzzle together.

Shadow people are immortal souls who haven't accepted death.

Now Zain is one of them, lost between planes of existence.

I glance over my shoulder at the tower, squinting my eyes from the glare. At the window is Sharnique. She is too far away to read her expression, but I imagine a smug smile.

Zain's shadow flickers in and out from sight, before disappearing entirely, his body disrespected by a mortal who uses it to spring up onto a doggan to pierce it from behind.

Waiting for my ghost friend proves useless. She doesn't appear to be in control of the body anymore, and she isn't reappearing.

Several immortals note Zain's spontaneous death. Some are genuinely devastated, while others look dazed, as if a mystical spell has been lifted. Refusing to fight, those with weapons throw them to the ground and run. Others are still caught up in the moment, dedicated to the cause and battling until the bitter end.

"Feel that?" Sharnique's voice echoes in my head. *"The land is healing oh-so slightly. We still have a way to go, granted. Somebody needs to stop that fire burning the prison."*

"What happened to my friend?" I ask.

"The dead immortal who possessed Zain?" she clarifies. *"I was keeping her from the shadow realm while she served a purpose. It was the last ounce of power I could tap into. She has served her purpose. I've allowed her to move on now."*

"To the shadows?"

"No. She will find the light. I have rewarded her for a service. Not many immortal souls have that luxury, Malin. Look at Zain. He shall be cursed to wander the shadows for all time. Nothing more than a lost soul with nobody to cling to. Pathetic."

I don't agree with her. I doubt I ever will. My transparent ally was an unwilling sacrifice, and it reminds me far too much of my time spent in the north. She wasn't even granted the privilege of seeing the outcome.

"My son," I ask. *"Return him to me."*

I jolt at the sudden bellow of an elephantano. Exposed, I frantically search for something to hide behind, but there's nothing. Keeping low to the ground, I gape in awe at the giant animal once cast in stone swaying towards the flaming prison. Atop the ginormous creature are Cheralin and Adalin, each with the head of a stoned water folk dangling from their throat like an ugly necklace.

How did they manage this feat? I wail at the sight of the innocent beings, cast in stone and used as a cruel fashion statement.

The sight of my sister makes me physically ill. She looks skinnier and less composed than our last meeting. Strands of hair have fallen into her angular face, her usual pristine skin bruised and cut. Her jewel-like eyes have a manic glint, contrasting well with Cheralin's exhausted, beaten-down expression.

The magnificent arrival is enough to stop the fighting for a moment.

"Bow to your northern royals," Adalin shrieks from atop the elephantano. "Mortals, we will save you from these immortals if you promise peace and service. You are fighting a losing battle!"

Confusion ensues. Doggans turn on the elephantano, fighting alongside mortals who temporarily forget about their immortal enemies.

Cheralin throws stones at those who dare attack them, casting them instantly. Their statues would be considered a masterpiece if crafted by a talented artist, but knowing their fate only adds to the multiple tragedies.

I howl.

Alone and helpless, I watch on and prepare myself for a lifetime as a statue, no doubt used as a tale of caution years from now when my sister takes over the land and indoctrinates generation after generation.

"*Only one sister will survive,*" Sharnique utters. "*If she lives, this land will die. All species will be segregated. History will continue to repeat. If you live, there is hope.*"

"*That can't be,*" I say. "*I haven't contributed anything. I've merely watched death upon death!*" It's difficult to contain my thoughts when I want to shout at the top of my lungs.

"*Your actions, deliberate and accident, have all provided a new path. They have served as motivation for others. I never said you were the one who had to kill your sister. I only said you needed to survive. Will you give up so easily?"*

I consider the statement, flicking through various memories of conversations with Sharnique. What is she implying?

"Mum?"

I'm frozen. I can't bring myself to face the inconceivably low voice behind me. A grown hand rests on my shoulder, light hair beneath the large, swirling knuckles. Reluctant, I turn to find a tall man, his black and blonde hair swirling together like Yin Yang. His jaw is chiseled, his shoulders are broad, his stubble is unkempt. Covered in dirt and bruises, he wears what was left of his clothes around his waist, exposing his chest and stomach.

It breaks my heart to see him grown, but I my heart swells with relief as I fall into his arms and embrace him.

"Diarmuid! How?"

"I don't know. I fell and hit hard...the next thing I knew, my body was huge. Maybe it was the jolt, the impact that shocked my body into growing. It was instantaneous. Maybe it's a protective mechanism. Maybe it isn't. I can feel this electricity surging in my body, a power unparalleled to what my child body contained."

I don't like the sounds of that. "I don't have the answers, but it doesn't matter. I'm not letting you go."

"I can't stay," he whispers. "There is a voice in my head. A woman. A god. She's told me what I must do and only I have the ability to do it."

"Don't do it," I plead.

"I must. It'll end the war. This is my purpose. My father was on the verge of godlike abilities. My birth mother was an immortal fertility god. Couple that with the northern power to trade immortality and I can do things that others can't."

I stare into my baby's eyes. He's older. He's harder. But that joyous softness still lingers. Caressing his cheek, I choke on tears and nod. "Don't lose yourself in the process."

"I have you to come back to."

I recall my conversation with Sharnique. This war was never mine to fight; I only served as a vessel for others. I was the torch to light the way.

Diarmuid jogs towards the bloody show, his muscles defined in a way that doesn't make sense given the timeframe. I hope he stops aging now. If he's anything like the other immortals, then he *should*. I hope. I *hope*.

Keeping low to the ground, I peer through the grass, wiping away the sweat that rolls down my forehead. The prison is completely ablaze, including the tower. The fire feeds on the grass and is trailing its way towards my hiding spot. I don't have much time left.

Suppressing horrified squeals as Diarmuid avoids various attacks, I hold my breath when he stands confidently in front of the towering elephantano.

"Please don't hurt it," I murmur. "It didn't do anything."

Adalin doesn't notice Diarmuid; or if she does, she doesn't acknowledge him. He'd be nothing more than another prisoner in her eyes.

"Aunt Adalin!" Diarmuid cries, his authoritative voice bellowing even from this distance. "I ask that you stop this unnecessary violence. We can find peace."

She only flinches at the name 'aunt', a bewildered look on her face as she attempts to comprehend the relation. When she decides it doesn't matter, she throws a stone at Diarmuid who uses his palm to shoot a burst of lightning, shattering it into pieces midair.

It's enough to deter her next move. She gapes in horror at Diarmuid, stumbling over her words. "I implore you, sir. Get back! The north must rise again! Do not stand in our way!"

"That's the kid!" Cheralin cries, eyes wide. "That's the kid! The hair is identical!"

She says something inaudible and my attempt to read her mind proves futile. Sharnique may feel more powerful with Zain's demise, but I don't. I mostly feel sick to my stomach.

It's never worked before, but I willfully summon any positive thoughts to protect Diarmuid, who stands stoically still betwixt the ongoing battle. Zain's demise barely stopped the revolution. Both sides are still madly encompassed, eager to thwart one another without any idea as to what happens once they emerge victorious. The win will be a loss. That's always the way with war.

"Last warning," Diarmuid shouts once more. "I don't want to hurt you."

He's taking too long and giving too many chances. He doesn't know Adalin like I do. He doesn't recognize that subtle stiff back or the way she touches her chin with her index finger. She is about to do something aggressive and extreme. Panicked, I scramble from my hiding spot and charge closer so that he can hear me.

"Just do it, Diarmuid!" I scream.

It all happens so quickly.

I reach Diarmuid just as Adalin nudges the elephantano to raise its front leg. I push him out of the way while he focuses on Adalin.

We roll together, narrowly avoiding collision, the stomp causing the earth to quake. Now curled beneath the elephantano's body, we huddle together to keep from getting trampled.

The elephantano storms forward, squashing anything in its wake. A shrill cry sounds, followed by a thud as a female drops beside us.

I stare in horror at my sister's lifeless face, electric sparks flickering from her wide eyes.

"Don't touch it! It could be catching!" A mortal warrior shouts. It's enough for Diarmuid to clear his throat and rise from the ground, helping me to my feet. As a doggan approaches us ready to strike, he raises his hand and the doggan collapses, sharing Adalin's same vacant, electrified eyes.

Cheralin gracefully slides down the trunk of the elephantano and slides to her knees next to Adalin, hands to her cheeks.

"Oh, no no no no! Addy? Addy, wake up! Adalin!"

"She's dead," Diarmuid says coldly, those close enough to hear stopping in their tracks.

As word begins to spread, mortals, immortals and doggans come to a mutual halt. Zain's death went virtually unnoticed due to his internal struggles. It looked like a heart attack, a pre-existing condition that he struggled with and might eventually overcome upon awakening. But an immortal northerner ejected off her giant mount by a half-naked man with the flick of his hand? It was enough to stop any sane person in the middle of war.

The fire fills the silence as the enemies process the scene. Blood blankets the dirt and grass, their leaders reduced to mere shells.

"Addy?" Cheralin sobs. "Don't leave me. I've lost my brothers. You're all I have left!"

"She is no longer your leader," Diarmuid says. "You needn't maintain the pretense. You follow power, not loyalty. She was *not* in line for the throne. If you want to follow your true leader, turn to Malin."

I frown. "No, no. I'm not taking the throne."

"He's right," Cheralin says glumly, staring at my lifeless sister. I can't bear to make eye contact. "You're the rightful heir."

"It is not happening," I say, formidable. It doesn't seem to matter. The doggans, despite their instruction to attack, have always respected northern royalty. Upon hearing the news, they drop to their knees and bow out of respect. Even the ones far away from the commotion follow suit when they see their comrades.

Immortals from the west and south do the same, but the mortals and immortals from the other corners remain upright, conflicted as to what to do. The battle is at an instant standstill, all eyes on me.

A spark of power ignites within, almost as if the land is grateful for the fighting to be over.

"*Interesting,*" Sharnique's voice echoes in my head. "*See what happens when you try to mess with a god? Welcome to the exclusive club, Malin.*"

"I'm not a god!" I throw my hands in the air and scream, forgetting for a moment who I'm speaking with. "Do *not* address me by that title! Or any title!"

Diarmuid quickly searches for my hand and links arms, pulling me closely into his body. I find comfort in his warmth, but feel strange that I'm now the little one he can embrace so easily, when only a few days ago I was the one carrying him. It's a sense of pride and melancholy I can't describe.

He distracts the others by speaking on my behalf. No doubt my irrelevant outburst has disturbed the others. I look unstable, potentially unfit to be a northern leader.

"She should not be expected to take the throne, however there are other options. Better options. As the living heir, Malin can choose who should take her place. Her brother, for example."

Oh, goodness no. I can't imagine a worse choice. He admitted he seeks power, and I fear he'd accidentally go down a route similar to my sister. Diarmuid reads my expression and continues to speak once he uncomfortably clears his throat.

"Technically speaking, I could also be next in line."

"Is that what you want?" I ask.

He shakes his head. "I'd do it for you, but I want to be free. I want a childhood. I want a home."

A mortal warrior steps forward, keeping a suspicious eye on a decapitated immortal writhing on the ground. "The north is a fallacy!"

"What does the north resurgence solve?" an immortal asks, her voice coated in blood.

"Nothing," I confess. "Not with another immortal at the helm. I am tired of segregating the corners and ignoring species that I never even knew existed. There aren't many of my kind left, but if we can prove that northern mortals and immortals can coexist, then it may serve as a stepping stone for the other corners. We can set an example."

"And why would we need an example?" A wounded mortal shouts from the ground, barely able to lift his head. "You are filthy torturers with a superiority complex! We don't want to coexist!"

"We have all hurt one another in some form. We are all guilty and we are all victims," I say. "There have been a lot of misguided actions and miscommunication over the generations. What if a mortal northerner ruled?"

The same warrior snorts. "No mortal northerners exist. Especially not one that would be allowed to rule. Your entire family are immortals!"

Diarmuid and I exchange glances.

"Not all of them."

CHAPTER XXII

"Absolutely no chance," a mortified Taylin announces.

The battle has taken a brief hiatus with the stipulation of consulting the future ruler of the north.

The armies tend to their wounds, after agreeing to tentative peace, while the elephantano uses its mighty trunk to extinguish the blazing fire. It eases the intense heat and allows us to breathe without choking.

Diarmuid, Taylin and I are privately huddled away from the masses, having found a small sanctuary within ourselves.

"Why does the north even need a leader?" Taylin continues. "Didn't you want to see that place buried and forgotten?"

"Because Lei will take it by default," I say. "He won't be able to help himself, the temptation will be too strong, and he will unintentionally run it into the ground. He relies too heavily on prophecy and is obsessed with power. Without realizing it, he is following in the path of our parents."

"*You're* the princess!"

"By birth, not by choice," I say. Exhausted, I stretch out my tired limbs and slump my aching body into the dirt. "I will do it if nobody else will. I can make that sacrifice. It was something to consider. How is your injury?"

Taylin dismisses my poor attempt to deflect. "Never mind that. What does that mean you must do? There is no north."

I consider the question. "I suppose word would spread and northerners in hiding might feel free to relocate and we would rebuild. It could be a home for outcasts, those who don't fit in anywhere. For beings like Torg or Diarmuid. I hazard a guess there are more than we realize. I would meet with the other corners to permanently shut down the Immortal Cells and prevent others like it from ever happening again. In exchange, I would put an end to mortal sacrifices. That would ensure the continuation of both species."

Ironically, immortals are the endangered species. Mortals continue to find a way, living life to the extreme because there is an end. Immortals seemingly go on to become gods, or give up immortality due to boredom or even waste away in volcanoes and underwater due to their inability to be killed effectively. It's a strange concept.

"It sounds like you finally have a good grasp as to what it takes to be a leader, Malin." Taylin scrutinizes my body, her eyes hard. "Maybe it is time to step up to the plate. Tell them how you will conquer and calm."

My heart sinks, but she's right. This isn't her burden; it was always mine. I've been running from my destiny for as long as I can remember.

"I would have to take charge immediately to prevent calamity," I say slowly. "Would somebody please ensure Nellabix's safe return?"

Taylin nods fervently.

Diarmuid maintains a very stoic expression, having not mastered the ability to mask emotions on his face. "What does this mean? Are you certain I can live with you in the north? Will I be rejected because of what I am capable of? My own aunt doesn't like me."

Taylin groans. "Ugh, I *like* you. I might even love you, all right? I'm *scared* of you. And I have every right to be! You should be living far away on an island somewhere; at least until you know for absolute certainty you can control your extreme power."

"I *can* control it," he mutters. "I've only ever killed on purpose and with great precision. My concern is Lei will come after Malin, regardless. He wants the throne, doesn't he?"

"I believe he does," I say after a long pause. "He's unpredictable, but good at heart. He might give his blessing."

Arms folded, Taylin shrugs like an uninterested juvenile. "Won't know until you try."

I wouldn't dare voice it, but I'm disappointed. Linking arms with Diarmuid, I lift my chin. "No more time to be wasted or blood to be shed. Let's do this."

Like death row, I walk miserably towards the armies, avoiding a grieving Cheralin who is slumped over my sister and wailing. I don't know why she hasn't left. Morbid curiosity as to my decision? Paralyzed by the devastation? It's hard to tell. All I know is I'm deliberately compartmentalizing to survive. Despite the poor relationship, I never wanted to see Adalin dead. If I stop to process it, I might just find myself sitting next to an inconsolable Cheralin.

I position myself on one of the slopes so that everyone can get a clear look at me. In a sea of anguish, there's the slightest glimmer of hope in their eyes that reminds me why I'm making this sacrifice. I try to glimpse over the gore and decapitation, but I fail. Swallowing back bile, I activate my diaphragm and project as loudly as I can.

"I understand the corners here only represent a small minority of the land's population," I begin. "We have forgotten or been misled as to who inhabits our areas. Due to pain and ego, history has constantly been rewritten or forged. I have met beings I never knew existed, destined to live in secrecy due to their limited abilities or way of life. Their existence lived in shadow while the feud between immortals and mortals in the four corners ravaged our homes. My kind, the northerners, are on the verge of extinction due to a civil war. By rebuilding the north and claiming the throne, we can show you that peace is possible within our own corner. If we can prove that, then it will serve as evidence that the remaining corners and species can also live as one."

There are rogue cheers from various warriors; predominately immortals. The doggans remain silent and the mortals appear suspicious.

"Mortals will lose this war. I'm sorry, but you will," I remind. "Immortals are angry. They're powerful. They live for eternity. If they don't come after you, they'll come after your grandchildren. It's time to stop hunting us down. It's time to trust us. And immortals, when they do cooperate, we cannot be petty. We cannot do unto them, otherwise the cycle will never end. A true compromise is when both parties are unhappy." I attempt to joke, but it clearly isn't the right time or place. In fact, most of them nod in agreement.

"We can't trust an immortal ruling," a mortal warrior pipes up, pointing his spear in my direction. "We can't have you!"

"You don't have a choice," I lament. "It's me or—"

"—me," Taylin says, limping forward. I frown at her, unsure where she is going with this. "I was born a mortal and am a descendent of Princess Malin. Not only am I genetically entitled, but I have also lived the life of a mortal after many generations flushed out the immortal trait. I've understood hiding away for all of my life due to my heritage. I am living proof of the best and worst. I, Taylin, will be your future ruler of the north."

I dig my nails into Diarmuid's arm, my heart leaping into my throat. *Why?* Why is she doing this? I scramble into her mind, wondering if she'll explain. She senses me knocking at her mental barrier and lets me in.

"What? I can't multitask well, so make this quick."

"Why?" I mouth.

"Because listening to you gives me hope. You have spent several lifetimes being punished for altruistic deeds. I only have one lifetime and it's time I made it count. You have inspired me to help this land, and you deserve the freedom you've never had. Worst-case scenario, I'll quit after ten years and then you can take over. We share immortality; why not share the pains and privileges of royalty? I owe you that. We all do."

I don't think I've done anything remarkably special to be owed anything. It isn't until I look up at Diarmuid, fully grown and eyes heavy with responsibility that I yearn to give him a childhood he missed out on. I long to be shielded from the prying eyes of the public and I crave the privacy of my own mind, my own thoughts.

"Thank you," I whisper.

Then the impossible happens. Mortal warriors bow. More follow. Immortals and doggans eventually do the same until, united, all sides taken a knee to show their respect to the future ruler of the north.

Diarmuid drops and motions at me to do the same. Hesitant, I lower and grin at a perplexed, albeit smug looking Taylin and am overwhelmed with gratitude.

My life sentence has finally been served.

XXIII

"Didn't think we'd see you again," an ogre announces. "And not so soon. You held your end of the deal, though. Torg just got back, skinny runt that he is. Forgot how humanoid lookin' he was."

"It was a disturbing sight, indeed," another agrees.

"I'm right here," Torg says, rugged up and snuggled into the hide of a wooly animal skin.

It's admittedly less stressful returning to the mountains without a baby in tow. Diarmuid may be shivering, but I feel less inclined to panic over a grown man's temperature.

"Are you happy?" I ask Torg, the large functionalist remarkably tiny compared to his family.

"I'm free," he says, the wrinkled smile unnatural on his face. Instead of hunching over a steel slab, he's hunched over a fire. "I can't live in these cold conditions forever, but I'm breathing fresh air. I'm laughing. I'm home. And if you think it's possible for the north to rebuild, then who knows? Maybe I can relocate there and design jewelry. Might be a commute, but at least it's not a prison."

"Speaking of!" Taylin awkwardly taps at her neck band, her lips the same color as her skin. Her mortal body isn't equipped to survive here much longer.

"Oh, right." Torg stands, flicking a tool out from his leather belt. With one hand clutching at the animal hide around his shoulders, he uses his head to motion at us to join him. Hesitantly, Taylin and I oblige. Offering myself forward, I nervously await the impact. I expect him to use brute force to bend the band off, but instead he inserts the tool into a tiny hole in the left side of the neck band and twists. Within a few moments, it drops to the ground and I take a deep breath—before regretting the sting of cold air that runs down my throat.

"I'm free." I sigh, echoing Torg's sentiments.

"The gold is good for you," he reminds, releasing Taylin from her brace next.

"Nothing is good for you when it's forced," I say, picking up the neck band. "I'd happily refashion this into a bracelet that I can put on and take off. It was awfully tight around my neck. Each inhalation rubbed. I couldn't sleep without it pressing into my vertebrae. Couldn't swallow."

"We get it," Taylin snaps, gently running her fingers over the crease where the neck band used to be. I wonder if my throat looks as red as hers. "Now for the unihorn."

"Please," Diarmuid and I say in unison. Taylin will need to work on her manners if she expects to rule the north efficiently.

The ogres exchange uncomfortable glances and my heart lurches. If they were bluffing about her, I might very well lunge at them.

"What?" I ask. "You promised her safe return."

"It's just that..." An ogre clears his throat. "We've become fond of her."

"Is she alive?" Taylin is quick to jump to the conclusion I was dancing around.

"Of course," the ogre with a clearer diction says. "We considered eating her, but she's become a fun pet of sorts. Does cute tricks. Sort of sings along with us. Feels nice to pet. We like her."

Taylin rolls her eyes and sticks out her hand. "Enough of this. I'm freezing and I'm tired. Get Nellabix now. A promise is a promise."

"Oh, all right!" The ogre throws his hands in the air and storms into the trees.

I wrap my arms around a shivering Taylin and offer my immortality, but she declines. She's been grumpier since arriving in the mountains, but the trip has been arduous. She was on a mission to retrieve Nellabix as soon as possible, having still felt guilty about losing her in the first place.

"You can settle," I assure. "She is in good hands."

"They would've eaten her," Taylin says through gritted teeth. "I saw the dream. A huge cold snap is coming, Malin. I didn't tell you about this. When the ogres run out of food during the cold month, Nellabix would have been the first to go. It's a cyclical occurrence in the mountains. Why do you think I wouldn't let us sleep for long last night? Or have a day's rest after the battle? Your unihorn's life depended on us getting here *today*. I didn't want to tell you because I know you're skeptical of those dreams."

My jaw hangs loose. She's right; I am a little suspicious of the dreams, but the whole thought of Nellabix being used as a food source sickens me. On edge, I bounce in the snow and anxiously await her arrival.

The wind whips at our faces as thick snow swirls around our feet. After what feels like an eternity, the ogre arrives, hand clasped around Nellabix's horn and leading her forward. When she sees us, she whinnies and squirms out of the ogre's grip. Bounding towards us, Taylin and I fling ourselves onto her and squeeze tightly.

Too exhausted to cry, I simply nestle my head into her shoulder. "Nellabix."

"I'm so sorry," Taylin says, exasperated. "I honestly never thought I'd see you again. I'm so sorry I let you down. I'm *so* sorry. We're going home now. We're going home."

"So Nellabix will return to the north with you?" Diarmuid asks, patting her mane which is covered in snow. "Are we all going to the north?"

I wish he hadn't asked. At least not now. Because I don't know how to tell Taylin I don't want to return.

As the weeks pass, Taylin, Diarmuid and I take turns riding Nellabix. For once, we don't feel rushed or like we are constantly looking over our shoulders. We treat our journey like a holiday; stopping to swim in lakes, to swing on vines and to relax.

Taylin's wound miraculously healed overnight, so I assume we must've been within Rune's radius once more. It was nice validation that he was still around.

"Do we drop by to see him?" I'd asked Taylin, who immediately shot down the question. Maybe I could see him once I help her settle in the north.

The further we trek, the less communicative I become; lost deep in thought. I recall a conversation with Sharnique, having met with her in private before we left.

"You'll need a fire," she'd said. "Or another elemental. Fire is the easiest to see and manage. Feed it and care for it well. It merges with you."

"I don't want it," I'd said firmly, my body buzzing with power.

"You may not want it, but you'll need it if you intend to not spoil your humanity. The fire contains our force and stops us from overextending our abilities. Gods go mad without boundaries. It's a little different once we have returned to our land."

Staring at the sun on the horizon, I replay the conversation, startled when Diarmuid speaks.

"Do you really think there's tentative peace?" Diarmuid says at dusk, as we set up a small campfire. The temperature is perfect, but the nights have been chilly. "How can we trust them?"

"Killing their leaders would've put a pause in any plan," I remind, massaging my feet. "Most immortals only wanted freedom; the others were brainwashed. Mortals were only doing their job. At their core, nobody *wants* to fight."

"And what about the gods? Sharnique and Garu?"

Taylin glances at me, braiding Nellabix's tail. We haven't spoken much since she volunteered to be princess. There's an odd tension between us and I don't know how to resolve it. I can't discern if she's the awkward one or if it's me.

"They're returning to their land," I say. "The land of the gods.

They seem satisfied with how events played out. Their powers are restored for the foreseeable future."

"They haven't left yet?" Diarmuid's tone is innocent enough, but there's a hidden agenda. It's like he's waiting for a confession I'm not willing to give.

I shrug, ashamed of my lie. I know for a fact the gods haven't left yet. I know because Sharnique is in constant telepathic contact.

I know because I asked them to wait for me.

"We're here," Taylin's distant voice announces.

Bleary-eyed, I stir, my head swaying side to side as I ride Nellabix. I'm unsure how long I've been asleep, but my mouth feels like cotton.

For a moment I forget who I am and where I'm going, but the shriveled remains of my home shoot me back into a grim reality I wanted to leave behind.

The sight is heart-aching. Clutching at my chest, I suppress the sobs as I stare at collapsed pillars blanketed in overgrown vines. Fountains which once trickled serenely are now still and flooded with a black goo. The flourishing city I remember is now completely abandoned, darkened by war, death and time. Wide cracks in marble steps make it near impossible to safely run up, the open terraces now home to poisonous animals watching from beneath the rubble.

"This is where you lived?" Diarmuid asks softly, his eyes heavy with grief. "It looks like it was beautiful once."

"It was," I choke. "The politics weren't, but every fiber of my being aches to see it like this."

"How am I supposed to rebuild *this*?" Taylin whispers, flinching when she accidentally steps on a detached jaw of a mortal from long ago. "This is impossible."

"*Have you reached the north yet?*" Sharnique asks telepathically, checking in like a concerned mother almost hourly.

"Yes," I respond. "But I feel you already knew that."

"Of course. Since the Immortal Cells have been destroyed, my abilities expanded. Love and connection is always key. I cannot wait to see what happens once the north is restored and beings unite. I can only imagine the power I will be able to draw on. It is quite an exciting concept, wouldn't you say?"

I ignore the rhetorical question. "And everything is all right there?"

"Yes, yes. Garu and I are safe, you needn't concern yourself with how we are spending our time. The prison is finally demolished and all remaining immortals are being relocated to the north in the coming weeks. From there, they can decide if they want to return to their homes or if they need rehabilitation. Zain's and Adalin's bodies remain in the coffin per your request. If you still intend on hosting a funeral for them, you best do it soon."

"I will, I will. I just need to sort my priorities. I know this probably sounds strange, but I am in mourning for both of them. They were villains from my perspective, but I don't hate them. I don't think they thought they were doing anything wrong. Did they deserve to die?"

"Nobody deserves to die; it is just luck of the draw."

"I don't want them to be lost in the shadow realm." I close my eyes and think of those lost souls. "Can you help them the way you helped—"

"—Malin, how many times do we have to go over this? Honestly, this altruistic side of yours is overwhelmingly frustrating at times. I am not the god of the afterlife. I guided your little friend because I foresaw that she was the only one who would not be affected by the land's lack of power and would stop Zain. Beyond that, I have no reason to aid Zain and Adalin. If they're lost, they'll be shadows. If they find peace within themselves, they'll move on. Stop asking me."

Rather than start a petty quarrel, I redirect the conversation towards something that might help Taylin. "Sharnique, how do we rebuild? It is so much worse than I was anticipating."

"Remember how Garu created illusions of fellow guards? I can *help you project an illusion of a healthier north. Over time I would encourage a physical restoration, but it can speed up the process. Whenever you are ready, envision how it should be and I will alert Garu so we can project the illusion into reality. I would strongly suggest you pull Diarmuid into it, too. That boy is extremely powerful."*

"Malin?" Taylin asks, irritated by my dreamlike state. "I swear, you have been off in la-la land lately. Please tell me you don't have post-traumatic stress, because I don't have time to deal with that. I need you. I am lost here. What am I supposed to do?"

It's a peculiar thing to say, but I find comfort in her panic. Taylin has always been so strong, so relentless, that when I see a dent in her armor, I'm reminded that she is nothing more than a young girl with a heart of gold.

"Have faith," I say. "I'm ready."

In my mind's eye, I restore the north to its former glory, but without the lavish adornments. I imagine a land of comfort, with grand buildings and beautiful views, but omit the statues of past leaders and pavement lined in jewels. Those unnecessary features would only hinder the true beauty of what's to come.

My entire body vibrates as I sense Garu's and Sharnique's combined power shooting through me. Awkwardly, I search for Diarmuid's hand.

"Trust me," I tell him. "Feel the energy and send it to me. You'll understand."

I know I needn't explain. I have a feeling he has been eavesdropping on some of my conversations with Sharnique, his quiet abilities advancing more and more each day. I get the impression he can invade any mental barrier with great stealth. There's no evidence of this; perhaps only a mother's instinct. Regardless, he merely squeezes my hand, and within moments I feel his power surge.

Taylin gasps as my vision leaves my imagination and enters the physical plane, replacing the dilapidated ruins of my old home.

When the illusion feels secure, the vibration ceases and I let go of Diarmuid's hand.

"What is this?" Taylin shouts, unmoving. "Can I move? Will this collapse around me?"

"No." I let out a breezy laugh, thrilled with the outcome. I'm almost tempted to stay. I jump up and down on the surface, secretly surprised by how sturdy the marble stairs are. Nobody would ever know it's made of pure energy. "It won't last forever. Ensure that you get people to build in its place."

"Malin." Her tone is a little too serious for my liking. "Seriously, how did you do this? I'm scared. Is it true you're a...a...*god?*"

I can't meet her gaze. "Gods aren't what we think they are, Taylin. Our history books had it wrong."

"But your brother! I mean, if Lei is the one who taught you all of these things and is Diarmuid's father, then does that means *he* is a god? Shouldn't we be concerned?"

I nod. "He is a wonderful researcher and teacher. Whether he is a god himself, I can't say. A lot of his work was theoretical, but he relies heavily on the promises of prophecies. Depending on what they show him will mark his future actions. Either he likes who he can become and will follow through, or he will remain in solitude if he thinks he will become too much of a threat. I believe he will make the right choice. When everything calms down, I will reach out to him once more. For the time being, however, I best show you around."

With a warm, reassured smile, Taylin links her arms through mine and follows my lead down the steps, through the hedge maze and into her new home. Overlooking a modest fountain with a view of the mountains is the open court where her new throne awaits.

She gulps at the sight of it.

"Nervous?" I ask, referencing the throne.

"I wasn't even considering that," Taylin says, her eyes wide. "Malin, you've given me a home. An actual home. It's so open. The balconies leading into the bedrooms. The sheer curtains in place of doors. There's no hiding here. There's no shame. It's pure freedom. Pure pride for who you are. It's everything I've ever wanted. Can you imagine all the other beings who were prosecuted for their identities when they arrive? The north will be a haven, nay, a sanctuary for so many! Your sister never had any intention of doing this if she were to take the throne."

"No. She only wanted what once was; wealth, glamor and power. Immortals back in power. It would have never worked." I cringe at the memory of my deceased sibling. "I'm not ready to talk about her."

"Sorry," Taylin blurts. "I will work on my charisma. I want to do you proud. You'll be around to guide me though, right?"

Diarmuid clears his throat, only validating my suspicions about his mental eavesdropping. Nervously, I pull on my thumb and wince at the deep crack it makes. "I will be around for a little while, yes."

"A little while?" Taylin cocks her head to the side. "What does that mean?"

Just like eating leftovers or telling somebody unpleasant news, life is all about timing. Sometimes you can be in control and other times, the universe throws a surprise or two your way.

This is one of those surprises. Fortunately for me, the gift of interruption presents itself at an opportune moment.

"Talk about an extreme makeover. This place looks great!"

Donning an uncharacteristic beard, wearing thick boots and shifting a bulky backpack slung over his shoulder, is the ever optimistic and ever animated Rune. Standing at the foot of the fountain, he takes in the sights.

I can't contain myself. I bound towards him and hold him close, his healing powers involuntarily released as I do so, his touch like a warm massage throughout my entire body.

"I wasn't sure if I'd ever see you again," I cry, unable to let him go. Part of me fears he's nothing more than a convincing illusion. "What are you doing here?"

Weary-eyed, Rune lifts a hand to his face and wriggles his fingers. "I had a dream, of course. Once news reached about your success, I wasted no time. I wanted to be a one-man portable healing center. I figured most of the war-torn and ex-prisoners would call the north their home, even if it's temporary. I want to heal all of them. The girls have been calling me a god, funny things. I've learned so much. I've brought animals on the brink of death back to life. I've regrown limbs. I can do anything. Sounds a little arrogant, but it's true. Did any of my distant healing help?"

I wipe away a stray tear, unable to express enough gratitude. "You have no idea."

Rune notices Diarmuid and offers a hand. "That's a relief. Oh, I haven't introduced myself. I'm Rune. And you are?"

Diarmuid and I exchange glances, laughing. He does the polite thing and extends his own hand while I explain. "He's the baby we rescued."

"No he's not. A baby is a baby. Where *is* the baby?"

"Here." Diarmuid points at himself. "I'm the result of mixed genetics. How are the birth parents who wished me dead?"

"Quite regretful, actually," Rune says, agape. "They almost followed after you but didn't know where to start. *Wait*, this can't be right. Are you *sure* you're the baby? I know they say it goes quickly, but you're what? Six months old? You're in your twenties!"

"Only physically."

Rune has difficulty processing the concept, stammering over his words. He leans against the fountain while I explain, staring at Diarmuid the entire time. When I finish, he shakes his head.

"I have questions. A lot of questions, but I'll come back to them. And the unihorn!" Rune notices Nellabix, his eyes alight with excitement. "She's safe! I have questions about her, too! No, no, I'm getting ahead of myself. Taylin? Tay, I can't stand another second without acknowledging you. I've missed you. Please look at me. We have so much to talk about."

Taylin purses her lips and shakes her head. "We have *nothing* to talk about."

"I don't understand why you're so angry at me. I did what I had to do, and it was advantageous for us all."

"You abandoned us by choosing to stay behind!"

Rune begins to argue, inhales and adjusts his tone. "Justifying my actions will prove useless in your eyes. Fine. I see your side. I truly do. I left you alone to raise a baby in the wilderness with maniacs hunting you. A true friend would've come with you. I was wrong. The best apology is changed behavior, so allow me to apologize profusely by devoting myself to your cause entirely. I only ask that you allow me to set up shop here to heal the wounded. Is that plausible?"

I want to applaud Rune's efforts. He has made it near impossible to argue with, which is ultimately a favorite pastime of Taylin's. Visibly put out, she huffs and rolls her eyes, which is the closest thing to forgiveness Rune will ever receive. Mollified, he smiles and lowers his bag to the ground.

"Well then. Do I have a room to call my own?"

It's strange to be sleeping in an illusion of my old home. I couldn't bring myself to find my original quarters, instead opting for my neighbor's dwelling. It is slightly understated compared to my lavish bedroom, which is exactly how I prefer. It helps me feel, I don't know, *normal*? If normal is even possible. Obviously, I never want to be a prisoner or homeless again, but the princess lifestyle never sat well with me either.

Here I have a roof over my head. Soft pillows. Diarmuid and Rune only meters away in their own rooms.

I'm safe.

"You did well."

I'm unsure if it's tiredness or a sense of contentment which stifles my surprise. I pull myself into a sitting position and tap the blue crystal next to my bedside so that it illuminates a little brighter.

At the foot of my bed, hovering ever so slightly, is my transparent ally. She is a vision of beauty; golden hair curled by her waist, bosoms rounded and perky, lips full and lush.

"Is this your new projection?" I ask, amused. "Seems I'm not the only one with a healthy imagination."

She smiles, radiating a soft glow. "As much as I'd love to take credit for this look, I did not intentionally choose it. Apparently gods of the afterlife are depicted as beautiful."

The statement is jarring. I feel my forehead crinkle as I gape at her. "What do you mean?"

"Do you remember how I said I think I might be a god? It turns out, you helped me become one. By learning those techniques, clinging to your humanity and avoiding the shadow realm, I became something far greater. I was intent on destroying Sharnique, but I suppose she always saw my greater purpose. I just wanted to let you know that I am all right and to thank you for your companionship."

"I am so relieved...and stunned," I admit. "What does your new role entail?"

"Oh, now that's a need-to-know basis." She raises a cheeky finger to her lips and winks. "Now, rumor has it you don't intend to stay here. Is that true?"

Somewhat petulantly, I shrug, as if confronted by an inquisitive parent. "Does it matter?"

"No. You are entitled to do what you please. Do you think Taylin will thrive on her own?"

"She won't be on her own. She has Rune. She might even be better without me."

"She might," she says, her tone neutral. "Will you bequeath your immortality to her?"

"Yes."

"I would advise that you don't. Where you're planning to go requires immortality. The waters conduct lightning you have never seen before. The electricity will fatally shock any mortal."

"Oh." My gaze drops to my infinite tattoo. "Now I *really* feel like I'm abandoning her."

"You can always come back," she says, her tone calm. "Even if you won't."

In the low light, I take in my surroundings, as fake as they may be. "Why am I so disconnected?"

"It isn't such a mystery," she says, almost bored with the conversation. "You have moved on. It's what all healthy beings do. You have simply begun the preparation for the next chapter in your life. Is that such a bad thing?"

When she puts it like that, it seems positively imperative for me to take the plunge into my new life. "But I feel selfish."

"Allow me to repeat myself: is that such a bad thing?"

Her glow slowly diminishes until I'm left alone within my illusion, contemplating my choices and considering her not-so-rhetorical question.

Why do we always assume that selfishness is a negative quality, when *sometimes* selfishness can be another term for survival and self-care?

Maybe it's time for me to be selfish.

CHAPTER XXIV

I love the hour between dusk and twilight. Sitting atop one of the pillars above the throne room, I have a picturesque view of the northern city and the pointy hills in the distance.

It was easy enough to climb; climbing has never been particularly difficult for me. I used to sit here at midnight as a child and stare up at the stars, wondering about life beyond the northern walls. That version of myself seems like a fictional character, blissfully unaware of trials and tribulations I'd yet to face. I have absolutely nothing in common with that young me; only the adoration for the sky and the inner sanctuary of sitting atop my pillar, far away from everyone else.

I've kept to myself over the last couple of weeks as more and more immortals flock to the north to be healed and find solace in the alleged haven.

Taylin is anything but a princess. She is abrupt, she doesn't dress the part, and she assigns chores to everybody so that the northern illusion can solidify into something more permanent.

She is perfect.

Diarmuid swiftly shimmies up the pillar to join me. We're a tad squished up here, but he dangles his legs over the ledge to give me more room.

"Nice view up here," he says, the warm hues reflecting in his eyes. "Serene."

"Almost too serene," I reply, sighing wistfully at the scene. "They won't wait much longer."

"I know."

"You know a lot." I shake my head. "How long have you been able to tap into people's minds?"

"Honestly?" He stares vacantly at where the sun was before it melted into a puddle of blues and pinks which now sweep across the sky. "I think birth. There are vague memories from then. I could understand the language even though my mind had trouble processing all the words. I knew I wasn't wanted and there was a frenzy. I remember finding comfort in you. I remember...hearing things that weren't said. Like whispers in the wind."

I smile. "Many might think you're a god."

"Oh, most definitely. I have a lot of the qualities. That's why I'm coming with you."

This is news to me. I shoot him a confounded expression and am met with a cheeky smirk. "But you... I'm not sure if you can invite yourself like this! I mean...yes please! You'd really come?"

He throws his head back and laughs. "Mum, I don't believe for a second that you thought you'd be leaving without me. I don't belong to this land. I was born for a purpose, even if I seemed like an accident. My father might rely on crystal dreams to the point of obsession, but they haven't led him astray yet. My abilities are scary if used incorrectly, but I used them for the right reason. Look at this place. Look at the potential. My work here is done. It's time for me to leave and find a new purpose."

I rest my head on his broad shoulders and hug his waist. "You mean the world to me, Diarmuid."

"And you're my best friend. My savior. My hero. My mother. Forever."

As the lights fade and darkness blankets the sky, we telepathically thank the universe for all of its happy accidents and deliberate mistakes.

"I'M TERRIFIED OF TELLING TAYLIN," I confide in Rune, who has finally shaved off that ridiculous beard of his. He is much better suited to a clean-shaven face to show off his animated expressions.

"I would be too," he says with mirth, but he isn't joking. "It took a couple of days before she'd even look me in the eye again, but we're making amends. She sat down with me in the courtyard and was telling me all about Diarmuid and how proud she was of him."

I raise an eyebrow. "She rejected him when she found out about his abilities."

"She didn't discuss that," Rune says. "Taylin is a big softie beneath it all. She hurts deeper than we do, which is why she acts so cold all the time. It's nothing more than an act. That is a concept I've come to accept over time. Those who are more sensitive tend to mask it with a more aggressive temperament. The ones who appear timid are the ones you need to look out for. They're tougher than stone."

"It'd be much easier if people didn't hide."

He hesitates. "Not necessarily. We evolved to be complex for a reason. Enough philosophy. Do you know what awaits on the other side of the sea? Are you nervous? Are you scared? Can you ever come back? How are you selected? Is it an exclusive invite? Why now?"

Unable to answer half of the questions, I merely pull Rune in close. "I'm going to miss you. Who would've ever thought you'd be a god of healing?"

Darting his eyes nervously, he motions for me to be quiet. "I don't know if we are progressed enough to flaunt that title yet. Maybe in another hundred years."

Smiling, I cherish his good nature and ache when I think of having to be apart from his enthusiasm once more. "Maybe then."

Taylin's reaction isn't what I expected.

She sits on her throne, looking out of place, with her chin to her chest, her arms folded and her legs crossed. She glares at me, her bottom teeth on show. After a couple of awkward moments, I disturb the silence with a nervous knuckle crack.

"I can't believe this."

"I know."

"I offer to take this princess role so you don't have to. Sure, I'm crushing it. Sure, I am delighted to see so many species, mixed and forgotten all in one place. Sure, I kind of enjoy bossing people. Sure, it's a nice place to live. But I still did it *for you*. You said you'd be here to help me. Now you're *leaving*?"

"In my defense, you haven't needed my help at all."

"It doesn't mean I won't require it in the future! And let me state the obvious here," she says, her voice rising with each syllable, "I love you, Malin! Both you and Diarmuid! It's your company I'm going to miss! I'm mortal! By the time you return for a weekend visit, I'll be geriatric or dead! Time actually means something to me!"

"I've lived as a mortal too," I remind. "I understand time and its importance. I plan to return regularly. I just can't stay here."

"But *why*?" Taylin asks, her voice quivering and her lower lip trembling. "What's so bad about here? Is it *me*?"

I clutch at my chest, holding back tears. "Taylin, no. You mean so much to me, but this goes beyond my feelings for you. I don't feel *right* here. I'm out of sync, out of step. I'm reminded of my sister, my parents and my brother every morning I open my eyes. I've returned to a place I ran from, and despite all the good that's to come from it, I'm only reminded of the bad. I have learned abilities that I don't trust. With a mere thought, I can eavesdrop on thoughts and control another's body. I need to be in a place where others are more powerful than I am so that I don't feel the urge to intrude. The truth is, it's getting easier and easier to hear thoughts, to control actions, to project illusions. Soon, I won't know the difference between what's real or not. Living with the gods will prevent that from happening. They can normalize me again."

Taylin turns away from me, but I catch the stray tear running down her cheek. If she weren't so proud, I'd hold her close. "I thought we were forever, Malin. I thought we were a family."

"This doesn't change what we are. Distance never changes that."

"Yes it does! First Rune—"

"—he's back! For good! And if he hadn't been *selfish*, he wouldn't be here being *selfless*. Sometimes you need to do the wrong thing to be in the right place."

"Well look where selfless got me!"

"Exactly!" I throw my hands out. "Look at where selfless got you! You said yourself you enjoy it here!"

"But now I'm on my own!"

"But you're not!" I protest, growing frustrated with the martyr; especially considering she once accused me of being one. "You have Rune. You have Nellabix. You have everyone here."

Eyes squeezed tight, she speaks through gritted teeth. "I don't. Have. You."

"I don't know what else I can say, Taylin," I admit, after a bout of silence. "If I stayed, it'd be out of guilt. I need to do this for me. This isn't goodbye forever, but I need to recharge and reset. I need to get a handle on who I am as a person and who I am as a god. These abilities alter your perspective."

She doesn't respond. I attempt to remember Rune's words, but my emotions overwhelm any rational thought. Infuriated, I storm out of the throne room and prepare to leave the north for good.

"*Lei?*" I focus on my brother, wondering where he could possibly be. I can't seem to track him, his energy distant. It's getting harder to find his mind. The last time I contacted him, he felt more present. He was inviting and chatty. This time, I've had to pound on his mental wall. "*Lei, can you hear me?*"

"*Malin? Is that you?*" His thoughts halt. "*I thought I was dreaming.*"

My stomach churns. "*What do you mean? Lei, you're addicted. You can't live in the dream world.*"

"*I what can wish I do.*" The words are jumbled, nonsensical.

"*Please tell me you are all right.*"

"I am better than all right. I am at one with everything. I see everything. I understand everything. I know you are leaving. You are making a beautiful choice. The right choice. I envy you."

"But what about you, Lei? Where are you?"

"I am home."

"And where is that?"

"Where my heart is."

If he were here physically, I think I would consider slapping him. He frustrates me in the way only a brother could. *"What are you going to do next?"*

Silence. Just as I go to repeat myself, the weak words echo in my mind. *"Whatever the dreams tell me to do."*

And I'm kicked out of my brother's thoughts.

THERE WERE no belongings to pack—I've been without possessions for so long that I don't typically feel like I own anything.

Sharnique transmitted a message to meet along the northern coastline to ensure a quicker trip for us. They have been riding the elephantano, which was apparently gifted by the gods to serve as protector of our land. It was never supposed to be cast to stone, but the water folk were scared of its power. It's the same old story no matter where I travel. Fear leads to violence and mistreatment, and thus creates a vicious cycle.

Diarmuid and I hop aboard Nellabix, and Rune rides on a dubclair, a borrowed mount that one of the central corner immortals brought with them. Its golden feline body slinks with ease over any surface, its silver mane emitting a sweet scent.

My stomach churns at the thought of leaving Taylin like this, but she left me with no choice. The gods refuse to wait another day, so it's now or never.

The sunrise serves as a beautiful metaphor as we approach the coastline, the rays tickling the fuchsia sands. Ankles deep in the tide stand Sharnique and Garu, looking ferociously majestic. They never seem to tire. This time of morning always lends to puffy eyes and poor posture for me, but they seem refreshed and esthetically perfect. Perhaps it's a godly ability I haven't stumbled upon yet.

"This is really happening, isn't it?" Rune says, his mount automatically coming to a halt. Nellabix waits for my cue before she stops. She makes a disgruntled sound and lifts her hooves, seemingly disgusted by the sandy sensation. Her mannerism makes me laugh, and I mourn her once more. I hope I'm making the right decision.

"I think so," I say, swallowing the lump in my throat. "It doesn't have to be permanent. I'll be back."

"You keep saying that," Rune says. "It is all right if you don't come back. Don't get me wrong; I want you to stay forever. Just know that you don't owe us anything. Do what you need to do."

His words reassure me slightly, but Taylin's cold expression flashes in my mind's eye. What if I'm making a mistake?

"Come on, Mum." Diarmuid jumps off Nellabix and offers me his hand. "It's time."

Reluctantly, I accept his gesture and land in the sand which kisses my toes. Sharnique waves elegantly, while Garu maintains his stoic stance.

"Lei won't give you any trouble?" I ask Rune.

"No. He has seen the future. He is a man of his word."

"I'm worried about him. He is living in his dreams. Can you keep an eye out for him? Or contact me if I need to return?"

"Malin, relax. Your brother is grieving. This is temporary. I have been healing him daily from a distance since your last exchange."

"He won't speak to me. I tried again, and he only said good luck and goodbye."

"Have faith in Lei. Have faith in me. I won't let anything bad happen to him. I promise when he is in a better mindspace, he will reach out to you. We tend to act strangely when we are feeling low. It's nothing personal."

I nod, various loose ties flitting through my mind. "And you'll stay in the north with Taylin? And you know what to feed Nellabix? And to continue rebuilding so the illusion doesn't falter? And watch out for shadow people? My ghost friend might be able to protect you. And don't let mortal sacrifices happen in the north!"

"Malin!" Rune chuckles gently, then reaches up to place his hands around my shoulders. "Everything is as it should be. This is *your* time now. Be free."

Shoulders tense, I follow Diarmuid's lead towards the gods and elephantano. "This creature will take us across the waters?"

"Back to our land, yes," Garu says. "Its hide protects it from the electricity which strikes halfway during the trip. It will feel prickly, but it won't hurt you much either. It is nature's way of deeming you worthy of a godly title. Any inferior entity will not be entitled access through the threshold."

His words alarm me. "What if we aren't ready?"

"You are," Sharnique reassures, her blinks heavy. "Trust me."

Garu offers to help me climb the elephantano, but we are disrupted by a shrill, manic cry.

"*Wait! Wait!*"

I turn to find a perplexed and out of breath Taylin sprinting towards us, her evening robe flowing behind her like a cape. Hair wild and eyes bloodshot, she doesn't stop until she has thrown herself into my arms, breathing swiftly down my neck. She is sweaty, but I don't care. I hold her close and allow my tears to stream.

"*I couldn't...let you...go...without...*"

"I know," I say, hoping she will preserve her breath. I am forever panicking that she, as a mortal, will collapse from a heart attack or stroke.

"Really, one moment." She catches her breath and pulls away, locking eyes with mine. "I understand. I truly, truly do. I'm sorry for yesterday."

"No, I'm sorry."

"No, Malin. Let me talk. I've always given you a hard time. I've always said you should make a decision, and when you finally do, I swoop in and tell you it's the wrong one. That wasn't fair of me. You have given me a home, a family and a purpose. I'm beyond proud to be part of your clan and I'll be right here whenever, if ever, you choose to return. I'm grateful for our time together, always."

I'm at a loss for words. All I can do is hold her tight until Sharnique sighs impatiently and signals at the sun. Despite our eternal life, time is apparently still of the essence.

"Forever," I whisper, tapping my chest.

As we climb and settle upon the grand elephantano, I shuffle behind Diarmuid and hold his waist. Gazing down at Rune, Taylin and Nellabix, my heart fills with love and gratitude.

"Can you believe it, Mum?" Diarmuid whispers over his shoulder as Garu and Sharnique pull themselves into position. "You're finally free. You get to start your life over. I can't wait to see what it's like!"

"Neither can I," I admit.

Redirecting my gaze to the sea, my mind floods with various images of what lies ahead.

"Oh!" I pat my pocket, remembering the dream crystal. Tossing it down to Rune, I smile. "I almost forgot."

Fumbling as he catches it, he holds it up. "What's this?"

"A crystal. I never used it."

"Why?"

"The past is a memory. The future is imagination. All that matters is the present, because it is a gift. I didn't want to know about a future that didn't exist. Maybe you can tell me about what you see when I return."

Rune smirks, pocketing the crystal. "Consider it a promise. Thank you, Malin."

"Are we just about finished here?" Sharnique asks, increasingly impatient. "This is highly un-godlike. You have a lot to learn, Malin."

Her comment doesn't bother me. All I know is I'm at peace with my decision and I'm at peace with those I love—a sensation I can't remember ever experiencing before.

"Ready," I announce, nuzzling into Diarmuid's back. "To the next chapter."

"To the next chapter!" Diarmuid replies enthusiastically.

As the elephantano makes way, I squeal with delight as we lurch forward into the tide. I wave farewell as we merge into the sea, basking in the warmth of the sunrise as it welcomes us towards a new land and a new home.

In this pure moment of peace and freedom, after centuries of terror and entrapment, I can finally say:

I have everything I have ever wanted.

Acknowledgments

The concept of Immortal Cells came from a throwaway joke in my paranormal comedy book, Colt Harper: Esteemed Vampire Cat.

Two years ago, I happened to be reading through the book in an attempt to find lines I could use to incorporate into a monologue my drama student requested to perform. I noticed the Immortal Cells line and thought that this is clearly a story waiting to happen (I can't believe I'd forgotten about the concept while initially writing Colt Harper!).

A few months later, the book was complete and Malin was alive.

There's a lot of ways to interpret the Immortal Cells, as it's a metaphor for various social, emotional and political issues. At its heart, I believe we can all relate to Malin in some way, as we can be victims of imposter syndrome, self-doubt, indecisiveness and guilt. Yet, it's Malin's determination and quiet strength that saves the day -- something a lot of us forget we have locked deep inside.

I want to thank everyone at Immortal Works for their tireless efforts to get this book out into the world!

I am sincerely grateful for my family, my friends and my students for constantly inspiring, motivating and encouraging all of my crazy creative endeavours. I am extremely blessed.

Here's to all of our Immortal Souls.

About the Author

Tyrolin is the #1 bestselling and award-winning author of over a dozen novels in the sci-fi, fantasy, comedy and visionary genres. As the recipient of multiple Australia Day awards for her contribution to the arts, Tyrolin writes for the stage and for the page.

A performing arts teacher by day, a writer by night and a hypnotherapist by weekends, Tyrolin is currently enjoying her favourite story of all: her own.

This has been an
Immortal Production

www.ingramcontent.com/pod-product-compliance
Lightning Source LLC
Chambersburg PA
CBHW020754190726
48285CB00006B/2029